PRAISE FOR *WHO DID YOU TELL?*

"Instantly immersive, then intriguing, then insanely suspenseful, then ... the truth. Believe me, Lesley Kara knows what she's doing."

—LEE CHILD

"I couldn't put it down! If you loved *The Rumor,* you'll love this one too."

—LAUREN NORTH, author of *The Perfect Son*

PRAISE FOR *THE RUMOR*

"In this chilling tale of paranoia, suspicion, and accusation, Lesley Kara keeps you guessing until the final page."

—PAULA HAWKINS, #1 *New York Times* bestselling author of *The Girl on the Train*

"A great debut with a slyly clever premise and a roller-coaster ride to the very last sentence."

—FIONA BARTON, *New York Times* bestselling author of *The Widow* and *The Child*

"An intriguing premise, a creeping sense of dread, and a twist you won't see coming . . . Everyone is going to be talking about *The Rumor*."

—SHARI LAPENA, *New York Times* bestselling author of *The Couple Next Door*

"A brilliant premise with a killer twist, *The Rumor* depicts the prejudices and secrets that simmer in a small seaside town to devastating effect."

—COLETTE MCBETH, author of *An Act of Silence*

"Lesley Kara's gripping debut offers a series of red herrings and twists. . . . The evocation of the way in which idle chatter can spiral into something potentially deadly is beautifully done and fans of page-turning suspense novels should lap it up."

—*The Guardian*

"Well-developed characters and a twisty plot will keep readers turning the pages. Those who stay to the very last sentence will be doubly surprised. Kara is off to a promising start."

—*Publishers Weekly*

"This mystery has an unusual and resonant theme—how a single rumor can morph into a completely unmanageable, deadly force. [There's] psychological acuity throughout and [an] astonishing ending."

—*Booklist*

BY LESLEY KARA

The Rumor

Who Did You Tell?

Who Did You Tell?

Who Did You Tell?

A NOVEL

Lesley Kara

BALLANTINE BOOKS
NEW YORK

2020 Ballantine Books Trade Paperback Edition

Published in the United States by Ballantine Books, an imprint of Random House, a division of Penguin Random House LLC, New York.

BALLANTINE and the HOUSE colophon are registered trademarks of Penguin Random House LLC.

Originally published in hardcover in the United Kingdom by Bantam Press, an imprint of Transworld Publishers, a division of Penguin Random House LLC, in 2020.

ISBN 978-0-593-15690-2
Ebook ISBN 978-0-593-15689-6

Printed in the United States of America on acid-free paper

randomhousebooks.com

2 4 6 8 9 7 5 3 1

Book design by Caroline Cunningham

For anyone whose life has been affected by addiction

Who Did You Tell?

Just because you imagine yourself doing something, and enjoy the way it makes you feel, doesn't mean you actually want to do it. It doesn't mean you're going to do it. Of course not. Because sometimes the very opposite is true and something you never in a million years could imagine yourself doing is done in the blink of an eye and changes your life forever.

So if, in my head, I'm grabbing a handful of her braids and slamming her head into a brick wall till her skull's smashed in, it doesn't mean that that's what I'll do. It doesn't make me a bad person just thinking about it. In fact, I'd go so far as to say it's normal to have the odd violent fantasy about someone you hate so much every muscle in your body contracts when you think of them. I mean, everybody does it sometimes, don't they? Don't they?

Seven slams, if you're interested. That's how many it takes till her braids run red.

Part One

1

I smell him first, or rather the aftershave he used to wear. Joint by Roccobarocco. A '90s vintage scent—masculine and woody. A discontinued line.

I spin round, but no one's there. Only a girl in a puffer jacket squatting to tie her laces. I almost trip over her. Then I see him, sprinting toward the sea, the furry flaps of his trapper hat flying in the breeze like a spaniel's ears. Simon.

My knees give way. I stare after him, but he's disappeared into the night. That's if he was ever there in the first place. Maybe it's all in my head. A hallucination. I've had a few of those in the past.

Whatever it was, I scurry home. A small, frightened creature, suddenly afraid of the dark. Afraid of *him*.

Mum pounces on me like a sniffer dog the second I walk through the door.

"Where've you been? I've been worried sick." Her fingers dig into my arms and I have to shake her off.

"It's only ten o'clock, Mum. You can't keep doing this. You've got to trust me."

The snort is out before she has a chance to think better of it. "Trust? You're talking to me about trust?"

She crumples onto the bottom stair with her head in her hands, and something inside me crumples too. I kneel down beside her and bury my head in her lap.

"Sorry." My voice is muffled in the folds of her dressing gown and the years roll away. I'm in my first year of secondary school and someone has upset me. Mum is telling me to rise above it.

Now, as then, she rubs her hand in a circle between my shoulders.

"I just don't understand why you have to walk when it's so late," she says, and I want to explain that if I have to come home and sit in this dreary little cottage night after night without drinking, my head will explode. I want to tell her that I walk to stay alive, that I have to keep on the move, doing things, going places, even when I've nothing to do and nowhere to go. Especially then. But all I can do is shed hot, silent tears into her lap.

It's been five months since I woke up in hospital, Mum standing at the foot of my bed with "That Look" on her face. A fortnight since my spell in rehab came to an end. It was she who suggested this arrangement. If she hadn't, I might have been forced to ask, wouldn't have had the luxury of indignation.

"Move in with *you*? In Flinstead? You've got to be joking."

Simon and I had laughed about the place on the few occasions it cropped up in conversation. Said the day we ended up somewhere like Flinstead was the day we gave up on life. It's got this reputation as being somewhere you go to die. Like Eastbourne, only smaller and with nothing to do of an evening.

"What are your other options?" Mum said. That must have been the moment she decided to adopt the dispassionate tone of a counselor. She's been using it ever since, when she can remember. Open questions. No hint of disapproval. I'm not fooled for a second. It's just another of her strategies. All that anger and frustration, all that *disappointment*—it's still seething beneath the surface, ready to boil up and spit in my face like hot fat.

It's past midnight now. I'm lying in bed, curled on my side, facing the window. My braids feel tight and itchy and I have a sudden urge to unpick them all, but they cost so much to put in, money I can ill afford, and besides, it'll take ages. I don't have the energy for it.

A sliver of moonlight seeps in through the gap in the curtains. I roll onto my other side and hug my knees against my chest, finally allowing myself to think of Simon. My mouth goes dry. There's a strange whooshing noise in my ears and a prickling behind my cheekbones. It couldn't have been him earlier. It was just my mind playing tricks on me.

We met in a bar. Where else? One of those cavernous London pubs with paneled wood walls and massive mirrors etched with the names of beers. Packed to the rafters on a Friday night, but depressing and sepulchral at four fifteen on a Tuesday afternoon. Was it a Tuesday? I don't really remember. Back then, the days were all pretty much the same. They are now, of course, only in a different way.

I just walked right up to where he was sitting and told him he had an interestingly shaped head. That's what drink does. *Did*. Gave me the gall to approach complete strangers, to bypass all the meaningless chit-chat and get straight to the point. Whatever point my fucked-up head was currently obsessing over. I thought I was being witty and flirtatious.

"No, Astrid. You're being foul and warped and ugly. Drink isn't your friend. It's your enemy. Your poison. Can't you see what it's doing to you?" Jane's words ring in my head. Jane, who was supposed to be my friend. My ally. I'd lost her by then, the latest in a long line of friends and acquaintances who couldn't hack it anymore.

Then I met Simon and none of it mattered. We drank cider till the men-in-suits brigade swaggered in and we slunk off back to his place. A dingy bedsit on Anglesey Road in Woolwich. His sheets were rank, but I didn't care. He already had a girlfriend, but I didn't care about that either. We weren't just a couple of drunks hitting it off; we were kindred spirits. Soulmates. Two sides of the same coin.

Must have been a bad penny, then, says that little voice in my head. The one that sounds just like Mum.

He can't have come back. He just can't.

2

The next morning I get dressed quickly, determined to put last night out of my mind. I loop my key chain round my neck and go downstairs. It's still early but Mum's beaten me to it, as usual.

"There's a banana needs eating," she says. "If you want that with some toast."

"Not that black spotty thing that's been moldering in the fruit bowl all week?"

She picks it up and gives it a squeeze. "Nothing wrong with it."

"You eat it, then. Toast will be fine."

"There's always porridge," she says. "I could make you some if you like."

"I don't like porridge, I've told you."

I take the last sachet from the box of green tea and pluck my favorite mug from the mug-tree. The one that says: *I don't like morning people. Or mornings. Or people.* It's one of the few things I haven't lost or broken over the years.

Mum sighs. "Oh, Hilly, it doesn't have to be like this."

I rip the sachet too fast and tea-leaf dust spills all over the counter. "Mum, I haven't been called Hilary in over seventeen years."

She touches my arm. "Sorry, darling. Sometimes it just slips out." She opens the cupboard above my head and draws out another box of green tea. "Here, I noticed you were running low so I picked some up."

With the flat of one hand, I sweep the spilled tea leaves into the cupped palm of the other. It's gone everywhere, but I'm glad of the distraction. It's something to focus on, something other than the horrible clogged sensation at the back of my throat. The one I always get when she does something kind.

"Thanks, Mum."

Hilary. It comes from the Latin *hilarus*, which means "cheerful." Mum said she and Dad chose it from the *Pan Book of Girls' Names*. They opened that treasure trove of possibilities and stuck a pin on a page to give them the title of my life. I'm assuming, of course, that if the pin had impaled itself on Beryl or Mildred, they might have tried again. But Mum *liked* the name Hilary. "As a baby, you had a very sunny disposition," she once told me, a wistful look in her eyes.

I've since worked out that I was born on a Wednesday, so what chance did I have? Woe is my default. Anyway, "Hilary" sounds like something out of the '50s. Head girl at a posh boarding school in Surrey. Captain of the hockey team. All-round jolly good sport. *By George, Hillers, you are a good egg!*

"Astrid" was the perfect antidote to all that, the antithesis of everything I was running away from. It's a rebellious, rock-and-roll kind of name that carries a hint of the stars, a wildness. There was Astrid Kirchherr, the woman who photographed the Beatles in Hamburg, and Astrid Proll, an early member of the Baader–Meinhof gang. Then there's Astrid Lindgren, author of the superstrong and thrillingly outrageous Pippi Longstocking stories. The list goes on. Queens and princesses. Sculptors and shot-putters. Skiers and porn stars. Troubled fictional protagonists. The name means "divine strength."

Changing my name changed *me*. It made me visible. Gave me the balls to get wrecked with the bad girls on Peckham Common. To suck Danny Harrison's cock in a mausoleum in Nunhead Cemetery. To get my nose pierced and a tattoo of a flame snaking up my inner thigh. Sunny disposition, my arse.

The tide is way out this morning, beyond the metal markers, and it's warm enough to believe that summer's on its way. I take my trainers off and walk barefoot on the flat, wet sand, dangling them by the laces. I've counted five small jellyfish, like transparent fried eggs, before I see the guy in the wetsuit clambering over the slimy spit of algae-covered rock. The same guy I've seen swimming from here for the last two weeks. The one who's nodded at me and said hello a couple of times. It's what people do in Flinstead. For someone who's spent most of their life in London, it takes a bit of getting used to.

"There's a whole ecosystem right here," he says, as if we're in the middle of a conversation. "Sea squirts, limpets, barnacles. An-en-om-es too." His teeth flash white against his tanned face. "I have to really concentrate to say that," he says.

My laugh peals out before I can rein it in. Too loud. Too eager. *Shut up, Astrid.*

He jumps onto the sand. Pale blond hairs curl at his ankles, where the legs of his wetsuit end, but they don't extend to the tops of his feet, which are smooth and golden brown with evenly spaced toes.

"Are you local?" he says.

I hesitate. "Not really—well, kind of. For now, anyway."

We're walking toward the sea, squelching through shallow pools left by the retreating tide. "I'm between jobs at the moment," he says.

"Me too. I'm keeping an eye on my mum." A gull screeches overhead—a harsh, mocking sound. "She's . . . a bit depressed."

Guilt snakes through me. I can hardly tell him the truth. Someone like him—so healthy, so *wholesome*—he'd run a mile. And I don't want him to. Not yet.

We've reached the water's edge.

"Listen," he says. "If you fancy a coffee sometime . . ."

"Yeah, sure." It's just his way of ending the conversation. If he meant it, he'd suggest a time. A place.

He turns away and strides into the water. I don't know whether I'm disappointed or relieved. Relieved, I think. The last thing I need is the complication of a new relationship.

"Eleven o'clock tomorrow all right for you?" he calls over his shoulder. "In the Fisherman's Shack on Flinstead Road?"

Nervous laughter bubbles up at the back of my throat. I feel sick. "Okay. See you then."

I watch as he commits his body to the cold and pushes off into a front crawl. It's remarkable, the distance he's already covered, the relentless rhythm of his strokes. It takes courage to head straight for the horizon. I nearly drowned once, doing that. Got caught in a rip current. I screw my eyes shut and clench my knuckles, trying to block out the memory of my panic, the sour burn of seawater at the back of my nose and throat.

And that's when it happens. The unmistakable scent of Simon's aftershave in my nostrils. Just like last night. My eyes snap open, but by the time I've registered it, it's gone, carried away by the breeze. I twist my head over my shoulder, bracing myself for what I might see: the old donkey jacket, the faded jeans, the rage in his eyes. But apart from a smattering of early-morning dog-walkers and a jogger with earplugs, there's no one else about. No one who looks remotely like the kind of person who'd be wearing Joint at half past eight in the morning. Or smoking one.

My gaze returns to the sea. Wetsuit Guy seems to have disappeared. Maybe I imagined him too.

Oh shit. I need a drink.

3

By the time I arrive at AA, I'm wired. All I've done since this morning is drink endless cups of coffee and smoke myself stupid. I've also been researching barnacles. Apparently, they exude an adhesive-type substance that binds them to hard surfaces and cements them in place. It's similar to the clotting mechanism in blood. I need facts like this to occupy my mind. To fill up the spaces where the bad stuff clings on. Anything to quell the compulsion to drink.

And now I'm here, hugging my chest to keep my heart from exploding. It's the first meeting I've been to since coming out of rehab. Mum's been on at me for days to go.

I take the chair nearest the door and do that thing I used to do on the Underground. Quick, furtive glances at the other passengers. Just to get a sense of them. The cross section of people in the vestry of Flinstead parish church on this chilly May evening is, in fact, remarkably similar to that of a London Underground carriage. I just wish I could get off at the next stop.

A woman with peroxide hair and a ravaged face gives me a knowing smile. The crowns on her front teeth are so old they're black at the gum line. She looks like she's in her sixties, but dresses younger, probably is. Drink ages a person. She's wearing tight black jeans, a gray vest over a black T-shirt, and one of those long, shapeless cardigans, which trails over the tops of her ankle boots. Every time she shifts position I catch a whiff of stale cigarettes. Do I smell like that too? God, I hope not.

"Is it your first time?" says a cultured voice to my left. Its owner wears an expensive-looking charcoal-gray suit and polished brogues. He has the air of someone distinguished. A lawyer or consultant, perhaps. It's a great leveler, this addiction of ours.

"First time *here*, yes." My voice is hoarse from too much smoking and there's an annoying twitch in my left eyelid.

He nods politely, and I sense that he's holding back another question. I'm glad. I'm not here for the small talk.

More people drift in and take their seats. A gaunt-looking woman with bulging eyes and long, fidgety fingers sits opposite me. Her eyes veer in their sockets like pale-blue marbles. Every so often they settle on me, before spinning off in another direction. I stare at my knees. When I look up, I find her watching me. And she isn't the only one. I'm clearly this evening's main attraction. A youngish man with bad acne keeps looking at me too.

This is unbearable. I could be out of that door and back home in ten minutes. Except then Mum will know I didn't come and I have to prove to her that, this time, I'll do it. This time, I'll quit for good. It's my last chance—she's left me in no doubt about that.

A noticeboard with AA literature pinned all over it has been propped on a table against the wall, no doubt so it can be whisked out of sight when the mother-and-toddler group takes over in the morning. My gaze drifts over the neatly typed list of the Twelve Steps, not that I need to read them again. After three months of rehab and daily meetings I could probably recite them by heart. Actually working them, step by step, is a different matter.

I can just about get my head round the first one and admit that for most of the time I'm powerless over alcohol, that my life has become unmanageable. But the next two are pretty major stumbling blocks: believing that a power greater than myself can restore me to sanity and, here's the killer: turning my will and my life over to the care of God. I mean, I know they say it doesn't have to be the old-man-in-the-sky kind of God, it can be anything I feel comfortable with—the cosmos, the power of the group itself, even—but it's hard to get down on your knees and pray to the collective wisdom of a random bunch of drunks.

I close my eyes. The room has that old-church smell: stale and musty. It prompts a memory I thought I'd forgotten. A Sunday-school classroom. Being shown how to write a capital "G" for "God" and pressing down on the paper so hard my pencil broke. Even as a small child, something inside me resisted the notion of a higher power.

Someone to my right clears his throat. He looks like the sort of man who might play the church organ or organize the local Neighborhood Watch. Dull and worthy. He looks like my old physics teacher, Mr. Staines. Semen Staines, we used to call him, poor bugger.

"Good evening, everyone," he says, his voice as watery and colorless as the rest of him. "My name is David and I'm an alcoholic."

And so it begins.

David is in the middle of the usual preamble when the door bursts open and a latecomer hurtles through. A tall middle-aged woman in a beige raincoat and red court shoes. Her messy hair is shoulder-length, mousy-colored.

"Sorry," she says, her face flushing as red as her shoes. Her flesh-colored tights have gone all bobbly round the ankles.

I give her a small smile. She looks so vulnerable, standing there in front of us all, and I can't help noticing that tremble in her hands. I bet she's still drinking. Poor woman. She looks like she'd rather be anywhere but here. I know just how she feels.

. . .

After the meeting, people drink coffee and chat. Some of them hug each other. The peroxide woman with gray skin—Rosie, eight years sober, AA evangelist—tries to hug the woman with red shoes, who clearly doesn't want to be hugged. I've met Rosie's type before. Homing in on the newbies. Oh God, now she's heading straight for me. I hold out my hand instead and the woman with red shoes rolls her eyes at me over Rosie's shoulder. I can't reciprocate, not without Rosie cottoning on, but I think she can tell from the way I look back at her that we're on the same wavelength about inappropriate hugging.

When Rosie finally slinks off to accost someone else, the man in the suit gestures at me with a cup. He's standing next to the man with acne, who's now openly staring at me. I shake my head. I have to get out of here. Now. But as I turn toward the door I bump straight into the woman with red shoes. We both say sorry at the same time.

"My fault," she says, flustered. "I wasn't looking where I was going."

Her voice is soft, tremulous, and though I haven't come here to make friends I feel as if I ought to encourage her. Reaching out more, helping others—that's how this whole fellowship thing is meant to work. *Be nice, Astrid. Be nice.*

"See you next week?" I say.

"Maybe." Her eyes glisten with tears. She rushes to the door and stumbles out into the corridor, her exit as sudden and clumsy as her entrance.

I imagine her running all the way home, then opening a bottle of red wine and drinking the lot. Opening another. I pack the thought away before it takes hold.

Outside, wind hurls itself from the sea end of Flinstead Road. I tug my coat across my chest and walk straight into it, chin pressed down, the musty smell in my nostrils blown clean away.

The street is deserted. Out of season, Flinstead is dead after nine o'clock. Actually, that's a lie—it's dead after eight. When I pass the alleyway that leads to the little cluster of overpriced boutiques, the ones only the tourists go in, I stop and stare into the shadows. This was the exact spot where I saw Simon last night. In the daylight, it looks enticing, with its coral-painted walls and that glimpse of courtyard at the end, the metal bistro tables and chairs, the hanging baskets. Now it looks like the kind of place a girl might get strangled.

I walk straight down it and sit on one of the chairs, the cold of the metal burning into the backs of my thighs. It's a matter of pride. To prove to myself that I'm not scared. That I don't believe for one second that it was really him.

Once, I would have said he wasn't spiteful enough to come back. But that was before.

I've lost count of the number of times I've killed her. The number of ways.

Yesterday, it went like this: we were standing on the pier at Mistden Sands and I just pushed her in. She was wearing those stupid Doc Martens she clumps about in and, what with them and her big, heavy coat, she couldn't keep afloat. I stood there, watching as she thrashed about, and waited for her to sink. Her braids spread out on the water like long fingers of seaweed.

The last thing I saw were those little blue beads at the ends, bobbing on the surface like fishing floats.

It was too easy, though. Too clean. I prefer it when there's blood.

4

I've passed the Fisherman's Shack almost every day since I arrived, but I've never been inside before this morning. I see at once what I've been missing. Creaky old floorboards and mismatched tables and chairs. Vintage, but only because they've been here for years. They haven't been specially "sourced" or painted in Farrow & Ball and roughed up with a sanding block. And, most impressively, they just serve coffee (instant or filter, not a macchiato or ristretto in sight), tea, Fanta, or Coke. Egg-and-bacon butties. Toasted tea-cakes.

It's an inspired choice. I love it.

The barista has arms like Bluto. The devil in me wants to ask for a skinny latte, just to see his face, but I order a filter coffee, black, and take it over to a table in the window. I'm ten minutes late and Wetsuit Guy's not here, which either means he isn't coming or he couldn't be bothered to wait. I don't even know his name. For all his chatter on the beach yesterday, he forgot to introduce himself.

I rub a circle in the steamed-up window and watch the good folk of Flinstead go about their usual business. Coming out of shops with papers tucked under their arms, waving to someone on the other side of the street or nodding their endless hellos. Sometimes

I think it's like *The Truman Show* and all I've got to do is find the perimeter of the set and break out through the papery screen to the real world on the other side. The messy, chaotic world of noise and pain and sharp-faced strangers who look straight through you.

Then I see her, the hugger from AA. Rosie, or whatever her name is. She's wearing another of those long, trailing cardigans, only this one is black, and she's dragging a rotating card stand out of the Oxfam shop. After she's wrestled it over the step and wheeled it into position in front of the window she swivels her head round and looks straight at me, almost as if she's sensed me watching her. For one awful second I think she's going to wave, but then she turns away and goes back into the shop.

My shoulders soften. There's no way she could have recognized me from this distance and, even if she did, there's an unspoken rule at AA that we don't acknowledge each other in public, especially in a town this size.

A girl in a puffer jacket emerges from the newsagent's. She's tucking into a huge block of chocolate, biting straight into it as if it's nothing more than a snack-size bar. My mouth waters. If Wetsuit Guy doesn't turn up soon, I'm going to buy some chocolate too.

I watch as she positions herself in front of the card stand, spinning it listlessly. Something about her looks familiar, but before I can work out what it is, she disappears into the charity shop.

I turn away and stare into my coffee. Why am I still hanging around in here, waiting for some fitness fanatic to show up? I might just as well finish this and go.

A door at the back, which has the word "Toilet" written on a piece of card strung round the handle, opens with a loud squeak, and there he is. For some stupid reason, I hadn't imagined him in anything other than a wetsuit but, of course, he's fully clothed. Faded jeans and a pale-green rugby shirt. Blond tousled hair. He's even more good-looking than I remember.

"You're here," he says, grinning.

For one awkward moment I think he's going to kiss me, but at the last minute he offers me his hand.

"I'm Josh, by the way."

"Astrid."

"Cool." He nods at my coffee. "Can I get you something to eat with that?"

I could murder an egg-and-bacon buttie but have visions of egg yolk sliding down my chin. It's not a great look for a first date. If that's what this is. Dating hasn't been part of my repertoire for ages. In fact, I'm not sure it ever was. Falling into bed, rat-arsed, with complete strangers is my usual modus operandi.

"A toasted teacake, maybe?" Christ, did I really say that? It sounds like something my great-aunt Dorothy would order.

"Toasted teacake coming up," he says, and saunters over to the counter, reaching in his back pocket for some money.

"One toasted teacake, one egg-and-bacon buttie, and a cup of tea, please, Bob," he says.

Bob nods and sets to work. I'm studying the back of Josh's head—the way his hair curls over his collar—when an involuntary shudder travels the length of my spine. I don't have to look out the window to tell that I'm being watched, and I instinctively know that, this time, it's not Rosie.

Josh pulls out the chair in front of me and it scrapes against the floor. "Are you okay?"

I swivel my eyes to the right. There's no one there. Of course there isn't. *Get a grip, Astrid. It's not him.*

"Yeah. Yeah, I'm fine."

Josh glances out of the window and frowns. Then he turns his attention back to me.

"So how long will you be staying with your mum?"

"Until she gets better, I suppose." There's just the faintest sensation of warmth in my cheeks.

"What do you do?" he says. "For a living, I mean."

My brain goes into overdrive. *Breathe.*

Josh screws up his face. "Sorry. That's a really annoying question. I sound like some tosser at a dinner party."

I smile. "I trained in scenic design. I work freelance."

What I don't tell him is that the last job I had that was anything remotely to do with design was over seven years ago. I had a reputation for turning up for work late, still pissed from the night before. A walking health-and-safety hazard. A useless drunk. Since then it's been a series of low-paid, temporary, or zero-hours contracts. Boring clerical positions, supermarket work, that kind of thing. For the last year it's been nothing at all.

I take a mouthful of coffee and scald the roof of my mouth.

Josh blows across the top of his drink, like I should have done. "I work in a university," he says. "Student services. At least, I will do, from the end of August. I was laid off from my last job."

"Oh, sorry to hear that."

"Don't be. I hated it. Anyway, it's worked out pretty well. My dad's bought a big old place overlooking the backwaters. So I'm staying here for the rest of the summer to help him out with the refurbishment."

He's looking right at me now. "So what made you want to be a set designer?"

Now, this I don't even have to think about. "I love painting on a big scale," I tell him. "Climbing on scaffold towers and transforming a plain old backdrop into a forest, or an ocean, or a busy street. Mixing the colors and textures together, flicking paint onto the canvas and getting my hands and clothes covered in it too. Makes me feel like I'm part of the painting, actually *inside* it—do you know what I mean?"

I haven't talked about any of this for ages, haven't even thought about it, to be honest. But now that I am, it's all coming back to me. The passion I felt before it all went wrong. Maybe if I hadn't been hell-bent on self-sabotage, I could have been on my way to being a respected set designer by now, or at least in regular work with good production companies.

Josh is nodding at me and smiling.

"It gets your adrenaline pumping too. Especially when you're working so high up. You've got to know what you're doing. And there's something really special about working in a theater late at night. The atmosphere, you know? Eerie and dark. Echoes bouncing off the empty auditorium. Always a broken light flickering somewhere in the darkness."

I stop. He must think I'm mad, rattling on like this.

He leans back in his chair. "I don't think I've ever seen someone so in love with what they do," he says. "Your face is completely transformed when you're talking about it."

I look down, embarrassed.

"Actually," he says, "I might pick your painterly brain, if you don't mind."

I give him a quizzical look.

"There's this weird little room in the middle of my dad's house that hardly gets any light. He's thought about knocking it through into the two adjoining rooms but there's something about it he likes, and I know what he means. It's like a secret chamber."

He pauses while Bob brings the buttie and teacake over and we move our cups aside to make more space.

"He's got this idea of getting someone to paint a window on one of the walls. You know, one of those realistic ones that looks like it's opening onto a beautiful garden, or something."

"A *trompe l'œil.*"

"I beg your pardon?"

"A *trompe l'œil.* It's French for 'deceive the eye.' A painting that tricks you into seeing it as a three-dimensional solid form. It's all about illusionism and forced perspective."

"You see?" Josh says. "You know about these things. Why don't you come and have a look, see what you think?" He winks. One casual movement of an eye and there's a strange fluttering sensation behind my breastbone. Between my thighs. I glance out of the window.

"Seriously, you don't have to if you're too busy, but it'd be good to have your input, and Dad's great. You'll love him." He blushes then. This six-foot-something blond Adonis actually blushes. "And it'd be really nice to see you again."

I wipe the palms of my hands on my jeans under the table. This is crazy. I've only known this guy five minutes and already he wants me to meet his dad. I was with Simon for almost three years and I never met a single one of his relatives. He'd lost touch with them all by then. It's hardly surprising, in the circumstances. I doubt Mum and I would still be talking if I hadn't agreed to rehab.

"Okay, then." The words fly out before I can change my mind.

5

Josh's text comes through later that week.

Hi Astrid. Meet you outside the Old Schooner in Mistden?
2pm Wednesday?

Shit! What have I done? I suppose I could tell him Mum's taken a turn for the worse and that I can't leave her too long on her own. Or I could do the easiest thing of all and ignore it. Not turn up. Pretend none of this is happening.

And yet, if I close my eyes, I can already visualize the small, dark room at the center of his dad's house. Its secret chamber. Part of my brain is already imagining myself there, doing the job for them. I can picture the bare plaster wall, smell the primer I will prep it with.

I stick my head round the living-room door. Mum's fallen asleep on the settee and her mouth's hanging open. She looks like a corpse. I close the door softly, then go upstairs and pull down the extending ladder that's attached to the loft hatch. My brushes must be up here somewhere, along with all my other stuff—the boxes and suitcases and trash bags that contain my worldly goods, or "a load of old rubbish," as I heard Mum call it the other day. She was speaking to one of her Quaker friends on the phone. I'm not the only one who goes to meetings.

I flick the switch and a dingy yellow light creeps into the darkness. It takes me a while to find them. They're in an old suitcase under a pile of winter clothes. I draw out the stained canvas roll and bring it toward my face, breathing in the long-forgotten smell of turps and linseed. Just the possibility of painting again makes me want to weep, but I wall in the emotion, seal it up tight. I'm about to pull the lid down on the case when something shiny and gold catches my attention. I peel back the jumper that's half covering it and gasp. It's one of Simon's old juggling balls. How the hell did *that* get here?

I pick it up and squeeze it into my palm, the beat of my heart loud, insistent. Simon was teaching himself to juggle when we first got together. He wanted to be an actor. He thought the more skills he could develop, the more roles he could play. The trouble was, he kept missing out. No matter how many auditions he went for, he never got the parts he wanted. Alcohol took the pain of rejection away.

I see him now, in my mind's eye, dropping the juggling balls and swearing. I'd pluck them off the floor and throw them back to him, and they'd be all warm and sticky in my hands. I'd say, "Go on, then, show us what you can do with your golden balls," and he'd give me that crooked little smile and start undoing his fly as a joke.

Did he have them with him that last time? He must have done. How else to explain one of them being here?

I stuff the ball back in the case, then take it out again and edge backward, my right foot dancing in the emptiness behind me, searching out the top step of the ladder. I turn the light off and climb down, watch the ladder retract into the dark black square in the ceiling.

Back in my bedroom, I put the ball on my bedside cabinet.

· · ·

In the early days, before it all went wrong, just seeing something of his would make me glow inside. Now my pulse races for entirely different reasons. Why on earth didn't I leave it in the loft? The last thing I need is reminding.

I unfurl the roll of brushes onto my bed. There's no way Josh's dad will ask me to do that painting. And even if he does, I won't agree. My tongue sticks to the roof of my mouth. It's happening again. The sudden swell inside me. The suffocating need to drink. My eyes flick to the travel clock perched on the windowsill, not that I need to check what my body knows with every fiber of its being. Four o'clock in the afternoon. The time I used to start drinking, or if by some miracle I was employed, the time I used to start planning for it in my head. Imagining the satisfying twist of the cap as the seal cracked, the glorious glugging sound as I poured it out. That first long-awaited mouthful.

The muscles in my stomach flutter. My scalp itches. I scratch it, or try to. Work my nails into the exposed areas between the braids. What the hell am I going to do? Is this what it's going to be like for the rest of my life?

Before I know what I'm doing, I'm ripping the beads off the ends of my braids. It's a long, fiddly procedure, unraveling every last one, detangling the clumpy bits at the roots, washing my hair over the bath, and combing conditioner all the way to the ends. But it's something to do. Something to fill the endlessly dry void. Besides, it feels good, dragging the teeth of the comb from my forehead to the crown of my head and down over the back of my neck. Over and over again, till my arm aches and my scalp tingles. Till the wave of longing finally breaks.

Mum widens her eyes when she sees my hair. "I was wondering when you'd get rid of those awful things. You look so much better without them," she adds.

She's scrubbing new potatoes at the sink with a nail brush. "Pam said she saw you coming out of the Fisherman's Shack," she says, not looking round.

Pam is her bridge partner and fellow Quaker.

"She said you were with a young man."

I sigh. It's no wonder I feel like I'm being watched.

"I'm surprised you haven't organized the whole town to keep an eye out for me."

The potato Mum's been scrubbing shoots out of her hand and plops into the washing-up bowl. She lifts it out and rinses it under the tap. "You know what they said in rehab, about not getting involved with anyone else. No major life changes."

"I had a coffee and a toasted teacake with him. We're not getting married."

Now it's Mum's turn to sigh. "Just so long as you know what you're doing."

If only I could confide in her that I have absolutely no idea what I'm doing, that each new day without drinking is uncharted territory, that I feel like a tiny boat, buffeted by waves. A boat that could sink at any minute. But we've left it a bit late for heart-to-hearts. The pattern of our relationship is already fixed, and it's prickly. Combative.

She runs cold water into a colander of lettuce and shakes it over the sink. "Omelette, new potatoes, and salad for supper. Is that okay for you?"

"Lovely, thanks."

She gives me a quick, tight smile. It's a truce, of sorts.

After supper, I open my copy of *Alcoholics Anonymous*. I've read the same paragraph three times and it still doesn't make any sense. It's no surprise that it's known as the Big Book. It's dated and repetitive and I seem to have been reading it forever but, right now, it's the closest I've got to a lifeline.

No wonder I can't concentrate. Mum's pushing a carpet sweeper over the rug and the squeaky noise is doing my head in. It's so like her to still be using a carpet sweeper.

"Someone at my bridge club is starting up a beginners' class at the community hall," she says, as if the thought has just that second popped into her head, as if she hasn't been planning on saying it to me all day. "It starts tomorrow. I wondered whether you might be interested."

"Not sure bridge is really my thing, Mum."

Mum's stopped pushing the sweeper now. "It's a fascinating game when you get the hang of it. And there's so much to learn, it might be good for you."

This is what she's like. She won't let things go.

"Seriously, Mum, I don't want to. I might start swimming or something."

The thought of plunging into cold seawater with Josh has been exercising my mind ever since we said goodbye and swapped phone numbers. I want to feel cleansed and invigorated. I want to learn about the tides. I want to learn what the hell a sea squirt is.

"I'm going to see Josh's dad's house next week."

She gives me a sharp look. "Who's Josh?"

"That guy I had coffee with. His dad wants some advice about a trompe l'œil."

A strange look comes into Mum's eyes. "I saw an amazing one of those in Quebec once," she says. "It was on the side of a house and it looked like the wall had been ripped off and you could see inside all the rooms."

I stare at her. It sounds like she's talking about the Fresque du Petit-Champlain. I remember it from one of the lectures at uni. "When were you in Quebec?"

There's a long pause. "After your dad died."

Dad. It's the first time either of us has mentioned him in ages. The words hang in the air like an accusation. No matter how many times I tell myself that he had a heart condition and would have died anyway, I'll never stop torturing myself about the stress my drinking gave him. It might not have caused his heart attack, but it didn't help. I know that's what Mum thinks too. I can see it in her eyes, hear it in the things she doesn't say.

"How come you never told me you'd been to Quebec?"

"I did."

"You didn't. I would have remembered."

"You think?"

I look down at my book, cheeks burning. Good point, *Mother.* I've missed too many things in my cobweb of a life. Black holes in my memory I'll never be able to fill, no matter how hard I try. Not that I want to fill them all. Some things are best forgotten.

6

The hair salon is warm and smells of hairspray. I made the appointment a few days ago. They're offering discounts if you don't mind letting a trainee loose on your head, and I don't. People who have to ask their mothers for pocket money can't afford to be too fussy about these things.

With each snip of the scissors, the curve of my skull is slowly revealed. My cheekbones look sharper. I feel lighter and freer than before, as if the weight of my past has also been shed. If only that were true. If only we could cut out the bits of our life we don't like. The bits that fill us with dread and self-loathing. If only we could excise them like warts or lumps and wait for the scar tissue to seal the wound.

I brush away the slivers of hair that sit on my gown-covered lap like pale wood shavings and try to steer my mind away from its usual course, the one it always takes when I start thinking like this. I read Josh's message for what must be the twentieth time. Wednesday has come around a lot sooner than I expected, and I still haven't decided if I'll go. It says to meet him *outside* the Old Schooner. Although there's still a chance he might suggest we pop in for a beer before we go to his dad's, so I need to have some excuses at the ready. Just in case I end up going.

Here's what I'll say: *I'm not that thirsty, to be honest.* Or, *Actually, I'm trying not to drink during the week.* No, not that, because then he might ask me at the weekend. What about *I've gone right off pubs lately,* or *The Old Schooner's a bit of a dive, isn't it?* or *I'm not really a pub person.*

The one thing I know for certain I *won't* say is: *The thing is, Josh, I'm a recovering alcoholic, so if you don't mind, I'd rather we didn't.*

Why can't I just say that? Why is it so damn hard?

"Wow!" Josh says. "You look fantastic. I nearly didn't recognize you."

He pecks me on the cheek, then falls in beside me. After all that worrying, he doesn't even mention the pub. It feels odd, having to match my pace to someone else's. It's as much as I can do to keep up with his long, easy strides. Still, at least there aren't any awkward silences. He has the easy confidence of someone who went to private school. He's got the voice too. Simon would hate him on principle.

They couldn't be more different, the two of them, and yet something about Josh reminds me a little of Simon. It's how he makes me feel, as if the two of us have known each other far longer than we have. It was like that with Simon too, before everything turned to shit.

My pulse quickens. Why am I still thinking about him? Now I can't stop myself glancing over my shoulder. Simon once said he'd kill any man who took me away from him. And then he'd kill me. It was only the drink talking, but still . . .

"Did you grow up round here?" I ask him. Anything to take my mind off the image that's just lodged itself in my head, of Simon watching me from the end of the road, tracking my every movement. My fingers tighten round the juggling ball in my pocket.

"No," Josh says. "I was born and raised in Berkshire. When my mum died, Dad sold the house. Couldn't bear the memories, I suppose." He pauses. "He bought a houseboat. Lived on it for years. It had been one of their dreams, to live on a boat, so I suppose he was doing it for her. Then he visited his aunt, who lived out this way, saw this place was up for sale, and that was that."

"I know what it's like to lose a parent. My dad died three years ago."

I don't usually talk about Dad—it's too painful. But after Mum's comment yesterday, he keeps coming into my thoughts.

Josh has the grace not to say anything, but there's a depth to his silence—a comfort to it.

Five minutes later we turn into a wide graveled driveway at the bottom of a narrow country lane. The driveway sweeps round in a curve toward a double-fronted Victorian villa that's about five times the width of my mother's tiny cottage.

The front door is on the latch. Josh opens it and waves me inside. As soon as I step over the threshold the house welcomes me and all the tension I've been holding in my lower jaw and shoulders falls away. My eyes travel from the high ceilings to the newly plastered walls and the bare gray floorboards.

"It's beautiful."

Josh laughs. "We've only just started."

"But the house itself, its dimensions and its . . . its aura. It's perfect."

A man in paint-splattered overalls emerges from the room on the right. He has the same facial structure as Josh, the same tousled blond hair, except his is finer and starting to recede. He also has tortoiseshell glasses perched on the end of his nose.

"It *does* have an aura, doesn't it?" he says. "See, Josh? It's not just your old man who senses these things." He comes toward me, hand outstretched. "I'm Richard. You must be Astrid," he says, his voice a fraction deeper than his son's, and I realize, in that split second, that I'm sexually attracted to both of them but that the new, sober Astrid will make a point of burying this thought and not returning to it under any circumstances.

"Come and look at the view," Josh says, and I follow him into one of the rooms on the left, a double parlor filled with light. Original fireplaces with marble surrounds are in both halves of the room. The walls in here have been painted white, the floorboards sanded.

"You can see all the way down to Langan's Creek and Brintock Island," Richard says, following us in. "Although the best view's from upstairs, of course."

I'm speechless. This beautiful house, the huge marshland skies merging with the mudflats. The birds circling overhead, the moored boats. I could stand at this window for hours and watch the tide creep over the salt marsh.

My voice, when it comes, is barely a whisper. "I love it."

"Come on, I'll give you the grand tour," Josh says, and now he's leading me through the house, each room a work in progress. The kitchen has been gutted. A cold tap sticks out of the wall over a washing-up bowl and the stand-alone gas oven has been left connected, but otherwise there's nothing but an old pine table that appears to be serving as a temporary food station. It's covered with plates and mugs and crumbs and half-empty packets of teabags, and salami and tomatoes. A small chrome microwave has been balanced on a chair and a massive fridge hums in the corner.

"This wall is being knocked down," Josh says, flinging his arm out in an expansive gesture. "Dad wants the kitchen to be one huge space with a long table in the middle and free-standing units."

I can picture it already. It will be stunning. Like one of those kitchens you see in glossy interior-design magazines. Josh's dad must be minted.

Upstairs, it's more of the same. High-ceilinged rooms with tiled fireplace surrounds and bare floorboards, some with the plaster still drying out, some already painted white.

"This is where I'm sleeping," Josh says, and for a few, excruciating seconds we're both staring at a king-size bed with the plumpest, whitest, most inviting-looking bedding I've ever seen. He must feel it too, this energy between us. It's almost palpable. I walk over to the window, my back to the bed, and focus instead on the view, which is, as Richard said, even better from up here.

When Josh comes over to join me, we don't talk. We don't even look at each other. But we both know what's going to happen. Maybe not today, or tomorrow. Maybe not even this week. But sometime soon.

If I let it.

"It was called 'the snug' in the property details," Richard says. The three of us are standing in the small, dark room in the middle of the house. "But somehow I don't see myself chilling out in here. It's too dingy. Too cramped."

"It's about the same size as my mum's living room," I say.

A fleeting look of discomfort passes over Richard's face. He must think I'm making a point, and I'm not. It was an observation, that's all. This is my problem. I blurt things out without thinking.

"But her room's much sunnier," I add. "And why would you want to be in here when you have all those other lovely rooms?"

Now I'm making it worse. Rubbing his nose in the fact that he's lucky enough to have this huge place while some people have to muddle through in poky little rabbit warrens. What's wrong with me?

"So what I was thinking," he says, "is that I could turn it into a piece of art instead."

"What sort of thing do you have in mind?"

"I don't know. A window, maybe? Or is that too clichéd?"

My eyes sweep round in an arc. "A *trompe l'œil* only really works from one point of view." I take a step back. "So in this case, you'd need to paint something on the wall that faces you as you come through the door. This one here." I pat it with the flat of my hand, enjoying the feel of cold plaster on my palm.

"You're the expert," Richard says.

"Hardly. But I have painted a couple in the past." The dim and distant past, but he doesn't need to know that. "To work best, the deceit needs to fit into the setting exactly." Heat floods my cheeks and I'm glad the room is dark. How would they react if they knew that I was deceiving them right now? That, just like a *trompe l'œil*, I'm one big, fat lie.

"I mean, there'd be no point painting a range of mountains, not when you live in one of the flattest counties in Britain."

Richard and Josh laugh.

"But if, for instance, you had a picture of an open door leading onto an old wooden jetty and a boat bobbing on some water, then that would match the existing landscape. Shall I play around with some ideas? Do some sketches?"

I can't believe I just said that. Art takes practice. It's like a muscle that needs to be worked. I haven't done anything like this for years. What if I've lost the ability to draw? And now that I've offered to do some sketches, there's every possibility he'll ask me to do the painting as well. Oh God! What have I done?

And yet there's a small throb of excitement I can't deny. I felt it almost as soon as I entered this room.

Richard pushes his glasses up his nose and smiles. "Would you? That'd be fantastic!" He glances at Josh and I sense their silent communication. "Are you staying for supper, Astrid? We could get some fish and chips if you like."

He's looking straight at me now, his pale-blue eyes unnervingly intense.

"I've got a rather nice bottle of red we could have with it," he says, and for one heart-stopping moment I have the feeling he sees right through me. All the way to my rotten core.

And now I'm mumbling something about having to leave. I'm stuffing my arms in my coat and retracing my steps through the house, aware of the shocked silence behind me, how odd I must seem to them, how rude and ungrateful. But I can't stay here any longer. I just can't.

She's in a real state—look at her.

I wait till she reaches the top of the lane before I set off in the same direction. Long, purposeful strides like I know where I'm going, like I've got someplace to be. By the time I turn onto the main road, she's way ahead of me, waiting for a gap in the traffic.

Why doesn't she just step out? That would really be something, wouldn't it? I can almost hear the screech of tires and the sickening thwack as her body wraps itself around the front of an SUV. See her shoot into the air then land on the tarmac like a broken doll, skidding along, her limbs sticking out at weird angles, her head all smashed in.

Better still, I'd be the one behind the wheel. The one who couldn't stop in time, who didn't even try. For one intense second, I'd see the look of horror in her eyes. Then she'd bounce off the windscreen with a dull thud and I'd drive straight over her. Hear the crunch of her bones.

7

"As soon as he mentioned the wine, I just mumbled my excuses and left. God knows what they think of me."

I stare at my lap. I never intended to tell them any of this, but that's what happens at AA. It's like a mutual bloodletting.

"I know I did the right thing, but I still wish I was there and not here." A fat tear lands on my knee. "That's it. That's all I want to say."

David smiles. "Thank you for sharing that with us, Astrid." For a second, he looks as though he might offer me some words of comfort. I can tell he wants to, but he's sticking to the rules. People like him always do.

"Does anyone else want to speak?" he says.

The tearful woman with the red shoes from last time—tonight she's wearing boots—folds her arms then unfolds them and clasps her hands in her lap. Will she pass again? It's her prerogative; of course it is. No one's forcing her to share—there are more than enough people at these things who enjoy the sound of their own voices almost as much as they used to enjoy a drink or twenty—but at some point she'll have to, or why come at all?

I try to send her a telepathic message. *For Christ's sake, just get it over with.*

"My name is Helen," she says.

Damn, I'm good.

Her voice is stilted, robotic. There are big red blotches on her neck. *Come on, love. Can't you feel the waves of goodwill radiating toward you?*

"And I'm an alcoholic."

The words tumble out in a rush. We all exhale in unison, or maybe it's just my own breath I hear. "Hello, Helen," we all chant back. One or two heads make those encouraging nodding movements. The woman with eyes like marbles (sixty-three days sober, had a "major setback after losing her son, but back on course now, God willing") makes a self-conscious little clapping gesture. Thank God we're not in America or we'd all be whooping. As it is, that woman from the charity shop is smiling her stupid fucking smile. Rosie. The name doesn't suit her. Too sweet and girly for a sixty-something alcoholic.

I cross my ankles and focus on my Doc Martens.

"Alcohol has stolen everything from me," Helen says. More nodding. I know what's coming next. It's the same old story. The blackouts. The hangovers from hell. The revolving-door cycle of ER visits. We're all just variations on a theme.

She's crossed her arms again and is rocking backward and forward in her chair. I want to tell her that sharing gets easier the more times you do it, but we're not allowed to interrupt or give advice or talk over people. Discussions so easily veer out of control, turn into disagreements, arguments. AA isn't the place for all that. It's a place to share, to listen.

"I've lost my home," she says. "My career." The rocking stops. "And the only man I've ever loved."

I squeeze the ball in my right pocket so hard I think it might split.

It happened again, on the way here. The smell of his aftershave in the air. More subtle this time—the merest trace—but it was there just the same. I'm losing it, I must be. How would he know where I am? I never brought him here. Not once.

I try to focus on Helen's share, tell myself it's just my subconscious warning me not to get involved with Josh and his dad, reminding me that I'm damaged goods, that I don't *do* normal. Certainly not "middle class, posh house, one room as a fucking art installation" normal.

"He was everything to me," Helen says. "I loved him so much."

My throat burns. That's what Simon used to say, in the beginning, that I was everything to him. "I love you heart, body, and soul, Astrid Phelps," he'd say, and then he'd grin and follow it up with: "Your body, especially."

How could I ever have thought I could leave him behind? He'll never let me go. Never. Wherever I go from now on, whatever I do, he'll follow me. I know he will.

"Sometimes I wonder what the hell is wrong with me." There's a catch in Helen's voice and for a second I think she might start crying, but she doesn't. She's found her voice at last. Except it's my voice too. It's as if she's tapped into my brain and downloaded all my demons.

"I can't function without alcohol. Not properly. I don't know what to say, what to do." She twists her fingers in her lap. "It's like I'm endlessly treading water, wearing myself out just trying to stay afloat while everyone else is effortlessly swimming length after length after length."

I stare at her. That's it. That's exactly how it is.

"I don't like the person I become when I'm drinking," she says. "But at least that person doesn't have to think, or feel."

She looks up then and I nod, my lips clamped together. If I open my mouth, I'm scared I'll make some kind of noise.

"At least I don't have to face the fact that I'm a complete and utter failure, that I've ruined every good thing that's ever happened, every chance I've ever had of leading a normal, happy life."

Our eyes meet. She might be older than me and dress like a librarian, but for those few seconds we're exactly the same.

This time, I stay on for a coffee. The little "after-the-meeting meeting." The silver-haired man in the charcoal suit—Jeremy, fifteen years sober, Christ, that sounds like a life sentence—hands me a carton of semi-skimmed milk. I shake my head, so he passes it to Helen instead. Her hand trembles as she pours it into her cup. I can't be the only one who's noticed.

Jeremy turns to face me. "Are you new to the area, Astrid?" I know he's just being friendly, but there's something about him that gives me the creeps. He's too charming. Too *nice*.

"Yes. I used to live in London."

Rosie materializes at his side. She does one of those slow nods, as if she already knows this about me, as if I've got the word "Londoner" engraved on my forehead.

"Me too," she says, tucking a strand of hair behind her ear and hoisting an overstuffed patchwork bag farther up her shoulder. "I moved here when my mother died."

She looks like the sort of person who might be expecting me to respond with something sympathetic, but I've never been much good at platitudes, so I tend not to bother. It's either that or say the wrong thing.

Jeremy clears his throat. The silence between us lengthens.

"Flinstead's a funny old place, isn't it?" he says.

My neck feels all hot and sticky. This is turning into a dry version of a cocktail party. I blink away the image of a classic daiquiri, a wheel of lime clinging to a salt-rimmed glass. I should never have stayed on. What was I thinking?

"It is, yes."

A strange expression flickers over his face, as if he wants to say more but can't find the words. I look away in case he does, and the woman with funny eyes who tried to start a round of applause earlier gives me a sly glance from across the room. She's been doing it all evening.

"Your hair looks lovely," Rosie says. "Not that it didn't look good before, but . . ." She makes a nervous clicking noise at the back of her throat.

I touch my head. I feel naked without my braids. "Thanks."

"So whereabouts in Flinstead do you live?" she says.

"With my mother."

It's an instinctive, passive-aggressive response, I know it is, but I don't elaborate. For some reason, Rosie grates on me. She blinks, slowly and lazily, like a cat.

Jeremy hands her a mug of coffee. "Did you manage to find somewhere to stay?" he asks.

Rosie shakes her head. "Still looking, I'm afraid. But I've found somewhere temporary."

Just as I'm heading for the door, she puts her arm out to stop me. Her fingers settle on my shoulder like a little bird. "You don't happen to know of any flatshares in the area, do you, Astrid? Or anyone who might need a lodger?"

"Er, no. Sorry."

My hand is on the door handle.

"Astrid?"

I turn round.

"Keep coming back," she says. "It works if you work it."

I'm standing in the alleyway by the side of the church, trying to light a cigarette in the wind, when Helen comes out. She cups her hands round my lighter to shield the flame.

"Thanks," I say at last.

I offer her a smoke, but she declines. "That's the one vice I *have* managed to resist. Although sometimes I'm sorely tempted to take it up. There's only so much coffee you can drink."

"The stuff in there's revolting," I say.

Helen nods. "The coffee's shit too."

We both laugh, just as the young man with acne appears at the top of the alleyway. He stops, momentarily startled, then hurries on past, eyes down, collar up.

Helen's forehead puckers into a worried frown as we watch him disappear into the darkness. "I hope he doesn't think we were laughing at *him*."

"Well, if he does, I'm sure he'll soon get over it."

"By the way," she says, "what did Rosie say to you when you were leaving?"

I tilt my head to one side and look at her from under my eyebrows. "*Keep coming back. It works if you work it.*" Helen widens her eyes. "Some people add another bit on the end: *So work it, you're worth it*. It's an AA slogan," I say. "There are loads of them out there."

We're walking away from the church now. Apart from the click of Helen's heels on the pavement and the faint roar of the wind coming off the sea, it's eerily quiet. No revelers shouting. No music spilling from bars. No cars whooshing by. I miss the noise and bustle of London. The way it barely takes a nap. Not like Flinstead, with its slippers on and cocoa warming, its curtains drawn against the dark.

"So what do you *really* think of AA?" she says.

I slide my eyes to the side. I'm pretty sure she's as cynical about the whole thing as I am, but maybe she's just testing me out.

"Well, you read all sorts of stuff about it being like a cult, don't you, and I have to admit, I'm not convinced it's for me. But I'm giving it a try." I don't tell her that without Mum forcing me to go I probably wouldn't.

"So are you working your way through the Twelve Steps?"

"Kind of."

Should I tell her what I really feel? That I have an issue with just about every single one of those damn steps and that, even if I could get beyond the God thing, which I'm not sure I can, I still don't buy into the notion that a set of non-medical principles is the only cure for what is meant to be a disease, for Christ's sake, a neurobiological condition.

"I guess I have a problem with the whole God thing," I tell her.

"I know what you mean," Helen says.

We're coming up to Mum's turning in a minute. I could say goodbye and shake her off if I wanted, but something keeps me walking. There's a connection between us, even if it is just a healthy skepticism about AA.

"You'd better watch out," I say. "Now that I've given Rosie the brush-off, it'll be your turn next week."

"If you ask me, she's already decided you're her pet project. Did you see the way she was looking at you when you were talking?"

"No, but then I try not to make eye contact when I'm sharing. It puts me off."

"God, yeah, I know what you mean."

We've cut through into Flinstead Road now and are heading toward the sea. A small group of drinkers spills out of the pub ahead of us and, instinctively, we both cross the road and quicken our pace. We don't say anything. Don't need to.

"Right, then, this is me." Helen stops outside a block of flats near the front. "See you next meeting?"

"Try keeping me away."

I watch as she taps a security code into a panel and opens the heavy glass door. As soon as it clicks shut behind her my confidence evaporates and all I can think of is Simon creeping up behind me. The hairs on the back of my neck stand on end. This is ridiculous.

I set off in the direction of the sea. It's that same compulsion I had the other night, to push myself out of my comfort zone, refuse to be frightened.

Down on the beach the moon silvers the sand and I can't tell whether the tide's going out or coming in. I shouldn't have come down here. I should have gone straight home, but that's part of the attraction. Maybe that's always been my problem. Doing things other people don't do. Being fearless.

I have this fantasy of breaking in to a beach hut and setting up camp there. Living like a fugitive, venturing out only at night, when Flinstead sleeps. I could probably get away with it too, for a while. I slept on a beach once, somewhere in Spain. Before things started to go wrong, back in the days when I thought I had a plan. When I was managing my relationship with drink perfectly well, thank you. Simon and me, tanked up on cheap wine. There'd been a barbecue, music, people dancing. I had sand in my hair and filthy feet. We'd just done it under an opened-out sleeping bag, on our sides, thrusting silently against each other. It was the happiest I've ever been.

The thought of Josh's muscular, tanned limbs splayed out on that big white bed flashes into my mind. I try to block it out, but I can't. It seems like a betrayal. How stupid is that, after everything that's happened?

The creeks will be filled to the brim now, the tidal flats submerged. And downstairs, on the pine table in that dark, echoey kitchen, an empty bottle of red and the remains of a fish-and-chip supper. Did I even say goodbye?

The wind is whipping up the waves. The tide's definitely coming in. It's creeping farther and farther up the sand. Fast and stealthy. In another half-hour it'll be slapping against the sea wall. Inky black against the worn gray stone. I'm aware of its brooding presence, teeming with alien life-forms. Nothing between me and the vast expanse of the North Sea but a thin stretch of silvery-gray sand. Nothing between me and the past but a racing heartbeat and a dry mouth.

The moon disappears behind a cloud and something about the rasping sound of the waves on the sand makes me shiver. What am I doing here? It's not thrilling anymore, it's frightening. I'm all on my own in the dark and I'm vulnerable. Defenseless. If anything happened to me down here, nobody would hear me scream. I'm not even sure my voice would work.

I hurry to the next set of steps and grab hold of the rail, haul myself up, visions of a fifteen-foot wave crashing over my head and dragging me back down. The steps are slippery with algae and for a second I think my feet are going to disappear from under me. When I reach the safety of the promenade, a yelp of relief erupts out of my mouth. When did I become such a scaredy-cat?

But as I'm heading back toward the cliff path, the unease returns. I have the sense that I'm not alone, that someone or something is watching me. It's the exact same feeling I had in the Fisherman's Shack when Josh was at the counter. Goosebumps swarm from my elbows to my shoulders. My breath is like ice at the back of my throat.

I glance over my shoulder, but the prom behind me is empty, as far as I can make out. I press on toward the path. I won't run. I won't. But just as I'm approaching the bottom of the slope, I see the dull orange glow of a cigarette. The nape of my neck shrinks. Someone is leaning against a beach hut about twenty-five yards ahead: a man, barely visible in the darkness.

He steps out of the shadows and my insides plummet. That same old donkey jacket. That hat. This isn't some figment of my imagination. He's there, right in front of me.

I run, or try to, my legs heavy and cumbersome, each step like running through water. The slope is steeper than I remember. Steeper and longer. My heart knocks against my breastbone. My DMs slip and scuff on the concrete as I lurch and scramble up. For one appalling second I think I'm going to pitch forward face-first, but I right myself just in time. I mustn't fall. If I fall, he'll catch up with me.

I'm nearly at the top now. Another few seconds and the ground will even out. I'll be on the greensward and it'll be easier. I listen for the sounds of pursuit, but all I hear is the heaving of my lungs, the pounding of blood in my ears. I plunge onward, my chest ragged with pain.

Somehow, I make it to the road without stopping. It isn't till I've crossed to the other side that I dare to look back. A man stands, motionless, at the top of the path, staring after me. No donkey jacket. No trapper hat. Just a regular guy in a fleece and beanie. I can't see his face from here, but something about his posture tells me he's alarmed by my behavior. He won't approach me. Not now. He'll already be feeling guilty. For being a man. A man who's had the temerity to be having a smoke and watching the sea at night, who's managed to terrify a woman just by being there.

I slump against the wall of someone's front garden. What the hell is wrong with me?

8

Overnight, the wind has died down and the skies have cleared. I pull the covers back and swing my legs onto the floor, astounded, as I am every morning, that—physically at least—I feel fine.

I open my bedroom window and breathe in the fresh morning air. I slept, eventually, but traces of last night's fear and confusion still linger. I need something to occupy my mind and stop all this weird shit clogging it up. The sooner I start working on ideas for the trompe l'œil, the better. Plus, I can prove to Josh and his dad that I'm not a complete idiot.

The art shop is closed and, for a minute or so, I'm consumed with rage and resentment. What's wrong with the shopkeepers round here? They seem to make up their opening hours as they go along. Why is it shut on the one morning I need to buy a decent sketch pad and some pencils? It's so unfair. Now I'm going to have to make do with a bog-standard one from the newsagent's, and if it's that cheap, shiny stuff it'll be worse than useless.

I'm aware of the tension in my jaw and that stupidly fast walk I always do when I'm stressed out. I need to calm down. Breathe. It isn't the end of the world. It's just a minor setback. I have to get things into perspective. Stop being so uptight all the time. No won-der I keep seeing things that aren't there. I'm a nervous wreck.

All these feelings are so destabilizing. For years, I've drowned them in alcohol. Now they're clamoring to the surface and gasping for air. A tsunami of emotions and sensations. This must be what it's like for a blind person who's suddenly able to see. I have to sep-arate out the shapes and colors of my changing moods, learn to recognize them for what they are.

By the time I reach the newsagent's, I'm breathing normally again and, as luck would have it, their stationery section is better than I thought and I find a pad that's halfway decent. The woman behind the counter smiles at me and I smile back. It's easy, really. I just have to practice mindfulness and live in the moment. If I keep on acting as if everything's fine, then maybe it will be. Maybe it's as simple as that.

I'm still smiling to myself like an idiot when I come out of the shop. I don't know what makes me turn right toward the sea in-stead of left toward home, but I do. Maybe it's intuition. My foot freezes mid-air. I can't believe my eyes. The mannequin in the Oxfam window display is wearing a Cranberries *No Need to Argue* world-tour black T-shirt. Simon had one just like it.

It's not his. Of course it isn't. How could it be his?

I inch toward the window, compelled to look closer but dread-ing what I'll see. Because if it's there, the small bleach stain near the hem on the left side, then I'll know for sure. I'll know it's the same limited-edition vintage T-shirt he bought off eBay. And if it is . . . ?

I peer at it, my eyes devouring the photograph printed on the front. It's the very same one. Noel and Mike Hogan and Fergal Lawler sprawled indolently on the grass and Dolores O'Riordan—the tragically *late* Dolores O'Riordan—with her elfin haircut, standing in the foreground. Simon's voice whispers in my ear. "Ev-erybody else is doing it, so why can't we?"

My stomach contracts. I stand, motionless. It isn't real, it's in my head. It must be. Just like all the rest of it. It's what he said that first time I met him, and I'd smirked, thinking it was a come-on. Then I heard what track was playing and felt like a right twat. It was "I Still Do" by the Cranberries and what he'd just said was the name of their debut album.

I can't see whether there's a bleach stain on the T-shirt from here because of the angle of the mannequin's arm. I'll have to go inside and take a closer look. But as I'm moving toward the door a deep voice calls my name from the other side of the street.

It's Richard Carter, Josh's dad. He's hurrying toward me, grinning from ear to ear. "Hi there, Astrid. I see you've bought a sketch pad."

Flustered, I hold it out in front of me, as if I've only just realized it's in my hands.

"Yes, I'm going to make a start later today."

"Fantastic. I can't wait to see what you come up with." He slides his glasses up his nose with his finger. "To be honest, I was worried I'd scared you away last night."

My cheeks burn. "Sorry about that. I'd promised my mum I'd go with her to the doctor's." The lie slips out automatically. "I only just got back in time."

"Ah, I see. Maybe another time, eh?"

"Yes, that'd be nice."

"It's a good thing you're doing, Astrid. Looking after your mother. Lots of young people wouldn't put their careers on hold the way you have."

I force a smile and watch as he raises his hand in a mock salute and marches off. He has the same confident, loping stride as his son. Now he's stopped to talk to a woman with red hair. She turns and looks in my direction. Is he saying something about me? No, of course he isn't. I'm being paranoid, as usual. She's probably just keeping an eye out for a traffic warden. Why do I always think everything's about me?

I turn back to the shop, bracing myself for what I'm about to do. I'm going to go inside and check the hem of that T-shirt. The T-shirt that can't possibly be Simon's. It's a coincidence, nothing more. But in the short time I've been talking to Richard, someone has hung a "Closed" sign at the door.

Josh's text comes through just as I'm hurrying back to the Oxfam shop to see if it's reopened.

> Hi Astrid. Dad said he bumped into you earlier. Hope your mum's ok? Let me know if you fancy going out for a drink. Or maybe I'll see you down on the beach sometime? x

I stop to tap out a reply.

> A walk on the beach would be good. What about Saturday? x

I could suggest tomorrow, but I don't want to sound too eager.

> Great. Ten o'clock at the spit? x

> Ten is good. x

I fire off the last message just seconds before I reach the shop. I stop dead in my tracks. This can't be happening. The mannequin is wearing the same black jeans and blue trainers as before, but the T-shirt is different. It's a plain gray crew-neck. I've only been gone half an hour and the shop was shut. Surely someone hasn't bought it already?

I open the door and go in. The sight of Rosie behind the counter gives me a start. I'd forgotten she volunteers in here.

"Hi, what happened to the Cranberries T-shirt in the window?"

Rosie lifts a pile of books from a chair and places them on the counter between us, starts scribbling prices in pencil on their in-side covers. "If it's not there now, then we must have sold it. I've only just got in."

Why do I get the impression she's lying?

"You don't happen to know who donated it, do you?"

She carries on writing. "Sorry, no. Sometimes people just leave things outside in bags." She looks up then and fingers the silver locket at her neck. "What did you say it was?"

"A Cranberries *No Need to Argue* T-shirt."

She makes an "O" shape with her mouth. "I don't remember see-ing it. Doug must have dressed the mannequin this morning and sold it before I came in."

"When will he be back?"

"I don't know. He's gone home sick. That's why I've had to come in on my day off."

She carries the books over to a set of shelves and slots them into the gaps. Then she turns and gives me that sly smile of hers, as if we are conspirators in a secret, which of course we are. We are mem-bers of a secret club. What's that Groucho Marx quote? "I don't want to belong to any club that will accept me as a member." AA is the sort of club nobody really *wants* to join. We might not have a special handshake, but we have our own literature and our polite little rituals and, thanks to our founder and his insistence on ano-nymity, we have our secret code. We are all "friends of Bill W."

"How *are* you?" she says.

"I'm fine."

She's got that strange look on her face again, as if she knows things about me, or thinks she does. This is what some of these old-timers at AA are like. Just because they've been round the block a few times. Just because they've laid themselves bare and dished themselves up to God on a plate, they think that gives them the right to your secrets too. Perhaps it's like Scientology. Tell them all your shit and they've won. They've got you.

"I'd better go," I say.

She reaches out and rests three fingers on my wrist. "You will come back? To meetings, I mean."

I nod. Her fingers are still on my wrist.

"He wants you to," she says. "He's watching over you."

I give her a blank stare. Then it dawns on me. She's talking about God. She withdraws her hand and I turn away. I don't want to offend her, not if she really believes in all that, but I can't stay and listen to it. I really can't.

Outside on the street, I stare once again at the mannequin. There's something menacing about its faceless white head, the way it's cocked to one side. Could someone really have bought that T-shirt and this Doug person have re-dressed the mannequin in the short time it took me to go home and come back again? It's possible, of course it is, and anyway, there's no reason to think the T-shirt was Simon's. There must be a fair few of them knocking about, limited edition or not. But what are the odds of one of them turning up in a charity shop in the very same town I'm now living in and of me seeing it?

Could I have imagined it? I haven't had a drink in months. I'm stone-cold sober, but my mind's still playing tricks on me. What with thinking I saw him down by the beach huts last night and now this . . .

But what if I'm *not* imagining it? What if it really *was* him and he's deliberately trying to freak me out? I hurry away from the shop window, trying to convince myself that the mannequin with no eyes isn't watching me as I go.

If only I'd been able to check for that bleach stain.

9

As I walk home, I try everything I can to get that mannequin out of my head. I watch my feet pound the pavement. *Left right left. I had a good home and I left. I left on my own and it served me right. Left right left.* It's a marching song my nan used to sing—something her nan had taught her. Funny the random things that pop into your head. Things you thought you'd forgotten rising to the surface like bubbles. Dear old Nan.

I'm so deep in thought I almost walk straight into a pushchair, swerve out of the way just in time. The young mother tuts and I mumble an apology and keep going, head down, heart thumping. I know what's coming next and there's nothing I can do to shut it down. There's a painful lump at the back of my throat as all the bad things crowd into my mind at once. Things my nan would struggle to believe. I blink away the tears of shame and hurry toward the cottage, narrowly avoiding a dead baby bird splattered on the pavement like a tiny fetus.

My stomach lurches. It's so unexpected and horrible, so pink and raw. The poor, helpless little thing. I cringe at the thought of what it would have felt like if I'd trodden on it. The soft squelch. The splintering of tiny bones. Maybe if I was wearing my DMs I'd nudge it off the curb into the road so that nobody has to go through that, but I'm wearing my cheap plimsolls today and can't bear the thought of its limp little body rolling against my toes, gathering the grit of the pavement in the folds of its skin.

Mum's sorting through a pile of post in the porch when I arrive.

"Anything from the DWP?" I say.

She gives me a blank look.

"Department of Work and Pensions. My benefits letter?"

She shakes her head. "It's all junk mail."

She hands me the pile of leaflets and flyers to dump in the recycling box by the front door. Are they ever going to sort out my claim? It's so demoralizing living on paltry handouts from my mother at the age of thirty-two.

She notices my sketch pad. "Oh, that's good, darling. I was going to suggest that you start drawing again, but I didn't want you to think I was nagging."

I tell her about the sketches I've offered to do for Josh's dad.

"I think I've still got some of your old charcoal and graphite pencils somewhere," she says. "Do you want me to look for them?"

I nod and her face softens in pleasure. It's so rare to see her smile these days and, before I know what's happening, my eye sockets are tingling. Mum used to be so proud of my art. She used to pin my pictures on the kitchen wall when I was little. She even got a couple of them framed, the ones I did for my art GCSE. They're still on the wall in the living room.

I look away. It's one of those charged moments that seems to encapsulate everything that's gone wrong between us, one of those moments when either one of us might reach out and say something profound, something that spans the chasm between us, and I know it should be me who says it.

But now I'm sliding my plimsolls onto the shoe rack in the porch and Mum steps back into the hall. The moment has passed.

. . .

It's ten past ten on Saturday and Josh is standing by the spit, gazing out to sea. He hears me approach and turns, a slow smile spreading across his face. He didn't think I was coming.

I like that about him, the visibility of his emotions. His openness. Simon was always so guarded, so secretive. I used to ask him what he was thinking, and he'd just narrow his eyes and say, "You don't want to know." But I did. I always wanted to know. Even when I didn't.

"I wasn't sure whether to give up on you," Josh says.

"Sorry. Lost track of the time." In fact, I was ironing my jeans dry, then cleaning my teeth a second time and swilling my mouth out with Mum's extra-strong mouthwash (alcohol-free, it goes without saying), holding it there till my tongue burned. No way am I going to smell like Rosie.

He puts his hands on my shoulders and draws me toward him, so close I see flecks of gold in the green of his irises. He brings the palms of his hands to my cheeks and cups my face.

"Your cheeks are cold," he says. It's intimate, and a hundred times more exciting than a kiss, but I wish he'd kiss me anyway. Especially after all that effort. A mouth this fresh deserves to be kissed.

"How's your mum today?"

I swallow hard. Lying used to come so easily I didn't even have to think about it. Perhaps if the notion of my hale-and-hearty mother succumbing to depression, or any other illness come to that, wasn't so outrageous, I wouldn't be having this much of a problem. My mother is not the sort of woman who needs looking after. She might be small and thin, but she has wrists and nerves of steel. I've seen her advance upon a gang of youths with nothing more than a wooden spoon in her hand. I've seen her wrestle a live rat from a drain.

"She's not too bad at the moment," I say.

"I'm glad you got back in time for her appointment."

"Yes. Me too." I clear my throat. "Which way shall we walk? Toward Mistden?"

"Why not?"

The sea looks gray and uninviting today. Large rollers sweep in at a curve and break noisily on the shore. Even on a weekend, at this time of morning on an overcast day there aren't many people about. The odd dog-walker or jogger. A mother making sandcastles for her toddler, who promptly kicks them over and shrieks with high-pitched giggles. That girl in the gray puffer jacket again, marching along the esplanade, head bowed against the wind. But for long stretches of time we have the beach to ourselves.

Josh makes a sudden detour round the name "Billy," which has been written in the sand in big, shaky letters.

"Did you used to do this?" he says. "When you were a kid?"

"Not that I can remember."

"I did. And I used to get really angry when people walked over my handiwork."

"I hated my name so much I wouldn't have wanted it scrawled across a beach for everyone to see."

"Really? I think Astrid's a lovely name."

"So do I. But it isn't the name I grew up with."

He spins round to face me. Why am I telling him this? It's as if I'm approaching the truth from an odd angle. Feeling my way toward it in stages. Trying to make up for the lies.

"Well, come on, then. Don't keep me in suspense. What was it?"

Me and my big mouth. "Hilary."

He narrows his eyes. "You don't look like a Hilary."

"Do I look like an Astrid?"

He puts his head on one side and squints at me. "Yes," he says. "You do." He stoops down to pick up the pointy piece of driftwood that Billy probably used as his pencil. Oh God. I hope he's not going to do what I think he is. *Please don't turn this into a scene from a cheesy movie, Josh.*

He runs his hand over the smooth, bleached wood, then tosses it back onto the sand. I breathe a sigh of relief.

"How did your parents react when you changed it?" he asks. "Were they upset?"

"Mum refused to accept it at first. Thought it was just a silly phase I was going through."

I kick a pebble with the toe of my plimsoll and watch as it shoots across the sand and lands in a dip by the wooden breaker up ahead. Maybe if she hadn't rolled her eyes and tutted every time I refused to respond when she called me Hilary, the novelty would have worn off in time. As it was, her disapproval made me even more determined to go through with it.

"Dad was fine about it. He used to call me Asteroid, just to annoy me."

Dad's face flashes into my mind. Those amused, crinkly eyes. The gentle set of his mouth, always on the point of a smile. The image is so clear, so heart-wrenchingly familiar, it makes me gulp for air.

"I'm sorry," Josh says. "I shouldn't have asked."

"It's okay."

"No, it isn't."

He's standing in front of me now, hands on my shoulders again. His eyes are so kind. I look at them for only a fraction of a second and before I know what's happening it's too late. The grief is never far from the surface. It only takes a tiny trigger and down it comes like an avalanche, collecting all the other debris in its path.

Josh pulls me toward him and I bury my face in his chest. We stay like this for ages. Until his sweatshirt is damp through. Until he strokes my head and kisses my left earlobe. Then we start walking again, except this time we're holding hands.

Look at her. Crying on another man's shoulders. Starting all over again with someone else.

My fingers find the envelope in my pocket and curl around its stiff edges. I work one of the corners under my thumbnail and push it in till it hurts. I do that all the time now. I like the little V-shape it makes at the top of the nailbed. I like the pain—the way it throbs.

She thinks she can reinvent herself just by moving away and cutting her hair. She thinks she's leaving the past behind her. Getting better.

She needs to think again.

10

Somehow or other, we resurface at Josh's dad's house. The table in the kitchen has been cleared and scrubbed. Josh opens the giant fridge and brings out lettuce with dirt still clinging to the leaves, big beefsteak tomatoes, and a small, curved, dusty-looking cucumber, like the type you find in French supermarkets. He blasts the lettuce under the cold tap, then dunks it in a bowl of water before tearing the leaves off one by one and shaking them out with concentrated force over the quarry-tiled floor.

Now he's boiling two eggs in a pan and I've been presented with a glass chopping board, two tomatoes, and a razor-sharp knife. There's something comforting in this silent communication, the wordless allocation of tasks. I like the way the knife drops through the firm red flesh of the tomatoes and lets me slice them really thinly.

I feel like an invalid who's only just been allowed up. Someone who still has to be looked after but is now well enough to do a few basic chores for herself, as long as she is sitting quietly, within sight of the restorative water, gleaming like gray silk beyond the window. Perhaps this is how I'll heal, being here with Josh, in this beautiful house. Perhaps this is where my future begins.

I see it then, on top of the microwave. A half-empty bottle of red. My throat dissolves. They didn't even finish it off. One bottle between two grown men and there's still a couple of glasses left. How is that even possible? Unless, of course, it's another bottle. It must be, surely.

Josh disappears for a few minutes. My hands tremble. There's a roaring sound at the back of my head. The knife slips through my fingers and clatters onto the glass board. I pop the ends of the tomatoes into my mouth and suck the juice out of them, forcing my eyes away from the bottle and toward the tap sticking out of the wall, but its image is burnt into my retinas. If I'm going to tell him, it has to be now. The longer I leave it, the worse it will be.

But when Josh returns, his dad's with him.

"Hi there, Astrid," Richard says. "How are the sketches coming on?"

"Bloody hell, Dad! Give her a chance."

My laugh comes easily. More out of relief than amusement.

"I should have something to show you in a few days."

A few *weeks*, I should have said. A *few weeks*. Why am I putting myself under pressure like this? I haven't even started yet. Too scared I'll have forgotten how.

Richard grins. "Fantastic."

His eyes take in our food preparations. "Right, I'm nipping out to the yacht club for a quick pint and a sandwich. I've got to wait for the plaster in the bathroom to dry out." He taps the side of his nose. "That's my excuse, anyway."

When he's gone and it's just Josh and me, alone in the kitchen, my heart starts to thud because I know what I have to do. And I have to do it now, before my resolve wavers. I have to tell him why I'm really here in Flinstead. Why I'm back home with my mum again after all these years.

"I'm glad Dad bought this house," Josh says. "It's given him a new lease on life. He looks happier than he has in years."

I focus on cutting my hard-boiled egg in half. The bottle of red wine is still making its presence felt from behind my head. I really like Josh. I mean, *really* like him. I like his dad too, and I know he'll ask me to paint the *trompe l'œil* for him, just like I know I'll say yes. I can't wait to get stuck into something creative again, to prove to myself that I'm not completely washed up. The thing is, if I tell him the truth, then everything will be spoiled before it's even begun.

"It's funny," Josh says, "but everyone always thinks he's such a positive, energetic kind of man—and he is, he really is—it's just that they don't see what's behind all that energy, what's driving it." He rests his fork on the side of his plate. This clearly isn't the time to talk about me and my drinking. I should have spoken up sooner.

"My mum's name was Lindsay," he says. His eyes are somewhere else now, some place in the past. "She was a dance teacher." He looks down at his plate and pushes the salad around with his fork. "She died the year I started uni."

I don't ask him how she died. Maybe you have to have lost a parent to know what is, and isn't, the right thing to say. Maybe that's why Simon and I clicked so easily, because we'd both lost our dads. Josh will tell me if he wants to, when the time is right.

"I was twenty-six when my dad died." My throat has closed up and my voice sounds weird, as if it belongs to someone else. Josh reaches across the table and traces a little pattern on the top of my hand with his finger. We finish our lunch in silence, but there's nothing awkward or uncomfortable about it. That one simple gesture is all the communication we need and I wonder whether we'll go upstairs later and make love on that soft white duvet. I hope so.

Afterward, I wash the bowls and cutlery in a washing-up bowl on the table with hot water from the kettle and Fairy Liquid. Then Josh rinses everything under the cold tap over a bucket and hands me each item, one at a time, for me to dry with a stripy linen tea towel that has a clean, pressed look about it, and though part of me is disappointed that he isn't leading me upstairs to make the most of his father's absence, another part thinks how wonderful it is not to rush things, to take care over the preparation of a simple salad, to clean up afterward, quietly, methodically, the skin of our elbows brushing up against each other, the anticipation of more, much more, thrumming gently between us. Why have I never known this before?

That night I have a dream. A nightmare. I'm kneeling before the assembled residents of Flinstead and Mistden in the community hall. Josh's dad is reading a list of my transgressions, every last sordid one, in that weird, monotonous voice poets sometimes use. Every so often, he looks straight at me with those intense blue eyes and I shrink before his gaze.

There are gasps and tuts from the audience. My mum and my nan are both there and so are all the people from AA. Rosie and Jeremy and Helen, and all the rest of them. Josh is there too, sitting at the back in his wetsuit with his head between his hands, water dripping from the ends of his hair onto the dusty parquet floor.

I'm not aware of Simon at first, but then my skin begins to prickle and I sense his presence on the stage, glowering at me. And then at Josh. The hall is now a theater and he's an actor in a play. He's standing over a small heap of clothes on the floor. But then the clothes begin to move and it's a young woman, struggling to get up, her finger pointing straight at me. And all the while a child screams. My stomach turns over on itself.

"Haven't you forgotten something?" she says, her voice ringing out in the hall. Angry and accusing.

But when I wake up, instead of relief, I feel dread. Cold, creeping dread that runs in my veins like a bad drug.

11

Mum's already up and moving about downstairs when the clanging of church bells penetrates my sleeping brain. I didn't think I'd ever fall asleep again after that nightmare, but here I am, rubbing the sleep from my eyes and yawning. I should have kept my window shut.

There's a knock on my bedroom door. "Astrid? Are you awake?" She says it in such a way that, if I weren't already awake, then I would be now.

I pull the duvet over my head and don't answer. I know what she's going to say because she says the same thing every Sunday morning. She's going to ask me if I want to go to the meeting house with her and do whatever it is Quakers do. Sit around in silence communing with God. Holding things "in the light."

"Will you come with me today?" she says.

Why does she persist with this? Surely she must have got the message by now.

"I'll take a rain check, Mum, if you don't mind."

Her silence thrums on the other side of the door. I want to shout, *Isn't it enough that I'm going to AA?* but I press my lips together and wait for her to leave. I've nothing against Quakers—as far as religions go, it's the least offensive and I know it's helped Mum cope with losing Dad. She probably wouldn't have embraced it so readily if it weren't for that—but it's not for me and I wish she'd accept that.

"Well, if you change your mind, I'm not leaving for another half-hour."

"I won't change my mind. I need to get on with those sketches."

I hear her steps move away from the door, then stop. "There's some tea in the pot if you want some."

"Thanks."

She waits for a few seconds, then goes into her bedroom and shuts the door. How does she do that? How does she always manage to make me feel like such a shit? As soon as she opens her mouth, I'm catapulted back into bolshie-teenager mode. Jesus Christ, those bells are annoying!

When Mum's gone, I get up and go downstairs. It might be a sunny day, but the back of the house is dark and chilly on account of its facing north, so I take my sketch pad and pencils and sit outside on the front step, where it's warm and bright, and where the pressure to create something good won't be as strong because I can kid myself I'm a little girl again, doodling to pass the time.

Even so, my hand is unsteady and the marks on the paper are clumsy and childlike. I rip the first sheet up and crumple it into a ball. It should be like riding a bike, shouldn't it? A skill I already possess. I just have to start doing it again and trick my brain into remembering how.

It isn't till I've covered the second page with squiggles and swirls and random, interlocking shapes that I start to relax into it. I'd forgotten how good it feels to get lost in the moment, to feel the pencil moving almost of its own accord, to forget my own mind and its incessant babble. I'm out of practice, for sure, but if I spend this morning getting a feel for it again, maybe I'll go down to the yacht club later and try sketching some of the boats.

A young mother with a pushchair walks past the house. I don't think she's the one who tutted at me the other day, although she could be. She stops for a moment to comfort the toddler, who is whinging loudly and trying to undo the harness.

The grating sound of the child's cry and the sight of its back arching stiffly away from the seat of the pushchair make me remember my dream from last night, and the back of my neck feels cold and clammy. Somewhere in the distance, another set of church bells starts up, and when finally she settles the child and sets off again I turn over a fresh page in my sketch pad and exhale slowly. But any confidence I thought I'd regained has evaporated and my fingers are too sweaty to grip the pencil.

Monday morning. I stoop down and gather the post into my hands. Still nothing from the DWP. I open the front door, wondering if it might have slipped through the postman's fingers and be lying on the porch mat.

Shock roots me to the spot. Shock and fear. There's no mistaking it: the distinctive aroma of Joint by Roccobarocco trapped in the stuffy porch. He's been here. Simon has been to the cottage, stood where I'm standing now. I'm not going mad. This is really happening.

All of a sudden, lightness floods through me. My head falls back and I slump against the doorframe, laughing at my own stupidity. It's the postman I've been catching whiffs of all this time. A postman who likes to smell nice, drawn to a scent that's a little bit different, that as far as I know you can only get online. This isn't Simon's smell after all. The scent in my nostrils is mixed with the chemicals in another man's skin, a swarthy, thickset man in standard-issue Royal Mail T-shirt and gray trousers. It explains why I've smelled it out and about too. I must have seen him loads of times, trundling his red trolley along the streets.

I open the porch door to release it and take a lungful of fresh air. What a fool I've been.

Mum's finishing off her breakfast and doing a crossword in the dining room. I put the pile of post next to her plate.

"Still nothing about my benefits."

"Never mind. You'll hear from them soon, I'm sure you will." Her voice is light, friendly. We're both making a supreme effort to be nice to each other.

"I hope so. I hate not being able to give you any money."

She nods and takes a sip of her tea. "I meant to ask you about Saturday. You were out a long while."

"We went for a walk on the beach. Then he made me lunch."

"That's nice."

She wants to say more, I know she does. She wants to give me another warning about not getting too involved, but she focuses on her crossword instead. I can see that it's a huge struggle for her, not saying what's on her mind. I lay my hand on her shoulder and give it a squeeze. She tilts her head to the side so that her cheek rests briefly on the top of my hand.

In the kitchen she's laid a tea towel over the counter so that half of it is hanging off. This is what she does to let them dry out. It's one of those hard cotton ones with pictures of herbs and their names on it. It must once have been white but now it's dull and gray. It's perfectly clean, but there are old tea stains on it. I think of the soft linen one in Josh's dad's house, how even though they're in the middle of a major refurbishment and the kitchen is a shell, they still have lovely things. Well-sharpened, good-quality knives, pretty crockery, and pristine tea towels.

"By the way," Mum calls out, "don't be surprised if someone pops round in the next day or so to have a look at the house."

"Why? You're not thinking of selling up already, are you?"

She comes into the kitchen and gives me an incredulous look. "Why would I want to do that? No, it's someone who used to live here when she was a child. A young woman. I've seen her standing across the road looking at the house a couple of times lately, so when I saw her this morning I called her over and had a few words. She said she'd be interested to look round, for old times' sake."

Mum dunks her breakfast things in the washing-up bowl. "I was in a bit of a hurry to go out, though, so I said she could drop by next time she was passing."

"Bet you wouldn't have said that if she'd been a man. You want to be careful. She could be anyone."

Mum stares at me. "What do you take me for? A fool?"

"No, of course not. But there are some desperate people out there."

She gives me a level look. "You think I don't know that?"

12

"I was expecting them to be good, but not *this* good," Josh says, peering over his dad's shoulder. "I've never seen such intricate sketches. They're works of art in themselves."

My cheeks flush at the compliment. "Don't be daft. They're really rough. I'll do better ones if you're happy with these designs."

"Happy?" Richard says. "I'm delighted. So when can you start the painting?"

Josh shoots him a look. "Don't you think you should ask her if she wants to first?"

Richard lifts his glasses up and wedges them on top of his head. "Astrid, I'd very much like to commission you to produce this painting for me. Would you please do me the honor of accepting the job? You'll need to tell me what it will cost, of course."

Even though I've been expecting this, I'm still tongue-tied. Agreeing to do privately commissioned work isn't something I've ever done before. I'm not even sure I can competently execute a *trompe l'œil*. Will I really be able to create something that stands up to daily inspection? I mean, it's one thing painting a backdrop in a theater which the audience views from a distance. Their attention is focused on the forefront of the stage, on the actors and the play itself. The words, the music. But taking on something like this, something Richard Carter will have to look at every day of his life, something that will, by its very nature, be scrutinized by guests and visitors—it couldn't be more different.

"I'll need to have a think about the cost. I'd probably paint it onto canvas first, then transfer the image to the wall once you're happy with it. I'll need to see if I can find an easel from somewhere."

"No need," Richard says. "There's one in the attic." He looks at Josh and the room stills. "It used to belong to my wife—a hobby she never quite took up. In fact," he says, now bright and jolly again, "why don't I give you some cash for the materials right now?"

He puts his hand in his pocket and draws out a fat wallet. "Will a hundred and fifty do for starters? Get the best paint you can buy, and whatever else you need. I'd recommend the new art shop on Flinstead Road."

I stare at the wad of notes he's thrusting toward me. I know I should be more professional about this and tell him to wait till I've done an estimate, but my brain is all scrambled. I can't think straight. I'm meant to be a freelance set designer, for God's sake. I should have got my act together yesterday and worked out some figures.

"It's okay," Josh says. "Dad wouldn't be flinging money at you if he didn't trust you."

Richard is still holding the notes out in front of me. It seems too much, but if he wants top-quality paint, that doesn't come cheap. I'll need some new brushes too. It might not even be enough. I take the warm bundle of notes and zip them into my coat pocket.

"You're not going yet, are you?" Josh says. "You'll stay for coffee?"

Richard holds out his hand again, this time for me to shake. "Welcome to the Carter family decorating team." His hand is warm and dry. He smiles and the skin round his eyes crinkles. "Now, if you'll excuse me, I've got a Pilates class to go to. All this decorating does my back in."

Josh makes coffee in a cafetière. He presses the plunger down with the flat of his palm.

"It's decaf, I'm afraid. Dad usually gets proper coffee in for guests but the tin's empty."

"It's fine."

Decaffeinated coffee. Salad lunches. Swimming. Pilates. Bottles of wine that last more than one day. It's like an advert for healthy living. I don't belong here.

So why do I feel like I do?

I don't know whether I'm three or four sips in when I'm aware of Josh looking at me over the rim of his mug. Those kind green eyes drinking me up. Except it's not kindness I'm seeing now. It's desire.

"Let's take our coffee upstairs," he says.

His skin has its own perfume—sweet and warm and dry. I stand, my back against the white wall. He faces me, his hands pressing into the wall so that I'm caged between his arms. I see the shape of his muscles through the thin cotton of his T-shirt. Their strength. He leans forward and brushes his lips against mine. A light, feathery sensation. When I feel the heat of his tongue inside my mouth, I close my eyes, lose myself in the rhythm and intensity of the kiss.

Our coffee grows cold on the windowsill.

Josh is deliberate, thorough. Gentle. Insistent. I thought he'd be shy to start with. Tentative. I thought I might be the one to take the lead and coax the lover out of him, the one he's always dreamed of becoming, but I'm much too late to that party.

He maneuvers me onto the middle of the bed, my legs dangling over the end. Something about the stillness of the white room and the way the duvet billows up around me and the quality of the light from the uncurtained bay window make this seem more like a dream. Maybe that's why I'm just lying here, waiting, uncharacteristically submissive.

Now he's pulling off my trainers and peeling down my jeans and knickers, tugging them over my ankles. He's pulling my legs gently so that my bottom is right at the end of the mattress, and he's kneeling on the floor and he must have seen my flame tattoo, but of course he's not going to say anything about it because we can't speak now.

He can't speak now.

Josh insists on walking me home. "You've got all that cash, remember?"

How could I forget? It's like a living thing in my pocket, rustling and vibrating against my right hip. The sooner I can turn it into paint and brushes, the better.

We've reached the cottages now. "I can't ask you in," I say. "Mum's a bit . . . *anxious* around strangers." Heat surges into my cheeks. "Not that you're a stranger, but . . ."

"It's fine. I understand." He rests his hands on my shoulders and kisses me on my forehead.

"I promised Dad I'd help him sand some floorboards tomorrow," he says. "I'll text you when we've finished. It's a pity it's not warmer or I'd suggest you join me for an evening swim."

"I haven't swum for ages. I don't even know if I've still got a swimsuit."

"I know a place where you can swim naked," he says, holding my gaze. "It'll be bloody cold, though. Cold enough to put that flame out between your thighs." And before I have a chance to reply he gives me the sexiest wink I've ever seen, turns on his heels, and jogs away.

I watch him till he reaches the end of the road and turns the corner, one hand raised in a backward wave, then I float up the path to the front door, still smiling like a lovestruck teenager. Josh might be the most sensible, middle-class man I've ever hooked up with, but when he stood at the end of that bed naked, he might have been Michelangelo's *David* made flesh. If anything's going to expel Simon from my mind, it's having sex with Josh. And I feel safe when I'm with him. Safe and cherished and turned on all at the same time. I've never felt anything quite like this before. Simon turned me on all right, but safe? Nothing about our relationship was safe. It always had a dangerous edge to it. I found it exciting at first. Exhilarating. Someone kind and gentle like Josh wouldn't even have been on my radar. But after what happened . . . Besides, I've seen another side to Josh today. A stronger, passionate side.

Just as I think this day can't get any better, I see a brown envelope lying on the porch mat. My benefits letter. At last. I bend down to pick it up, but as I turn it over I see that it's not at all what I'm expecting. This isn't an official DWP envelope, it's an ordinary one with my name and address in green ink in strange, curly handwriting I don't recognize. Who would be writing to me here? Apart from the staff at the rehab center and the local GP surgery where I registered last week, and the DWP of course, nobody knows where I am.

I slide my thumb under the flap and tear through the top of the envelope. With trembling fingers, I draw out a photo of Simon. It's one I've never seen before. It's black and white and he's leaning against some railings and smiling into the camera. There's nothing else in the envelope. No letter. No note. Just this one black-and-white photo.

I turn it over in my hands and the world tilts. Someone has cut out a small picture of a woman's hand dripping with blood and glued it to the back of the photo.

My stomach twists with fear. Thinking I'm being haunted by my dead boyfriend is one thing, but unless ghosts can use scissors and glue and buy stamps, this is far, far scarier than that.

Someone knows. Someone knows I killed Simon.

Part Two

13

can't look at the photo again. I mustn't. But I do. Of course I do.

He looked like this the day I bumped into him in the park. I hadn't seen him for months, not since we'd split up. He'd never looked so healthy. His skin glowed. Sobriety suited him.

I trace the contours of his face with my fingertip. Those sharp cheekbones and intelligent eyes. The small bump on the bridge of his nose. I'd give anything to have him back. A tear rolls silently down my cheek and splashes onto his clean-shaven chin. Oh, Simon. What did I do to you?

I force myself to turn the photo over, praying that somehow the picture on the back won't be there, that I've imagined the whole thing. But there it is. A woman's hand, dripping with blood. A spike of fear runs through me.

I rack my brains to see if there's anyone who might somehow have got hold of this address. The only people I've told anything about my past are the people I met in rehab—the counselors and the other residents. But they all had their demons. Why would any of them do something like this?

I know I should tell Mum what's happened, but I can't. Because then it won't just be about Simon anymore. It'll be about Dad too, and I can't face that. I can't face seeing it in her eyes. No, there's only one thing that will make this go away.

I pick up the coat I've thrown onto the end of my bed and unzip the pocket, take out Richard Carter's money, the notes like old cloth in my hands. Ten pounds, that's all I need. Half a bottle of vodka, just to take the edge off my nerves. He won't even know. No one will.

My heart thuds with anticipation. My palms sweat. A couple of mouthfuls, that's all I'll have. I can tip the rest away. The nanosecond it hits me, I'll be able to think straight. None of this will matter.

The stairs creak as I tiptoe down them. Mum's in the kitchen and the blender's going. She's making one of her wholesome soups—I saw the recipe book open earlier and couldn't help noticing the 275 milliliters of dry white wine in the list of ingredients. I suck my tongue and swallow. She'll have substituted something else for that.

She won't hear me go out, but still, I can't take any chances. If she knows I've gone, she'll be on the lookout when I come back. She won't have me in the house if I've been drinking—she's made that patently clear—and I've nowhere else to go. Not anymore. No more sofas to crash out on. No more favors to call in.

But this time it's different. This time I'll be okay. I'll know when to stop.

Outside on the street, the wind is picking up. It's behind me, like a helping hand in the small of my back, propelling me forward. Vodka. Vodka. Vodka.

Whoever sent that picture is right. There's blood on my hands as surely as if I'd plunged a knife through Simon's heart. Somebody out there knows it. Just when things are finally working out. With me and Mum. With Josh. I know it's early days yet, but it's real, this thing between us. It means something. I know it does. I've even got the chance to start painting again.

A car swooshes by. A dog barks. The Co-op is just round the corner. I'll be there in three minutes.

I stop dead. This is insane. If I don't turn back now, it'll be too late. I'll be walking into the shop. I'll see the bottles behind the counter and I won't hear this voice anymore. My body will be screaming for that drink. It already is.

No. No. No! I force myself to turn round and head back for the house. The wind's in my face now, pushing me back, but I'm running into it. Gasping for breath, I snatch the key from under the front of my T-shirt, almost ripping the chain off. Now it's in the front door. I'm falling into the hall, lurching up the stairs, back to the four walls of my bedroom.

I stuff the tenner in my coat pocket with all the rest and zip it up. Then I hurl it on top of the wardrobe and fling myself facedown on my bed.

Down in the kitchen, I hear Mum singing.

. . .

"God grant me the serenity to accept the things I cannot
    change,
The courage to change the things I can,
And the wisdom to know the difference."

The meeting ends, as usual, with the serenity prayer. I haven't told the group what's happened. My aborted trip to the Co-op. I just couldn't find the words. I didn't want to come here in the first place. Someone is deliberately targeting me and, for all I know, they're following my every move. It would certainly explain that weird sensation of being watched I've had lately. But missing AA isn't an option, not unless I want Mum giving me grief 24/7, and I don't. Not on top of everything else.

I make a conscious effort to breathe slowly and deeply, try to overcome the shaky feeling that's started up in the pit of my stomach. How dare someone send that vile picture through the post? How dare they mess with me like this? A horrible thought takes up residence in my mind and spreads like a stain. What else might they know?

Helen tilts her head toward the door. I give a quick nod and follow her out, glad of the distraction. Rosie's clocked us, but one of the others is bending her ear about something. Her eyes latch on to me as I leave the vestry.

Outside, Helen waits while I light a cigarette, hold the smoke in my lungs for as long as possible, then release it in one long, slow exhalation. Nicotine is a poor substitute for alcohol, but I wouldn't be without it. Especially now. I need all the crutches I can get. The door opens and Rosie steps out. It's too late to shrink back into the shadows. She's already seen us.

"You okay, Astrid?"

"Yeah, fine."

"Mind if I join you?" she says, not waiting for an answer. She shifts her weight from one foot to the other. "I hope you don't mind me saying this, but I get the feeling you've been struggling lately. Am I right?"

Helen's eyes flick toward me as Rosie lights her cigarette and I wonder if she's thinking what I'm thinking, that Rosie's a nosy cow who needs to mind her own business. The meeting is over. If she thinks I'm going to start spilling my guts out here in the open, she's got another think coming. And what does she mean, *she gets the feeling*? As far as I know, I've been wearing my best poker face all evening. She's right, though, I'll give her that.

"No, I'm just tired, that's all."

She doesn't look convinced by the lie and I can hardly blame her for that. I'm so edgy I feel like I've taken some speed.

Rosie nods. "It's exhausting, isn't it, staying sober?"

"Even after eight years?" Helen says.

Rosie shrugs. "Eight years. Eight months. Eight days. Eight hours. It's all the same."

It might be Helen who asked the question, but it's me Rosie's talking to. Maybe Helen's right about her singling me out as her pet project. It certainly feels that way.

"Are you coming back in for coffee?" she says, that strange little smile playing at the corners of her mouth.

"No. I'm going to head back home now."

"You live with your mum, yeah?"

"Yeah." Why is she asking me that again? I've already told her all this.

Rosie reaches into her back pocket and pulls out a piece of paper. "My phone number," she says, sliding it into the top pocket of my shirt. "In case you ever need to talk and you can't get hold of me at the shop."

Halfway back to the church, she stops and turns round. "Sorry, Helen. I should have written it down for you too. Feel free to make a note of it."

Helen gives her a brisk smile but doesn't respond.

"At least I know where I stand," she says when Rosie goes back inside.

I take the piece of paper out of my pocket and stare at it. "Why did she put it in my pocket instead of just giving it to me?"

I scrunch the paper up and toss it into the rubbish bin at the side of the path.

"She's right about one thing," Helen says as we head out of the churchyard. "It is exhausting, staying sober." She does the buttons up on her coat. "Do you think she's right about it not getting any easier? I was kind of banking on that."

We walk for a while in silence and, though I wasn't going to make a habit of walking back with her after meetings, tonight I'm glad of the company. I tell her what Rosie said to me the other day in the shop, about God watching over me.

Helen snorts. "What, like some kind of stalker?"

The word "stalker" sends a shiver down my spine, only this time it's not the supernatural I have to be afraid of but the living, and that's got to be worse, hasn't it?

"You can come in for a coffee if you like," she says. We're almost at her block of flats now. "Proper coffee. Not like the stuff at AA. Or tea, if you prefer."

I hesitate. I should be getting back. Mum will only start fretting if I'm late. But suddenly I don't want to be outside anymore.

"Do you have any green tea?"

She twists her mouth to one side. "I *think* so."

"Then why not?"

I follow Helen through the wide glass doors. At the end of the path in the space between the tall hedges that separate the flats from the street, a figure flashes past in a gray blur.

Was that Rosie? Has she been following us?

14

"It's not mine, I rent it," Helen says, walking over to the window that looks out on a small concrete balcony and drawing the curtains. She turns a couple of lamps on.

It's a typical rental. Neutral colors. Plain, functional furniture. But dotted around the place are small splashes of color and personality. One of those Indian wall-hangings with tiny round mirrors sewn into it, brass candlesticks with half-burnt candles in them, an incense burner on a little circular table, and a huge weeping fig in the corner.

As I move farther into the room I see that it's an L-shape and that a small kitchen looks over the living area. Helen is already in there, filling up the kettle, taking tea caddies out of cupboards, selecting cups. On the draining rack next to the sink are one dinner plate, one bowl, and one upturned wine glass, which my eyes won't leave alone. What I wouldn't give for a good slug of red wine right now. That'd kick this fear, or at the very least dull its edges.

I watch Helen's hands as she tears open a sachet that contains a bag of green tea. No shaking tonight. Tonight she seems fine. I'd know if she'd been drinking. I wouldn't have come up if she had. Besides, you can drink anything out of a wine glass. Water. Fruit juice. Milk. I tend to avoid using them if I can, but that's just me. Just holding a certain type of glass can be a trigger.

"I've become rather obsessed with the whole paraphernalia surrounding tea and coffee," Helen says. "I've got at least four different teapots and more strainers and infusers than I'll ever be able to use. As for coffee . . ." She opens another cupboard to reveal shelves stuffed with cafetières, percolators, plastic filter holders, filter papers, a coffee-bean grinder, and various packets of coffee beans.

I lean on the counter and watch her set two cups on a tray. "Maybe it's all part of our obsessive personalities. We need something to fill the void that alcohol once took up. I eat far too many sweet things too."

Helen opens yet another cupboard, rammed with chocolates.

"Bloody hell!"

She pulls out a packet of red Bounty bars and puts it on the tray with the tea.

"I've become a bit obsessive about cleaning too," she says, setting the tray down on the coffee table in front of the sofa. "Something else to fill the days."

"You don't work, then?"

"I'm an accountant. *Was* an accountant. Well, still am, I suppose. An out-of-work accountant."

She looks round the room in distaste. "I used to have a really nice house, but then my work dried up." She puffs air through her nose. "Give you three guesses why. Couldn't pay my mortgage, got more and more into debt. Still, at least there was enough equity in the house to pay off the debts and start again. I've got just enough savings to live on for the next year if I'm *really* careful, but I'll have to find some work soon."

"Did you live alone?"

Her eyes cloud over. I've said the wrong thing.

"Sorry, I didn't mean to pry."

"No, it's okay. Honestly. I lived with my husband, but . . ." She lowers her eyes. "He couldn't cope with my drinking. He gave me an ultimatum." She pauses to stir her tea. "Actually, he gave me three."

I wait for her to continue. She'd started to share some of this at the meeting tonight but became too tearful and had to stop.

"One day I got back from wherever it was I'd been and he'd cleared out, taken every last one of his possessions. I haven't seen or heard from him since."

She sniffs and looks up, gives a sad little smile. "Think I'm ready for that Bounty now. Want one?"

I sink my teeth into the dark, coconut-filled chocolate. It's gone in a flash and I immediately want another one. I hardly touched my supper earlier. All I could think of were those bloodstained hands.

"What was his name?" I ask, trying hard to sound relaxed and normal.

She bounces her teabag up and down by the string, then lifts it out and lays it carefully on the little saucer she's placed on the table. Her mouth is pinched and for a minute or so I wonder if she's heard me.

"Peter," she says at last, her voice so soft I barely hear it. She's staring into the middle distance, almost as if I'm no longer there.

"My boyfriend was called Simon," I say, and before I know what's happening my eyes are brimming with tears. Seeing that photo of him looking so happy and healthy has unpicked a fresh seam of grief.

And guilt. Always the guilt.

"What happened?"

"How long have you got?"

"As long as it takes."

"It'll take hours," I say. "Days. Trained counselors can't cope with listening to this sort of shit for more than an hour, and they're getting paid."

The urge to confide in her is strong. While I've more or less convinced myself that the incident at the beach huts and the thing with the T-shirt were nothing more than concoctions of my guiltraddled mind, the contents of that envelope are something else altogether. I need to tell someone or I'll go mad.

I guess that's the whole point of making friends with other addicts. Knowing you can offload to someone who's also fucked up. Not just once, but over and over again. And Helen *gets* me. I know she does. All those things she said at the last meeting.

Then again, her fuck-ups aren't likely to be on the same scale as mine. She and I are from different planets.

"No, I'd better go. Mum practically has a seizure if I'm back late. I mean, I understand why and I can't really blame her, but . . ." I sigh. "It'll be too much hassle if I don't leave now."

"Can't you give her a quick ring and tell her you're with a friend from AA?"

"To be honest, that's not likely to reassure her. She'll worry that we'll egg each other on to have a drink."

I drain my last mouthful of tea and stand up. "It's ridiculous, isn't it? I'm a thirty-two-year-old woman and I feel like a teenager on curfew."

Helen carries our cups over to the kitchen. "I'd offer you my number in case you want to get in touch between meetings," she says. "But you'll probably just screw it up and throw it in a bin on the way home, like you did with Rosie's."

"I won't. I promise."

She puts the cups in the sink, then comes back over to the living area and scribbles it down on a sticky note. "You can put it in your pocket yourself," she says, smiling.

She walks with me to the front door and watches from the top of the stairwell as I go down.

"Astrid?" she calls after me.

I look up.

"Let go and let God," she says, her voice strangely solemn all of a sudden.

I stare at her in confusion. What the hell is she on about?

She grins. "I googled those slogans you told me about. You're right. There are loads of them."

Of course. She's impersonating Rosie.

I'm still laughing as I reach the main entrance, but when I see the black night waiting for me beyond the glass the laughter dies in my throat. Right now I don't care if Mum *does* have another go at me. I just want to get home.

I quicken my pace and take the shortest route. The background roar of the sea sounds particularly menacing tonight. My heart is hammering away so fast I feel sick. I don't want to look over my shoulder because that feels like giving in to the fear. Maybe whoever's doing this is behind me right now. Maybe that gray figure I saw earlier wasn't Rosie after all. Maybe it was the person who sent me that photo and they've been waiting all this time, skulking in the shadows.

I force myself to turn round just long enough to see there's no one there, then I keep on walking and don't look again.

She's scared. It's obvious from the way she's walking. Charging forward, chin pressed down onto her chest.

I imagine a circle under her left shoulder blade—an optic viewfinder on a rifle.

For a second I think she's sensed me, like an animal senses danger. She stops dead in her tracks and spins round. I shrink back into the shadows till she starts up again, then follow her progress with my eyes.

I reposition the viewfinder. My forefinger curls, then squeezes. The bullet hits its target and she slumps to the ground.

Game over.

Except it isn't. Not yet. The game's only just begun.

15

This time, Mum doesn't pounce on me in the hallway like a wild-cat; she stays in the living room, watching TV, or pretending to. I surprise myself, and her, by apologizing for not texting to say I'd be late. Then I perch on the edge of the settee and tell her about Helen and her cupboards full of chocolate and coffee.

"It's nice that you're making friends," she says.

She doesn't even warn me to be careful and take things slowly, and I know she wants to. It feels like something has shifted, that the ice field between us is starting to shrink. Just a fraction of an inch, but even so . . .

God knows, it's not easy living here with Mum again, but she's all I've got now.

Upstairs, I sit on my bed and stare at my top drawer, where the envelope with the photo of Simon in it is stuffed under my socks and knickers. I'm not going to look at it again. I'm not. It was stupid of me to get all worked up like that. I've never been scared of walk-ing alone at night and I'm not about to start now. The only thing I've got to be scared of is the darkness in my own mind. The black holes. My anonymous pen pal knows that too. They're clever, who-ever they are. They don't need to physically harm me. They just need to sit back and watch me lose my mind. Well, I won't give them the satisfaction.

I take off my clothes and get into my pajamas. Ten thirty at night and here I am, ready for bed like a good little mummy's girl. I'm even hanging my clothes in the wardrobe instead of slinging them on the floor. Routine and structure. They used to bang on about that in rehab. Keep busy. Create new habits. Good ones, like hobbies and chores. Don't give yourself time to get bored. Write in your journal every night.

But the exercise book I've been using is in the same drawer as the envelope. Panic swells behind my breastbone as soon as I see it lying there. I think about tearing it up and throwing it away, or burning it in the garden. I could kick the embers into the soil and that would be that. But I can't do either of those things because I can't bring myself to tear up Simon's beautiful, happy face and throw him out with the rubbish. I certainly can't watch him being devoured by flames.

Dust to dust. Ashes to ashes. Grief sideswipes me so hard it's like a physical blow. Sometimes I struggle to believe he's really dead. Maybe if I'd been to his funeral, I'd have had some form of closure, if there is such a thing. But I was so ill, so out of it. I don't even know if he was buried or cremated, or where his remains are. Why don't I know these things? Why didn't I try harder to find out? I should have said goodbye. It's the least I could have done.

I think about earlier, making love with Josh as if none of this had ever happened, and guilt presses down on me once more. But I can't help the way I feel, can I? It's chemistry, pure and simple. The need for love and intimacy, for sex. It's what makes us human. It doesn't mean I don't still love Simon. The memory of him.

I take hold of the envelope and go over to the wardrobe, stand on the tips of my toes, and give the envelope a firm push so that it slides toward the back, out of reach. The arm of my coat is dangling over the edge where I threw it earlier, so I push that back too.

I could have taken the photo out and had another look. I could have pulled the coat down and helped myself to a £20 note, then got dressed again and slipped out of the house when Mum wasn't looking and bought some gin or vodka, something I could pour into my water glass to get me through the night. I wanted to. I still do. But I didn't. I don't. I sit on the bed again and focus on my breathing till the tightness in my chest recedes. I won't be intimidated like this.

The next morning, after I've washed my face and got dressed—I can't face any breakfast—I reach up to the top of my wardrobe and grope along the edge till I grab a handful of coat and pull it toward me. The dreaded brown envelope comes down with it, but I put it up again, flicking it away from the edge. I hear it fluttering down the space between the back of the wardrobe and the wall. I exhale. I won't be able to reach it now, not without dragging the heavy wardrobe out. Just as well.

I put the coat on. The sooner I order those painting materials and get shot of this money, the better.

"You won't need that coat today," Mum says when I go downstairs. "It's absolutely gorgeous out there. They said on the news that a heatwave's on its way."

"Really?" I think of the last thing Josh said, about taking me somewhere I could swim naked. Maybe that'll happen sooner than I imagined.

"I've got a swimsuit somewhere I don't use anymore," Mum says. "You can have it if you like. Unless you've already got one."

"I doubt it. I can't remember the last time I went swimming."

Actually, I can. It was that holiday in Spain. I had a tiny red bikini that looked great with my tan. Simon had finally learned to juggle by then. I remember the crowd that gathered round to watch, the teenage girls fluttering their eyelashes at him and giving me envious, sidelong glances. He was so happy then, so alive. It seems like a lifetime ago. I miss him so much.

"Shall I hunt it out for you?" Mum says.

I shake my head. The thought of Josh seeing me in one of Mum's old suits is too embarrassing to contemplate. Does she seriously think I'd even *consider* wearing anything of hers?

I hang my coat on one of the hooks in the porch and transfer the contents of my pockets into my rucksack. "You couldn't lend me some money till my benefit comes through, could you? I don't know what's happened to all my summer clothes."

I hate asking her for more money; she's already spent most of her savings on putting me through rehab, but if I have to wear these old jeans for much longer, they'll be falling apart. Her eyebrows dip.

"Forget it. I'll make do with what I've got."

"No, you're right," she says. "You do need some more clothes. I could come with you if you like?"

"You can't keep treating me like a child, Mum. I'm not going to buy any alcohol, okay? Just give me twenty-five quid, if you can afford it. I'll pick up a few bits and pieces at one of the charity shops. But if you'd rather not, that's fine. I understand."

I have a sudden urge to show her the £150, to thrust it under her nose and say, *See? This is what Josh's dad has given me to buy paint. Don't you think I'd have spent some of it in the off-license by now if I couldn't be trusted?* But of course I don't. Because she's right. I came so close yesterday. So close.

She goes to where her handbag is hanging over the end of the banister and takes out her purse. It's small with a silver clasp. I swallow hard. It reminds me of another purse. Another time. Opening it up and scooping the notes out with shaky fingers. Blood on my sleeve.

The jagged images swim before my eyes like reflections in broken glass. No, don't go there. Shut it down. Shut it down fast.

"I'll bring you the receipts," I say, but she shakes her head and hands me four £10 notes.

"You can pay me back a tenner a week when your dole money comes through."

I lean forward and kiss her on the cheek, humiliated, resentful, and grateful all at the same time.

How has it come to this?

Even though it's broad daylight, I'm still anxious when I leave the cottage, my senses primed for anything or anyone out of the ordinary. But the fine weather has brought an influx of visitors and after a while I relax. Nothing's going to happen to me with all these people around.

An old-fashioned bell pings as I push open the door of the art shop. A seductive smorgasbord of familiar smells greets my nostrils: paint thinner and varnish, mint and lanolin from the bars of artist's soap, the clay-like aroma of crayons and the deliciously pulpy scent of new paper and freshly stretched canvas. It reminds me of being in the studios and workshops at university, of building sets in empty theatres. It makes me want to cry.

At first glance the shop looks thrown together, a higgledy-piggledy profusion of tubs and tubes and tins and brushes, all jostling for space on the shelves and display units. But as my eyes adjust to the gloomy interior, I know just by looking at the balding, brown-overalled man at the counter that he will be able to put his hands on anything I might ask for within a matter of seconds.

He raises his eyes above his half-moon spectacles and says good morning. He doesn't ask if there's anything in particular I'm looking for, or whether he can help me in any way, and for that I'm grateful. I know exactly what I need because I spent hours thinking it through last night and making a long, detailed list. I also worked out a fee for the job—it's probably way less than it should be, but it's still a damn sight more than I'll have earned in a long while. It was the only thing I could think of doing to calm me down after my scary walk home. The only thing other than drinking. But first I want to browse. I want to walk slowly up and down the aisles and feast my eyes on the glut of supplies.

I want to feel the smooth handles of the brushes and test the bounce of the bristles on the backs of my hands. I want to reacquaint myself with the poetry of their names: the fans and the flats and the riggers, the lily-bristle mottlers, the brights and the filberts. I want to slide my eyes over the oils: linseed, poppy, safflower, and walnut; oil of spike and copaiba balsam. Larch Venice turpentine. Dragon's blood.

I could stay here forever, soaking it all up, running my fingers along the shelves, gazing at the sponges and palette knives as if my life depends on memorizing each and every item. It's like a portal into my old life. If only I could step back in and do things differently this time.

An hour later, after I've agreed to collect my purchases later today and with just a handful of change out of the £150 in one pocket, and the £40 Mum's given me in the other, I head for the charity shops on Flinstead Road.

No longer under the spell of the art shop, the old tension returns and I can't help checking out every face I pass. Maybe one of them belongs to the person who sent me that photo. So when someone taps me on the shoulder as I'm waiting to cross the road, I flinch so hard I almost twist my neck.

16

"Astrid, I'm so sorry. I didn't mean to make you jump."

It's Rosie. So much for not acknowledging each other in public.

"Don't worry about it. I'm a bundle of nerves today."

"Let me buy you a coffee, then," she says, already pulling her purse from her bag. "It's the least I can do for scaring you half to death."

My heart sinks. "That's really kind of you, but . . ." I glance across the street for inspiration and see the steamed-up windows of the Fisherman's Shack. "It's just that"—I tilt my head toward it—"I'm meant to be meeting a friend over there."

Rosie lifts her chin. A faint tinge of pink colors her neck. She knows I'm lying. "Oh, okay, no problem. I'll see you around, then."

"Yes."

She goes to walk away, then stops and turns back. "I don't suppose I could wait in there with you, just until your friend arrives? My shift doesn't start for another half an hour."

For fuck's sake. She's not going to give up. I rack my brain for a good enough reason to say no, but nothing comes. Just as I've resigned myself to saying yes, a miracle appears in the form of Helen,

walking briskly along the pavement, eyes looking straight ahead.
She hasn't seen us yet.

"Hi, Helen," I call out to her, hoping she'll pick up on the look of
desperation in my eyes, the silent beam of communication I'm pro-
jecting onto her. "I was beginning to think you'd forgotten about
our coffee."

For a split second she looks confused, but she doesn't let me
down. "Of *course* I haven't forgotten. I was just popping into the
newsagent's for a paper first. Oh, hello, Rosie."

Rosie gives her a tight smile.

"Rosie was going to join us, but I've just remembered you
wanted to go for a walk first, didn't you, Helen?" I smile brightly,
hoping Rosie won't be pushy enough to tag along for that too.
"Maybe another time, eh?"

Rosie nods, defeated. "Of course."

I wait till she's walked far enough away not to hear us. "Sorry
about that, but I really couldn't face it."

"I do fancy a bit of a walk, as it happens," Helen says. "But I need
to eat first."

I twist my head over my shoulder. Rosie is nowhere in sight, but
I've the weirdest sensation that she's watching us from somewhere.
Then I spot the man with bad acne coming out of the chemist's.
This is ridiculous. I can't seem to go five minutes without seeing
someone from AA. Who'd have thought there'd be so many of us
in this sleepy little town? Although I guess not everyone in the
group actually lives here. There are lots of small villages and ham-
lets in the surrounding countryside with even less going on than
Flinstead. That's enough to drive a person to drink in itself.

I steer Helen across the road before he catches sight of us. Not
that he'd come over even if he did. He always keeps himself to himself in meetings.

"Come on, let's go and get an egg-and-bacon buttie."

Now that we're sitting opposite each other, steam rising from
our mugs of coffee, a couple of crumbs and the odd twist of un-

wanted bacon rind the only thing left on our plates, I notice the deep furrow between Helen's eyebrows and the prominent vein over her left temple. She's tried to cover it with foundation but hasn't blended it in properly at the hairline. And her lipstick's the wrong color for her face. It's too red and is starting to feather into the fine lines on her upper lip.

I stab the crumbs on my plate with my forefinger and suck them off. We're two people whose paths would probably never have crossed were it not for AA, but now that they have I'm kind of glad. I do need a friend right now. Someone who knows what I'm struggling with. Someone I can confide in without fear of being judged or misunderstood.

Simon's face creeps into my head. The healthy, handsome face captured in that photo. Which means it isn't long till the other picture—the one of the hand dripping with blood—floats across it like the grisly title sequence of a crime drama. What chance do I have of making something good happen with Josh when my past keeps rearing up to remind me of all my flaws, all my failures?

And what if that picture is just the beginning? What if there's more to come?

"Astrid? What's wrong?"

I jerk my head up and stare at Helen's concerned face. "Someone's trying to frighten me," I say, immediately wishing I hadn't. Because now that I've said those words, now that I've admitted it aloud, in the presence of another person, the threat has become more solid, more real. Someone *is* trying to frighten me. It's not just in my head anymore. And now that the words have escaped, it's inevitable that the rest will follow. A dam has been breached.

Helen leans forward and touches my forearm. "What do you mean, trying to frighten you? Who is?"

I look around at the other people in the café. One old man hunched over a mug of tea and the *Sun*. Two men in high-visibility jackets silently stuffing butties into their mouths, and Bob in his grease-splattered apron, wiping down the counter with a stained dishcloth. It's hardly crowded, and we're tucked away in the corner by the window. Nobody would hear me if I spoke in a low voice, but, even so, I'm self-conscious, wary.

"I can't do this. Not here."

Helen nods. "Let's finish our coffees and go for a walk, shall we?"

17

We walk along the tops of the cliffs, the sea a deep summer blue that sparkles in the sun to our right. After about five minutes I have to take my sweater off and tie it round my waist by the sleeves. Helen folds her raincoat over her left arm. Ever since leaving the café we've been chatting about inconsequential things: the unseasonably warm weather, the Thames barge on the horizon, and the way, on days like this, if you filter out the Englishness of the buildings and streets to our left, the North Sea looks almost Mediterranean.

But hovering below and between and on the edges of our words is the thing I'm not talking about. The reason we're now wending our way down the cliff path toward the wide expanse of sand where I can speak freely, with only the swooping gulls to eavesdrop.

At last, when we've settled into a comfortable pace across the flat sand, I tell Helen about the photo and the picture. The words spew out of me. A tide of broken sentences, ragged with emotion. God knows how she'll make sense of it. It's like someone's dropped a manuscript on the floor and I'm picking all the pages up and trying to put them back together, but they aren't numbered and I can't organize the story into any kind of coherent order.

So many scenes and images, so many memories. It all feels too sketchy and inadequate. The emphasis is all wrong, but I have to keep going. One by one, the facts emerge.

"He'd been dry for eight and a half months."

I stare straight ahead of me, but it's not the beach I'm seeing. It's Simon's face that day in the park. Proud, confident. Handsome. If he hadn't seen me first and come over, I doubt I'd even have recognized him. He could have walked straight past me while I sat on the bench in my beer-soaked reverie.

"I told him I was impressed, but really I was jealous. There he was, getting himself sorted out at last. He even had a job on a building site, only as a laborer, but it was clearly doing him good. He looked so fit and healthy it made me ache inside. I wanted him back."

I pause to take a few deep breaths.

"He was talking about some work he had coming up, as an extra on a film. It wasn't much, but he was so excited about it. He thought it might lead to something else." My voice breaks. "Maybe if he hadn't met me again, he'd have had the chance to make something of his life, fulfill his dreams."

I don't fight the urge to cry this time. It all spills out in snotty sobs and heaving gulps. Helen pats me gently on my shoulders till I recover enough to go on.

"It was a really hot day, a bit like today. I had six cans of ice-cold lager in my rucksack."

I take a deep breath. Even now, I can still see the little drops of condensation clinging to the outside of the cans. The sun beats down on the back of my neck. I sneak a look at Helen from the corner of my eye, see the tip of her tongue slide across her bottom lip. It isn't a great time to be talking about cold lagers, but I can't stop now.

"Maybe I had him at the hissing noise as I pulled back the tab. Or maybe it was when I took one long, greedy gulp. I was probably crass enough to waggle one under his nose. I can almost hear myself telling him that one little drink wouldn't hurt and that we should celebrate his good fortune."

Helen makes one of those cynical little noises in the back of her throat.

"The truth is, I don't know how it happened. But it was my fault. All of it. All I can remember is waking up, sick and jittery, God knows how many hours later, with Simon passed out on the floor next to me. He came to, eventually, but he kept throwing up and passing out again. He had it really bad, the worst DTs I've ever seen, thought his skin was crawling with maggots, kept tearing at his flesh with his nails."

We've reached the headland now and run out of beach, so we walk up the ramp and onto the promenade in front of the beach huts. Helen points to a bench and we sit down. I light a cigarette and draw on it deeply.

"I remember taking slugs of vodka to calm my nerves and then, the next thing I knew, two paramedics were hammering on the door. Somehow or other, I must have got myself together enough to phone for an ambulance. I don't even remember doing it, but I must have done. It was the only decent thing I did."

I feel light-headed all of a sudden. Nauseous. Instinctively, I lean forward and put my head between my knees. I take long, deep lungfuls of air and focus on the concrete between my feet and the crack that runs through it. Helen's hand is on the back of my neck.

"Go on," she says, her voice soft, encouraging.

"Two weeks later, after he'd been discharged, Simon threw himself off Seaford Head in Sussex."

Her hand falls away. "Oh my God! Oh, Astrid!"

"I read about it in the paper. That's how I found out. So yes, whoever sent me that photo is right. There *is* blood on my hands. I didn't push Simon off that cliff, but I might just as well have done."

I sniff to clear my nose, but it's completely blocked. Helen passes me a tissue.

"Everyone says I shouldn't think that way. Counselors, and people like that. But I can't help the way I feel, can I?"

"Of *course* you can't."

"And even if they're right and it isn't my fault, it doesn't make it any better. He's still dead."

Helen turns to face me. "Where is it, this photo? Can I see it?"

I think of the brown envelope gathering dust and bits of carpet fluff at the back of my wardrobe and my palms start to sweat.

"No, I left it at home."

"Have you thought about going to the police?"

I swallow hard. The very thought of walking into a police station makes me cringe.

"I doubt they'd take much notice of an ex-addict, do you? And if they start asking me a load of questions . . . well, let's just say I haven't exactly been a model citizen. I've . . ."

Shit. I wish I hadn't started this now. It's all coming out. The wreckage of my life, spilling out in a great ugly heap. I know if I'm going to do this Twelve-Step thing properly, then at some point I'm going to have to confess all this anyway, and the rest of it. It's one of the stages you have to work through. But some secrets are too shameful to share with anyone. Even more shameful than goading Simon to take a drink. In fact, they're so off limits that when they creep into my head at night I ward them off before they can torment me, crowd them out with other thoughts, other images.

"I've taken things that weren't mine," I say. *Keep it vague, Astrid.* "Things I could sell to buy booze. I know the police are never going to find out and there's bugger all they could do about it now, but still . . . I'd feel uneasy talking to them. Guilty conscience, I suppose."

Helen rests her hand on my forearm again. "We've all done things we're not proud of. I know *I* have. But remember"—she makes the inverted-commas sign with her fingers and adopts the familiar, smug tone that I instantly recognize as her impression of Rosie—"we're only as sick as our secrets."

It feels good to laugh after the emotional intensity of the last half-hour.

Helen pats my hand. "The sort of haters who post anonymous mail through people's letterboxes are usually cowards at heart. They're like internet trolls. They get pleasure from upsetting people." A crease appears between her eyebrows. "It's a particularly vindictive thing to do. Was there anyone else, do you know? Another woman, perhaps?"

"After me, do you mean? I don't think so. There was an ex who kept sending him Facebook messages. An old schoolfriend who used to have a crush on him. I think he was seeing her when he met me, actually, but it wasn't serious."

"Well, whoever it is, they've made their nasty little point now. I doubt you'll be hearing from them again."

"I hope you're right, Helen. I really do."

18

Filled with a fresh resolve not to be intimidated by some pathetic saddo's twisted mind game, I say goodbye to Helen and head for the British Red Cross shop. Flinstead has more than its fair share of charity shops so I'm bound to find something I like.

Soon, I've bought a pair of Next shorts that look almost brand new, some cropped linen trousers that'll look great with my trainers, and two Zara T-shirts—a real find. The only new things I've shelled out for are some Rizlas and tobacco—I can't afford to keep buying cigarettes—and a cheap bathing suit from Peacocks. Just in case Josh suggests a swim.

I was going to ignore the Oxfam shop so I don't have to face Rosie again, but I can't stop myself looking in the window. The creepy mannequin is now sporting white chinos, a navy blazer, and a panama hat. It still freaks me out, thinking about that T-shirt. It's amazing the tricks a mind can play, even without alcohol, and yet, now that someone's sending me nasty messages, someone who knows about Simon and me, I can't help wondering whether the mannequin was a message too. No, that's ridiculous. I'm just being paranoid.

My eyes wander over to a '60s smock dress on a dressmaker's

dummy. It's exquisite, and only £6.99. It's too much of a bargain. I'm going to have to go in.

The customer Rosie's serving says goodbye. Now it's just the two of us. Her mouth twists into a smile.

"Good walk?" she says.

I nod. Why the hell did I have to look in the window in the first place?

"It's lovely, isn't it, that dress you were looking at? My daughter used to have one just like it."

Her daughter. Somehow, I didn't imagine Rosie as a mother.

She comes out from behind the counter. "It's been a long time since I've seen her wearing it, though." She exhales slowly. "It's been a long time since I've seen her, full stop." She gives a wry smile. "She can't forgive me, you see. For ruining her childhood."

I don't know how to respond to this, or even if I want to. She acts as if we're already friends, assumes there's some kind of intimacy between us. As if the fact that we're both alcoholics automatically binds us together. Or maybe it's a ploy to draw me into conversation, and I know exactly what will happen if I let her. She'll start asking me questions and smiling at me in that smug way of hers, as if she already knows the answers.

"You can try it on if you like," she says. "There's a changing room at the back."

"Erm . . ."

"Go on. It'll look great on you."

She peels the dress off the dummy and gestures toward a changing cubicle at the back of the shop, just off the room where all the donations are stored and sorted. It's tiny and dark, with stained carpet tiles. I tug the flimsy curtain across, but it doesn't fit the frame properly so there's a gap of about an inch on one side.

"Don't worry," Rosie calls out. "There's nobody else here."

I squeeze out of my jeans and take my top off, then wriggle into the dress. It fits perfectly. I peer at myself in the mirror, but it's so gloomy in here it's hard to get a good look. I'm sure I noticed a bigger full-length mirror propped against the wall in the back room, near the workstation and the PC. I step outside and almost bump into Rosie. She must have been standing behind the curtain the whole time.

"Stunning," she says. "You look like a young Mia Farrow."

She stares at my body for a beat too long and my mind returns to when she pressed her phone number on me, tucked it into my shirt pocket, her fingers brushing my left breast. I feel her eyes on me as I pick my way past all the donations heaped on the floor. The fusty scent of old books and second-hand clothes is even riper back here. Some attempt has been made to freshen things up with one of those floral room sprays. There's an undertone of something else too, though I can't put my finger on what it is. It reminds me of some of the squats I've dossed in.

On a large table in the center of the room things are being grouped into categories: men's jackets and old suits, ladies' woolen pullovers and cardigans, a heap of shoes and strappy sandals. It makes me think of one of those hideous old photographs from the Holocaust—the possessions of the dead. I blink the image away.

It's been a long while since I've worn a dress. I feel exposed, vulnerable, although I know it looks good on me. Short, but not *too* short. Sexy, but not in an obvious, provocative way. I wish Rosie would go away and leave me to decide on my own, but she's still right here next to me, nodding and smiling. Telling me how great I look in it, how for £6.99 it's a *no-brainer*. Christ, talk about hard sell. Anyone would think we were in an expensive boutique and she was on commission.

At last, another customer comes in and Rosie goes off to deal with them. Her reluctance at leaving me here on my own is obvious. I take one last look at myself in the mirror. The dress is great. I'll buy it. But just as I'm about to return to the cubicle to take it off I hear Richard Carter's voice. He's dropping off a bag of old clothes. The second this week, by the sound of it.

"I think that's the lot now," he says.

I linger by the mirror, unwilling to walk over to the cubicle in case he spots me. The last thing I want is for these two completely separate parts of my world to collide.

My eyes drift round the room as I wait for him to leave. They settle first on the PC that's been left open on the Word template screen, and then travel down to the floor and Rosie's cloth bag, the one with the patchwork design she always has with her at AA meetings. It's stuffed behind the mirror and I can't help noticing that there's a rolled-up sleeping bag in there with a toothbrush and tube of toothpaste sticking out the top. There's something else in there too: a flashlight.

Didn't she say something a while back about looking for somewhere to stay?

At last, Richard leaves and I dash back into the cubicle to change. I suppose if you had the keys to a small shop like this and knew what you were doing, you could get away with it, as long as you covered your tracks and cleared out before the morning-shift person turned up. Is that what Rosie's been doing? Why else would she be lugging a sleeping bag and flashlight around with her? I know I've dossed on a fair few floors in my time, but to still be doing it in your sixties? How tragic is that?

When I come back into the shop she's sifting through a massive laundry bag, her dyed hair hanging in front of her face. She straightens up at my approach and walks toward the till. I put the dress down and rootle around in my pocket for my last tenner. Where the hell is it?

I empty my rucksack onto the counter, heat staining my cheeks: a packet of green Rizlas, a pouch of Golden Virginia, Simon's juggling ball, and a handful of screwed-up tissues. The ball rolls toward Rosie and, just as I'm about to grab it, she picks it up and gives it a squeeze. Damn. It won't be the same anymore, not now *she's* touched it. Why the hell did I have to bring it out with me in the first place?

"Here."

I place the tenner on the counter in front of her and put the tissues, tobacco, and Rizlas back into my rucksack. She's still playing with the ball, tossing it slowly and rhythmically from one hand to the other, a strange trance-like expression on her face. I want to grab it back, but all I can do is wait till she takes my money.

Eventually, almost reluctantly, she puts it down and I grab hold of it. It's ruined now. I won't be able to hold it for comfort anymore, or bring it to my face at night and kid myself it smells of Simon, because her hands have been all over it.

She drops the dress into a brown paper bag.

"I bet your new fella's going to love you in this," she says. "He *is* your new fella, isn't he? The good-looking guy with the blond hair?"

How does she know what Josh looks like? She must have seen me come out of the Fisherman's Shack with him that time, or else she's seen us down on the beach. That's the trouble with a town this small. Everyone knows your business. Thank God Richard isn't still here. I'd have died from embarrassment if he'd heard her say that.

"I guess so."

She folds the top of the bag and passes it over to me. She lowers her voice. "I hope you don't mind me saying this, Astrid, but when you were sharing the other week I got the impression that you've lost someone close to you recently."

I take hold of the bag. I need to be more careful at meetings in future. I must have said more than I thought I had.

"I know it's none of my business," she says. "But, well, you know, I lost my mother recently, so if you ever want to talk . . ."

"Thanks." I turn to leave, but she hasn't finished with me yet.

"There's a lot of guilt when someone dies, especially if it's . . ." She pauses. "Especially if it's a . . . *troubled* relationship."

I stare at her. "I don't remember saying anything about having a troubled relationship."

Her face reddens. "Oh, but you must have done. Maybe you

don't remember. You were very upset when you were talking. Was it someone close to you? A brother or boyfriend, perhaps?"

"A boyfriend." The words are out before I have a chance to think better of it. This is how they operate, people like her. They latch on to some little snippet you've told them and use it to reel you in.

"I'm sorry to hear that," Rosie says.

It isn't till I'm out on the street that I work out what it is about her I don't like, apart from the nosiness and the silly little sayings and the incessant attempts to befriend me. Her smile doesn't quite reach her eyes. There's something else too. Trapped behind that caring, sharing, successful sobriety act, I can still see the nasty, fucked-up drunk she once was.

Takes one to know one, I guess.

19

Mum holds my new swimsuit out in front of her. "This will suit you a lot better than my old one."

"Well, I didn't like to say anything, but . . ."

"That's not like you, darling. Not saying anything."

We both laugh. We haven't teased each other in this jokey way for ages. It feels good. Although the fact that it feels good is now making me feel bad about all the times I've been mean to her in the past. Which then gets me thinking that, actually, that wasn't always my fault because she can be so fucking annoying sometimes. So now the good feeling is all spoiled because it's got mixed up with guilt and resentment. That's the trouble with emotions; they zig-zag all over the place and leave you exhausted. Leave you wanting a drink to make them soft at the edges.

If I knew for sure that there was a bottle of vodka somewhere in this house, or wine, or beer. Sherry. Cider—anything, in fact—I'd drink it. I'd drink all of it, every last drop. And then I'd scrape together the last of the money in my pockets and anything else I could get my hands on, the contents of Mum's loose-change bowl for instance, and I'd go down to the Co-op and buy whatever I could afford. And I'd sit on the beach and drink it all and then I'd come home and I'd see Mum's face, all screwed up and angry, and I'd hear what came out of her mouth, but it wouldn't be words, it'd be noise. A harsh, jarring noise. The sort of noise that sets your nerves on edge and makes you want to drink even more so you don't have to hear it any longer and you don't have to see the way her mouth moves and the way her pupils dilate, and you don't have to feel her pain because it's your pain too. It's always your pain.

"Astrid? Astrid?"

"Sorry, what?"

"I said, what do you fancy for supper?"

Josh's text arrives in the nick of time. It saves me from the downward spiral of my thoughts.

I've just got back from my swim. Do you want to meet me at the chippie? I'm starving. xx

Sounds great. What time?

7 o'clock? I'm just going to have a quick shower.

Ok. See you soon. xx

It isn't till my hand's on the front door half an hour later that I remember Mum's taken a vegetable curry out of the freezer.

"Mum?"

"In here, darling."

She's watching the evening news in the living room. I keep my voice as light and friendly as I can. "You don't mind if I have that curry tomorrow, do you? Only Josh has asked me out for fish and chips."

She looks at my new dress and something unreadable flickers across her face. This really is like being a teenager again. Only now it's worse, far worse. Back then it felt like the power was all mine. I knew it all, had my whole life in front of me. Navigating Mum's moods was just something I had to do for a couple more years and then I'd be free. Now I'm back where I started. I've had my taste of freedom, and look where it got me.

"Of course I don't mind," she says. "Are you bringing it back here to eat?"

"No, we'll probably sit on a bench or something. It's a nice warm evening."

"You haven't told him, have you."

The way she says it, it's more of a statement than a question.

"I will do. When I'm ready."

She nods. *Don't say anything else, Mum. Please, just don't say anything else.*

"Don't leave it too long," she says. "You know what they said . . ."

"At rehab, yes. I know what they said. I was *there*, remember?"

Mum presses her lips together. One of those stupid Go Compare adverts with the twirly-mustached Italian opera singer has just come on. Normally, she switches channels the second it starts up. Now she just stares at it, stony-faced.

There's a queue outside the chippie, but I don't join it, just in case I get to the counter before Josh arrives. I sit on the wall of someone's front garden. That's the price they pay for living next to the chippie, having to put up with strangers' bums on their wall. Mum would hate it. She gets cross when mothers who've just dropped their children off at school gather on the pavement outside the house to chat. She says things like: "Why can't they have their mothers' meetings somewhere else?"

As I'm waiting, something she said a few days ago comes back to me, about the young woman she saw staring at the house, the one who said she lived there as a child.

I chew the inside of my lip. I don't like the thought of her turning up at the house when Mum's on her own. What if she's lying about it being her childhood home?

If it weren't for all the weird things that have been happening lately, I probably wouldn't be giving it a second thought. I mean, some people do things like that, don't they? Revisit the place where they grew up. Wild horses couldn't drag me back to Peckham Rye—too many memories. But what if she's connected to all this? What if this woman, whoever she is, is the one who sent me that photo?

Josh drops onto the wall next to me and grabs hold of my hand, brings it to his lips. I didn't even see him approach. He gives me a hug. His hair smells of shampoo.

"I saw you with your mum earlier," he says as we join the end of the queue.

I stare at him. How is that possible? Then I realize. He must have seen me with Helen down on the beach.

"I was going to come over and say hi, but you looked so engrossed in your conversation I thought I'd better not."

"That wasn't my mum. It was a friend of hers."

Why did I say that? Why didn't I just say it was a friend of mine? Why have I tied myself up in another lie? What's wrong with me?

"She was asking me how Mum was," I say. "Mum isn't socializing much at the moment." Now I'm making things worse, spinning another tale. It's completely unnecessary. He wasn't going to ask what we were talking about. Why would he?

"Depression's like that," he says. "Not that I've suffered from it myself, but I know people who have."

I nod. I'm trying to think what he might have seen. Was it when we were on the beach or when we were sitting on the bench? Was I crying? I can't remember. I was so immersed in my own problems I wasn't aware of anyone but Helen and myself.

The woman at the front of the queue is taking ages to make up her mind and the people behind her and in front of us are rolling their eyes at each other and muttering under their breath. Josh and

I are still on the pavement outside because there isn't room for us all in the shop.

"Where were you, when you saw us?"

He hesitates. Is it my imagination or does he look a bit cagey?

"In the sea," he says. "Well, just walking out of it."

Of course. That's why I didn't see him. For once, I wasn't focused on the sea; I was too busy regurgitating bits of my past to Helen.

I'm on the verge of saying that I thought he'd said in his text that he'd only got back from swimming a little while ago, but I stop myself just in time. Maybe he went earlier too, although didn't he say he was helping his dad sand some floors? Oh, for God's sake, why am I even worrying about this? Josh is a free agent. He's allowed to change his mind, isn't he? I don't want him to think I'm checking up on him. Maybe he already does. The dynamics in a new relationship are so hard to call sometimes, especially when there's no alcohol to smooth things along.

"The thing is," he says, taking hold of my hands and fixing me sternly with his eyes, "now I know your shameful secret."

20

Blood rushes to my ears. What does he mean, he knows my shameful secret? How does he know? *What* does he know? I try to swallow, but it takes ages. For a split second, I even wonder if maybe Josh has something to do with what's been going on. All those times I just happened to see him down on the beach—and it was him who approached me first, wasn't it?

I can't look at him for fear of what I might see in his eyes and yet . . . he's still holding my hand.

I'll brazen it out. What else can I do?

"Which one?" I say, forcing myself to meet his eyes, to smile. It's the standard jokey response. He can't possibly know how serious a question it is.

"The smoking one," he says, pulling an expression of mock-disapproval.

It's as much as I can do not to laugh out loud. I look down at my feet to compose myself, but Josh obviously thinks I'm annoyed, or embarrassed, or both.

He draws me into his arms and hugs me tight. "I didn't mean to make you feel bad," he says. "I was just surprised, that's all."

"I want to give it up," I say.

"Good for you. I tried smoking once, but I was always into my swimming so I never really got into it." He fingers the hem of my new dress. "This is nice."

"You can borrow it if you like."

Josh's shoulders start to shake and, before long, we're both giggling like a couple of schoolkids. I haven't laughed like this for ages. Not since Simon and I were on that park bench draining cans of beer, slipping beyond the point of no return. Things weren't so funny after that.

The chips are good. Crisp on the outside, fluffy on the inside. Josh put even more salt on his than I did on mine. It's nice to know he's got *some* vices, that he's not a complete health freak. We're sitting on a bench in the little garden near the seafront. The sun is still warm and the sky is tinged with orange and red. Gulls circle overhead, waiting to swoop down on a dropped chip.

"I bought the paints today," I say. "The man in the shop was really helpful."

"Charlie?"

"Don't know his name."

"Sixtyish. Bald. Glasses."

"That's him."

"Yep, that's Charlie. He and Dad go sea-fishing sometimes. Charlie's got a boat."

I take the last mouthful of my fish and lick my lips. I can't get used to this small-town life, everyone knowing each other. It's kind of nice, although part of me can't help worrying. Mum knows a lot of people round here. I don't know how many of them she's told about me, apart from her Quaker friend Pam, and Quakers aren't generally the sort to gossip. But then everyone does sometimes, don't they? It's human nature.

Rumors spread like wildfire in places like this. So how long will it be before one of them mentions something about June Phelps's alcoholic daughter? And then someone says something to someone who happens to know Charlie's wife and before long Charlie's wife tells Charlie and Charlie tells Josh's dad.

Josh shovels up the last of his chips with his fingers and scrunches his paper into a ball.

"Fancy a quick drink in the Flinstead Arms?" he says, holding his hand out for my rubbish.

My stomach tenses. Such an innocent, casual question. I should have anticipated this, should have prepared an answer, but it was all so last-minute I didn't even think.

"I don't really like leaving Mum on her own too long."

A look of disappointment flashes over his face. It sounds like a brush-off, I know it does. But what else can I say? It'll be weird just eating our fish and chips and saying goodbye. I can't invite him back to Mum's. It'll be unbearable, the three of us squeezed into that tiny living room. I'll be on tenterhooks the whole time. There's no way I'm inviting him up to my dingy cell of a bedroom with its squeaky single bed either, and he's not likely to suggest I go back with him to Mistden, not now he's just walked all the way here.

This is crazy. Surely I can walk into a pub without falling apart. I can have a Coke or a lime and soda. I can't spend my whole life avoiding places where people drink. I'll never be able to go anywhere or do anything.

"But I'm sure she'll be fine for a little while longer. She's probably watching one of her gardening programs."

For fuck's sake, what the hell are you doing?

"Great," he says. "I could murder a pint."

The Flinstead Arms is heaving.

"What do you want to drink?" Josh shouts over the noise.

My eyes dart toward the bar and the line of optics illuminated by spotlights. Smirnoff, Gordon's, Jack Daniel's, Archers, Pernod, Bacardi, Courvoisier, Captain Morgan, Teacher's, Grant's, Martini, Baileys. All the premium spirits glinting seductively. My knees tremble. My mouth is dry.

"A lime and soda, please." My voice sounds all muffled, as if I've got a bad head cold. I brace myself for his reaction. The jokey comment. The "Are you *serious?*" look.

"With ice?" he says.

"Yes, please."

"Look, there's a space near the window. Why don't you grab it?"

He wrestles his way to the bar and I head back toward the door and the small gap where there's space to stand by the windowsill. My heart knocks so fast it's painful. This is a huge mistake. Everything's too loud and bright, as if someone's put the volume on full blast and turned on all the lights. I'm drowning in noise and animated faces, in sloshing, sparkling, jewel-colored drinks, in the clinking of glass and drunken laughter. That musty, hoppy beer smell fills my nostrils. My mouth waters. My stomach flutters, then twists. I'll push through the bodies and catch up with him. Tell him I've changed my mind. I want a beer too. I'll be okay with a small beer. Just half a pint. Just to turn down the volume and dim the lights.

Fuck no! This is madness. I shouldn't have come. I can't stay. I have to get out. I have to breathe fresh air.

Josh finds me on the street, not with the smokers outside the pub but peering into the window of the gift shop next door, my forehead pressed against the cold glass. People are looking at me as if I'm some kind of weirdo. I know they are. And so is Josh.

"I thought you'd done a bunk," he says, handing me my drink. He peers at my face. "What's wrong?"

"Sorry, I just needed some air."

"There's a garden out the back. If you can face battling your way through."

"It's the crowds I can't stand. I hate being hemmed in like that."

"Me too. It was a stupid idea coming here. It's much nicer at the Old Schooner. Have you been there?"

"No. I'm not really a pub person, to be honest."

To be honest? Oh, Astrid, that's priceless.

"You should have said. We could have gone to the wine bar. It's much quieter in there. Do you want to go there instead?"

"No, I'd better get back to Mum. Sorry, I shouldn't have come out in the first place. I'm not very good company this evening."

Josh puts his beer on the pavement, close to the shop entrance.

"That's twice you've run away from me." He takes my glass out of my hands and places it down next to his. "Is it what I said about your smoking?"

"No, of course not."

"Only it must have sounded like I was spying on you."

"It's got nothing to do with that. It's me, it's . . . it's just a bit complicated, that's all."

Josh looks away. He's gone very still. "Is there a boyfriend back in London?"

"What? No. No. Not anymore."

"You don't have to talk about it if you don't want to. I understand."

He takes a step toward me and I wrap my arms round his neck, bury my head in his broad chest. His hands cradle my shoulders. He kisses the top of my head. Minutes pass.

"The other day," he says, his mouth so close to the side of my head I feel the warmth of his breath on my ear. "It was too soon. You were so sad about your dad. And you've got your mum's depression to deal with."

Oh God. He's such a lovely, sensitive man. So kind and tender. So heartbreakingly beautiful. He isn't the kind of man to enter into a relationship lightly. He's not like other men. If he thinks smoking cigarettes is my shameful secret, how the hell is he going to react when he finds out what I'm really like? The things I've done. The lies I've told. I have to stop this now, tell him he's right, that things are moving too fast for me. That I just want us to be friends.

So why are my arms still round his neck? Why am I kissing him, tasting the beer on his lips and tongue? Drinking him in.

21

The sun dips below the horizon above the sea, half of a giant orange ball. We sprawl on the grass at the top of the cliff and watch its slow descent. Now that there's distance between us and the Flinstead Arms, my heart rate has returned to normal. I've been inside a pub and survived the experience. I'm stronger than I thought.

Maybe I can conquer this thing after all. On my own terms. I'm not kidding myself that the worst is over. I mean, it's always going to be an ordeal, but maybe it'll get easier with time. Who knows, maybe one day I'll be able to drink normally, sip a glass of cold white wine outside a pub with Josh. All this stuff they say in AA, about people like me being *allergic* to alcohol, that we'll never, ever get better unless we turn our lives over to God—it can't be the *only* way, can it?

Maybe one day I'll look back on this evening as a turning point. Sitting here with Josh, gazing at this epic sky, all streaked with crimson and gold. One thing is certain: I'm not going to let some poison-pen writer throw me off course.

"Did you know that sunsets are an optical illusion?" I say.

Josh traces a pattern on the back of my neck with his fingertips. "And there was me thinking how romantic this was."

"I didn't say the sunset wasn't romantic. Just that it's not real."

"I remember learning about that at school," Josh says. "Something about the light from the sun curving upward so that by the time we see it on the horizon it's already disappeared."

"It's hard to believe, isn't it?"

Josh grins. "I'm hoping your 'trumpey loll' will be equally realistic. I'm looking forward to watching Dad's mates walk straight into the wall and bang their heads."

I give his shoulder a playful shove. He's so easy to be with, so laid back. I want him so badly there's a delicious ache in my groin. He pulls me toward him so that I'm sitting on his lap, my legs wrapped round his back. We kiss for so long I lose track of the time. The light fades. The air grows cool.

"Guess what I've got in my pocket?" he says when we finally stop kissing.

I raise an eyebrow. "Think I've already felt it."

"Not that, you twit! This." He slips his fingers into his jacket pocket and pulls out two keys on a ring. "Come with me," he says, levering me off his lap and scrambling to his feet.

"Don't tell me your dad's got a pied-à-terre on the front as well?"

"Sort of. Come on, I'll show you."

He pulls me gently toward the path that winds down to the promenade. The path that not so long ago I ran up in blind panic, convinced that Simon's ghost was chasing me. And even though I know it couldn't have been him, that none of it was real, the memory of him standing against the beach huts, cigarette glowing in his hand, is so vivid I can't help feeling scared all over again. Because whoever sent me that photo and the picture of the bloodstained hand is real. And for all I know they could be watching me right now.

I try to quiet my mind by telling myself it won't be someone who lives round here. It'll be some sicko in London, getting off on fright-

ening me from afar. I make a mental note to pull the wardrobe out
when I get home and retrieve the envelope, check the postmark to
see where it's from. Why the hell didn't I do that before? I hold tight
to Josh's hand. Even if I'm wrong and they've followed me to Flinstead, no one's going to try anything while I'm with him.

The hut is in the opposite direction from Mistden. It's one of the
ones on stilts with doors and decked platforms that look over the
golf course and fields beyond but whose large windows open out
onto the sea. Now, at high tide, the surf breaks against the stilts.
Soon it will flow right under the hut. Josh flings open the double
windows and I kneel on the single bed that serves as a sofa and lean
out over the black sea with its orangey glimmer. Now that the door
of the beach hut is closed behind us I start to relax.

"I wish I could sleep here," I say, looking over my shoulder at
Josh. He's stuffing something into one of the cupboards in the
kitchen area, his face flushed all of a sudden. Perhaps he's concerned it's not tidy enough for a visitor. Who'd have thought I'd be
going out with the sort of man who cares about such things?

"You're not supposed to," he says, his voice unusually brusque,
as if the suggestion has annoyed him. He straightens up and comes
over to join me at the window. "It's one of the conditions of the
lease."

How is it possible I've fallen for someone so inherently sensible
and cautious?

"But you *could*, right, just for the odd night? I mean, how would
they find out?"

He shrugs. "They wouldn't, I guess."

Something is wrong with him. His mood has darkened.

"Haven't you ever wanted to?"

I think of all the places I've slept over the years as a result of bra-
vado, romanticism, or, more often than not, sheer desperation:
beaches, cars, abandoned buildings, a bothy in Scotland, tents, bus
shelters. Cold, hard floors.

"It's crossed my mind a couple of times."

I get the feeling he's just saying this because he thinks it's what I want to hear.

"I dunno," he continues. "Maybe it's the thought of the stilts giving way while I'm asleep, of waking up in the water."

Our shoulders touch as we kneel on the bed next to each other, our arms resting on the window frame. The sea creeps nearer and nearer and for a few minutes we gaze at it in silence and awe.

"Is that likely to happen?"

"I guess not. Not unless there was a massive tidal surge."

"I thought you must be fearless, the way you swim so far out."

He frowns. "You'd be a fool not to fear the sea, Astrid. It can turn on you in an instant."

Then I tell him how I almost drowned once, how if I hadn't managed to scramble onto a concrete groin I wouldn't be here today.

"That was probably what got you into trouble in the first place, swimming too near the groin. The currents deflect off any obstruction like that. You were lucky."

"My legs got cut to ribbons trying to clamber on top."

"Talking of your legs," he says, slowly trailing the fingertip of his right index finger from my knee to my thigh like a feather. "That's some piece of ink you've got down there."

I grin. Whatever was troubling him back then seems to have passed. "Were you shocked when you saw it?"

"Surprised more than shocked. What with the braids and the Doc Martens, I guessed you might have one somewhere."

"You were looking for a discreet dolphin or butterfly on the hip or shoulder, weren't you?" I say, teasing him. I can just imagine some of the trendy middle-class girlfriends he's been out with in the past.

A slow smile spreads across his face. "I might have guessed you'd go for something more dangerous. There's something subversive about people who change their names."

Within seconds we're tugging each other's clothes off. The bed creaks as Josh lowers himself on top of me. His mouth closes over my left nipple and I wrap my legs round his warm, smooth back. Over his right shoulder I watch the darkening sky framed by the open window of the beach hut. In the top left-hand corner is a small circular patch still streaked with crimson. The last vestiges of the fraudulent sunset, like a bloodshot eye staring down at me.

Josh walks me home and I can't help noticing how relaxed I feel when I'm with him. How safe. The last time I walked home at this time of night, I was petrified, couldn't wait to get inside the cottage and be with Mum. Now I'd do anything to stretch time and make these precious moments with him last as long as possible.

We kiss goodbye in front of the neighbor's hedge, just in case Mum happens to look out of the window. But as soon as I turn my key in the door I know something's wrong. Mum is waiting for me in the hall, stony-faced.

"Pam phoned me earlier," she says. Her voice is cold, her eyes like small black bullets, boring into me. "She saw you go into the Flinstead Arms. You lied to me, Astrid. You said you were going for fish and chips."

I stare at her, open-mouthed. How dare she accuse me of lying? And how dare that wretched friend of hers spy on me like that?

"Did Pam also tell you I ran out of there literally five minutes later? Did she tell you I drank lime and soda? Did she? Well, *did* she?"

I walk right up to her and breathe out in her face. "Can you smell any alcohol on my breath?"

Her nostrils quiver. Her upper body bristles with rage. "What were you doing in a pub? What were you *thinking*?"

"Look, I made a mistake, okay? I thought I could handle it and I couldn't. I came straight out again. I promise you, Mum, I didn't drink anything. You have to believe me."

"Like I believed you all those other times, you mean?"

"That's not fair. You know it isn't. It's different now."

"Is it, Astrid? *Is* it?" She walks away from me into the living room and sinks down into her armchair. "How do I know it's not exactly the same?"

"Because I made you a promise, Mum, and I wouldn't break it."

"You made promises before, remember? And you broke them all. Every last one."

I perch on the edge of the coffee table and take hold of her hands. "I'm telling you the truth, Mum. Pam's right. I did go into the pub, but I was always going to have a soft drink. Then when I got inside and saw all the people drinking and laughing, I thought for a moment I could have one and it'd be all right."

Mum closes her eyes and shakes her head.

"But as soon as I thought that, I changed my mind. I got out of there as fast as I could. Please, Mum, please believe me."

She opens her eyes and they're full of tears. "Oh, Astrid."

I lean forward to hug her and, for a few seconds, I think she's going to push me away. Her body is hard, unyielding. But then she softens against me and I'm sobbing into her shoulder. "I'm so sorry for all those other times, Mum. I'm sorry for hurting you. I'm sorry for everything. But I didn't have anything to drink tonight. I didn't."

She squeezes me tight and we sit there for ages. Me still perched on the edge of the coffee table and her on her armchair, clinging to each other in a way we've never done before.

"I believe you, darling. I believe you."

Another week. Another Wednesday. Why does AA night always come round so fast? Because if there's one place I don't want to be, it's here, in the vestry of Flinstead parish church, sitting on a rickety wooden chair with this bunch of losers. But of course, I'm one of them, aren't I? I nearly blew everything by walking into the pub last week.

The man with acne is rambling on about his boring life. I

stopped listening after the first few sentences. I know I should be concentrating and making the sort of encouraging noises the rest of them are making—those little "mm" sounds when he says something they can relate to—but my mind's too scattered to take any of it in. I feel like telling him to relish the boredom, to make the most of the fact that he's not having his every move scrutinized, that he's not receiving threatening messages through the post.

I've been so jittery lately. Jumping at the slightest noise. Not sleeping. It's ever since I pulled the wardrobe away from the wall to check the postmark on that envelope. I think part of me was hoping there'd be nothing there except bits of dust and carpet fluff and that I'd imagined the whole thing, but of course, there it was. It was pretty faint, but I could just about make out that it said "London, EC2."

At first I was relieved it wasn't local, but then I realized that doesn't mean a thing. If you wanted to remain anonymous—and clearly, they do—you'd travel somewhere else to send it, wouldn't you? EC2 is a central London postcode. It'd be easy to travel into town and pop something in the post there. *Where* it was posted is irrelevant. What's more worrying is that whoever sent it knows where I live.

I hope to God Helen is right and that the person behind this is a coward at heart. Someone who gets pleasure from upsetting people from a distance. Why are there so many haters in the world?

A sudden burst of clapping brings me back to the moment. Acne Man must have finished. Should I go next and bring the pub thing up? What's the point of dragging myself here if I don't? And who knows, it might make me feel better, saying it aloud. After all, telling Helen about Simon and my twisted pen pal helped a bit. None of it's gone away, of course, but it's true what they say: a problem shared is a problem halved. Well, maybe not halved exactly, but certainly reduced. Confession is good for the soul.

At last the clapping dies down and silence settles upon us like a welcome breeze on a hot day. I know that if I don't speak now, someone else will pick up the baton and run with it and I'll have missed my chance.

"I went into the Flinstead Arms last week," I hear myself saying. The atmosphere in the room shifts up a gear.

"I couldn't think of an excuse not to and I thought I'd be fine."

The woman with protruding eyes leans forward slightly, as if she doesn't want to miss a single thing. As if my words are drops of neat vodka.

"I nearly ordered half a pint of beer."

Acne Man taps his right foot on the floor and stares at my knees. He's already knocked it back in his head and is ordering another—a pint this time. Helen smiles at me with her eyes, but she's twisting her fingers in her lap and making the knuckles click.

Only Rosie and Jeremy seem unfazed. It's as if they've been expecting it, just waiting for me to slip up so they can brandish the Big Book in front of me and say, *We told you so—now will you listen to us and do this thing properly?*

But I'm glad I've told them. I'm glad it's out in the open, even if it is only within these four walls. I just wish I could be as honest with Josh.

She's not beautiful, not by a long chalk, but there's something rather sensual about her mouth. And then there are those long, slender legs. Those pert little tits. I can just about see what he saw in her.

Why do I do this to myself? Why do I keep imagining them together? It's unhealthy. Masochistic.

Every day I tell myself I'm going to stop. But here I am again. Watching. Waiting. Biding my time till the moment is right. Till the perfect opportunity presents itself.

Revenge. The anticipation of it. The playing it out in my mind.

It's almost like . . . an addiction.

22

"Where do you want this set up?" Josh says. "I'm guessing the living room has the best light."

He's been up into the attic and brought down the old easel that used to belong to his mother.

"It's probably best if I paint it *in situ*. I need to get the colors right."

Finalizing the sketches and meeting Josh for walks along the beach that invariably end up with more sex in the beach hut have been the only things keeping me focused these last few days. But now that I'm finally ready to start on the preliminary painting, my nerves are in shatters. It's been ages since I've done this type of work. Would Richard have commissioned me if he knew I hadn't painted for seven long years?

Josh carries the easel into the small middle room where the only light comes in via the wall lights and the transom windows above the two internal doors. He helps me slot the canvas into place.

A couple of minutes later he returns with a portable radio.

"In case you fancy a bit of background music as you work," he says.

Alone in the room, surrounded by my brushes and sponges, my

tubes of paint and my plastic palettes, I take a deep breath. This is the moment I've been anticipating for days. It's also the moment I've been dreading.

I try to visualize the finished product. Once I'm happy with the painting on canvas—*if* I'm happy with it—and once I've got Richard's agreement to go ahead, I'll take a photo, print it out, and draw a grid over it. Then I'll draw a larger grid of equal ratio onto the wall itself so that I can transfer what I see in my reference photo square by square. It's like painting by numbers except it'll be my own painting I'm copying.

There is, of course, an easier way of transferring an image onto a large surface, and that's using a digital projector, but it's expensive and, besides, the grid method is a brilliant way of training your eye to break down images into small, interlocking shapes. I'll have to get the ratios spot on, though. There has to be the exact same number of equally spaced lines on the wall as there are on the photo—identical, perfect squares—otherwise the finished product will look distorted.

It's time-consuming, intricate work, but if it was good enough for the Old Masters, then it's good enough for me, and Richard has already said that I must take as long as I need. He's not after a rushed job, and neither am I. This house is a labor of love for him. He cares about aesthetics. He cares about the small details. Josh does too. I can tell from the quality of their workmanship. Which makes the task ahead of me seem even more daunting.

I can't begin to imagine what they'd make of Mum's house, with its dated textured wallpaper and popcorn ceilings. I've stopped suggesting she redecorate because, try as she might, she can't stop herself harking back to the squat thing. As if someone who's lived in a squat isn't allowed to have an opinion about home decor. I suppose one day the house will be mine—then I can do what I want with it. Unless she's left it all to Wells in India or Donkeys in Peril. I wouldn't put it past her.

Suddenly, I feel terribly ashamed. My mother is a good person.

A worthy person. She used to teach challenging children. Children who'd been expelled from school. She doesn't deserve a fuck-up like me. She wanted someone called Hilary. Someone who would have benefited from her steady influence, who would have followed her into teaching or social work or another public-spirited career. Someone who would have made her proud.

I swallow hard. She was proud of me once. Proud of the paintings I used to do. Maybe it's not too late.

We call it a day around three. Josh suggests a swim—he knows my swimsuit is in my bag because he saw it earlier, when I was searching for my lip balm—and although I'm weary from my first day's painting, it's that good type of weariness, the one that comes after doing something you want to be doing. Turns out I *can* still paint, after all.

I'm expecting it to be cold, but as I walk into the water it's still a shock to the system. The chill coils round my ankles and creeps up my calves like a pair of icy socks. It doesn't seem like such a good idea now that I'm actually here, even though the late-afternoon sun is warm on my back. But I'm not going to chicken out now.

"Don't just launch yourself in," Josh says. "Wade in slowly. Get your body and mind acclimatized first." He's up to his waist already, splashing water onto his arms. "It's the first time this year I've been in without a wetsuit."

As the water reaches my thighs I gasp. Josh laughs. "Told you it'd put that flame out."

Right, then: it's now or never. I dip below the surface of the water. It's even colder than I imagined, a real adrenaline rush that makes me gasp. I propel myself forward and, within seconds, Josh is swimming alongside me. I'd never have done this on my own, not at this time of year, but he makes me feel safe. There's never a moment when I think he might ambush me from under the water or splash me. For Josh, swimming is a serious business.

I have a sudden image of him teaching a child to float. Our child. Talking to her in that gentle voice of his, a reassuring hand under the small of her back. My God, what am I thinking? I can barely look after myself, let alone a child.

I keep swimming, but now another child threatens to come into focus. I won't let it. I won't. But it pushes its way through, its little feet kicking and thrashing against the footplate of its pushchair, its face contorted in distress. And then the noise of its cry. That panicky, staccato burst that makes my ears pound.

Not now, please. Not here. I turn back toward the shore, anxious to get out of the water and dry off.

"I don't want to get out of my depth," I manage to say between breaths.

"You won't," Josh says. "Not if you swim parallel to the shore."

At last, the image fades. The crying becomes the squawking of a distant gull and I feel strong enough to swim alongside him.

"How do you feel?" he asks.

Broken. Adrift. At the mercy of forces beyond my control. The sudden swell of an unwanted memory crashing into me like a wave.

"Freezing," I tell him.

But with each stroke it becomes just a little easier, till it's bordering on being strangely pleasant, in a sharp, biting, masochistically invigorating sort of way. The water is smooth and silky on my arms and shoulders. Every so often, I pause and stand up, just to reassure myself that I can still feel soft sand beneath my feet.

Josh dives under the water and surfaces a few feet in front of me. His wet hair clings to his head like a swimming cap and he runs his hands through it, pushing it back so that it's off his forehead.

"Maybe I should get a short back and sides like you," he says.

"No. I love your hair." Shit. It's too soon to be bandying words like "love" about, even if I am just referring to his hair. *Change the subject. Quick.* I take a deep breath through my nostrils. "That ozone smell's great, isn't it? Takes me back to being a little girl, on day trips to the beach."

The way my voice is coming out, all breathy with the cold and the physical exertion of the swimming, I must sound like a little girl to his ears.

"Except it isn't ozone," Josh says. His face glistens with water, drops of it trapped on his eyelashes. "What you're smelling is actually the gas that comes off decomposing plankton and seaweed. That's why it has that sulfurous whiff. It's called dimethyl sulfide."

"Now who's being romantic?"

Josh grins and launches himself headfirst into the water again. The last thing I see is the pink soles of his feet. I wait for him to reappear, but he doesn't. A stray cloud covers the sun and fear sneaks up my spine, vertebra by vertebra. How can he do that? How can he swim under for so long? I take a step forward. My foot slides across the slippery surface of a large smooth stone embedded in the sand, and as I try to right myself I realize my toes aren't touching the bottom and I almost lose my balance. Water rushes up my nostrils and before I can snort it out some of it's gone down the back of my throat.

I tread water till I've coughed and spluttered the pungent, briny taste away. A few yards to my right Josh's shoulders and arms, and then the long, graceful curve of his back, break the surface. At least he didn't witness me spitting and snotting into the sea.

I swim over to him in my pedestrian breaststroke.

"I want to be able to swim like you."

He pulls me toward him and encloses me in his strong, wet arms. "I'll teach you," he says. "I taught my mum how to swim too."

"Really?"

"Yeah, she had a mean front crawl."

"I can't do that."

"Sure you can. Go on, have a try."

I do my useless version for as long as I'm able, which isn't long at all, not in this choppy water.

"Hmm," he says, grinning. "We're going to have to do a lot of work on your breathing technique. You need to roll farther for your breaths and breathe on alternate sides, if you can. You've got to find a pattern that matches the waves and breathe as fast as you can, suck the air in quick. You are breathing out underwater, aren't you?"

"No, I'm holding my breath when my face is under."

"Well, that's where you're going wrong. You've got to exhale while your face is in the water, or you're going to get out of breath and tire too fast. The most important thing to remember when you're swimming in the sea is that if you get into trouble, try not to panic. Tread water for a while, or float. The more relaxed you are, the less oxygen you'll need."

"I'm not sure I'll be any good at it."

"Don't worry," he says. "By the end of summer I'll have you leaping through the water like a dolphin."

The end of summer. It sounds so final.

23

The second I turn my key and push open the porch door, I smell it. Joint, by Roccobarocco. Simon's aftershave. And even though I know it isn't his—of course it isn't, it's just the postman— the sudden and powerful surge of memories that come with it still makes me gasp.

I drop my bag on the hall floor and walk toward the living room and the clacking sound of knitting needles. The door is ajar and, as I approach, I see Mum, sitting in her usual armchair by the fireplace, balls of flesh-colored wool nestled in her lap like hairless kittens. On the coffee table in front of her are two empty cups and saucers.

Oh no, Pam isn't here, is she? Mum's informant. That's all I need. I've only met her a couple of times, and on both occasions she looked at me as if I were some kind of alien. Pam's daughter, it goes without saying, isn't a hopeless alcoholic without a penny to her name. Pam's daughter is a proper grown-up. A math teacher, married with two boys. Lives on the new estate on the outskirts of Mistden, which, if you listen to Pam, you'd think was the pinnacle of success.

And to think, all that could have been mine . . .

I walk farther into the room and turn, reluctantly, toward the sofa. But whoever was here is now gone. Only a slight indentation in the cushion remains.

"You've had a visitor."

Mum lances a ball of wool with her needles and drops it into the basket at her feet. "Yes, she came back. The girl who used to live here. Well, young woman, I suppose I should say. She kept saying how different it looked."

My eyes scan the room. Something about this doesn't feel right.

"When did she say she lived here?"

"Sometime in the early nineties, I think she said."

"Don't you think that's odd? I'd be surprised if the decor in here isn't exactly as it was twenty, maybe even thirty years ago."

Mum shrugs. "If you say so, dear. The furniture and curtains will have been different, though, and the layout. I expect that's what she meant."

"I thought you told me once that the previous owner was really old. A widower, you said."

Mum stands up and starts stacking the cups. "Yes, that's right. He got too frail and had to go into a home."

"So how could a little girl have been living here?"

"Oh, for heaven's sake, Astrid. I don't know. Maybe she was his granddaughter."

"Did she go upstairs?"

Mum walks out into the hall with the cups and saucers. "Of course. She wanted to see her old room. She was only up there a couple of minutes."

The hairs on the back of my neck stand up. I don't like the thought of a stranger coming to the house when Mum's on her own. She's too trusting. It could have been anyone.

I follow her out. "You mean she was up there alone?"

"Yes."

"Jeez, Mum! You let a complete stranger wander round the house on her own?"

Mum makes an exasperated snorting noise. "Astrid, why do you always think the worst of people?"

"I don't, I just . . ."

"She was only up there a few minutes, and then she left."

"Did she tell you her name?"

"Laura."

"Laura what?"

"I don't know, dear. She didn't say."

"And you didn't think to ask?"

Mum rolls her eyes. "Perhaps I should have checked her ID before letting her over the doorstep. Oh, by the way, I forgot to tell you. Your DWP letter's arrived. I've left it on the stairs on top of some other bits and pieces that need sorting through for recycling."

My stomach muscles tighten at the thought of another brown envelope and what it might contain, but when I see what she's talking about my fears dissolve. This is what I've been waiting for. I recognize the official logo. I tear the envelope open and scan the letter inside, relief flooding through me. Mum looks at me expectantly.

"They've given me a date to sign on. About time."

I scoop up the pile that's left and head for the recycling box in the porch, sifting through them as I go. A flyer about pizza delivery. The little magazine full of adverts for local services and tradespeople. Something from Flinstead parish church detailing service times and various other groups and clubs—nothing about AA meetings, I notice, although I guess that's not the sort of thing they tend to shout about—and . . . and another brown envelope with the same curly green handwriting as before. My ears begin to buzz. My gut feels as if it's being wrung out like a towel.

Mum's still standing there. "Did I miss something important? I thought the rest was all junk mail."

I force myself to think of a response. "It's from someone I met in rehab. I recognize her writing."

"Oh, I didn't realize you were keeping in touch with anyone."

"She said she'd drop me a line sometime." My voice sounds distant and tinny, as if it's being squeezed through a narrow tube.

"Right, I'd better get on with our supper." Mum heads toward the kitchen. "Could you close the window in the front room, please? I don't know what perfume that girl was wearing, but it was really overpowering."

Something niggles at the back of my mind. Like the trace of a dream I can't quite remember. The sense that I've overlooked something. An important detail. And then it comes to me.

"What did she look like? Can you describe her?"

Mum stops and turns round, an irritated look on her face. "Why are you obsessing over this? She was about your age, I think. Pale skin. Dark hair."

My scalp shrinks. There's a strange, tightening sensation in my chest. "What was she wearing?"

"What is this, Astrid? An interrogation?" She sighs. "Jeans, I think. Gray jeans. Oh, and she had a sort of quilted anorak on. I remember thinking she must be far too hot in it, but she wouldn't take it off."

The tightness in my chest intensifies. "Do you mean a puffer jacket?"

"I've no idea what a puffer jacket is, dear. It was gray and quilted, that's all I can remember. Why are you asking me all these questions?"

"Someone at AA mentioned there's been a spate of house burglaries recently and they all reported having strange house calls a few days before."

The lie sounds plausible enough.

Mum makes one of her little harrumphing noises as she sets off for the kitchen again. "I'm not in my dotage yet, dear. I'm perfectly capable of using my own judgment."

I stare at the green writing on the envelope. Why didn't I make the connection before? The first time I noticed the smell was the night I thought I saw Simon's ghost running past me. There was someone else there too, wasn't there? A girl tying her laces. A girl in a gray puffer jacket. I almost tripped over her.

I take the stairs two at a time and lock myself in the toilet. The handwriting on the envelope taunts me with its extravagant loops and curls. With its psychopathic *greenness*. This time, there's no postmark.

And that's not the only time I've seen her. I'm sure it was her eating chocolate when I was in the Fisherman's Shack waiting for Josh. And I've seen her at the beach too. Those times I've caught the scent on the breeze . . . the scent that must have acted like a trigger in my mind and made me hallucinate. All this time, she's been following me. It wasn't the postman after all. And now she's been inside this house! She must have slipped this into the pile of post on her way upstairs when Mum wasn't looking.

As before, there's just one piece of paper inside. Gingerly, I draw it out, unfold it slowly. It's a page torn from a local newspaper with the name blacked out—a family-announcement page—and there, in the deaths section, someone has crossed out one of the names of the deceased and written something above it, in tiny neat letters.

I peer a little closer. It says "Hilary Phelps."

The walls close in on me and my eyes grow fuzzy. Someone wants me dead.

The sheet of newspaper flutters to the floor. And that's when I see the large green letters scrawled on the back:

You'd better not get too comfortable in sleepy little Flinstead. You'd better keep your wits about you from now on. What goes around comes around. And now it's time. It's time to pay for what you've done . . . Because it's not just Simon on your conscience, is it?

24

I open my eyes. I'm scrunched up on the toilet floor, face squashed against the rubbery cork tiles. What the hell happened here? I must have passed out.

Then I remember, and it's like a switch has been flicked on in my brain. All the bad neurons firing at once.

You need a drink. It's the only way out of this.

I can't allow myself to listen to this voice, but it's so persistent. So persuasive.

You know how good it will taste. Just one little drink. You can handle it.

I can't. I really can't.

Oh, but you can. You'll know when to stop this time.

No! I just have to ride the compulsion out. I can resist it. I can. Whoever's doing this to me *wants* this to happen. They want me to fall apart. But I won't. I can't. Not this time. I've got too much to lose.

Too much to lose? Don't make me laugh. You've lost it already. You don't for one minute think this thing with Josh has got legs, do you? It's doomed, and you know it. He won't want anything to do with you once he knows what kind of person you are.

It's true. I can't deny that.

Pretending your mother's depressed and that you're here to look after her. How low can you get? Ha! Daft question. We both know how low you can get, and it's much, much lower than that. You're a disgrace, a pathetic excuse for a human being. A waste of space.

I snatch the piece of paper from the floor and rip it up, tearing into it till it's completely destroyed, till there's no way I could piece it together again, even if I wanted to. Then I scoop every last scrap of it into my hands and throw the whole lot down the loo and flush the chain.

It hasn't gone away, though. How could it? I'll never *unsee* those words.

Because it's not just Simon on your conscience, is it?

The young woman from my nightmare appears behind my eyes, struggling to her feet and pointing her finger. I shake my head to force the image away. Simon wouldn't have told anyone else. We made a pact when we sobered up. He was as disgusted with himself as I was. As I still am. The self-loathing. The guilt. These things don't lessen with time, they get worse. They fester inside you like a cancerous growth. It was the one thing we couldn't talk about, either of us, ever again.

What goes around comes around. And now it's time. It's time to pay for what you've done.

As if I don't pay for it every day. As if it isn't always hovering at the back of my mind, ready to ambush me at any given moment.

I take a deep breath. My mind won't stop now. It's doing what it always does, flinging me straight back to the horrors of that night—what bits of it I can remember. The pictures in my head collide and blur. The horrified shape of her mouth. Her knuckles white against the brown leather strap of her bag. The child in the pushchair screaming and kicking its legs.

Now that I've conjured the fragments of memory I'm piecing them together like I always do, trying to find the right order, to make sense of the noise and confusion in my brain. The pushing and shoving. That sickening crack. The rising note of terror in the child's wail.

My heart pounds. The rest is blurred, like a film on fast-forward. Simon pulling me away. The pain in my chest from running. The fluorescent light in the late-night Spar. More cheap wine. More cider. Then . . . nothing. I must have blacked out. When I came to there was blood on my sleeve, but it wasn't mine. *It wasn't mine.* What the hell did I do to that poor woman?

I force myself to breathe more deeply, to return to the here and now. I retch into the toilet. It's the patchy nature of my memories that's so hard to bear. The not knowing. It was down by the river somewhere. Blue railings, that's all I can remember. She must have fought back or she wouldn't have fallen. Why the hell did she fight back? She had a child with her, for Christ's sake!

Was it her head that hit the paving stones? She could have died! And what about the child? How long was it screaming before someone came to help? We scoured the news reports when we sobered up, desperate for information, but we couldn't find it reported anywhere, not even one small paragraph in the local news.

I unlock the toilet door and go into my bedroom. My eyes travel slowly round the room. At first glance, it looks exactly the same, but something in this eight-by-ten-foot space is subtly different. Like in one of those spot-the-difference pictures.

I draw back my duvet and stare at the bottom sheet and the pillow. I don't know what I'm expecting to see, but whatever gruesome discovery my subconscious anticipates—a dead rat; a horse's head—the bed harbors nothing but my own folded T-shirt.

I run my hands over my bedside cabinet. The small travel clock, my lip salve and box of tissues. What's wrong with this picture?

And then I see it, the Big Book with its marker sticking out, and something clicks into place. Of course! I grab hold of it and flip through the chapters with trembling fingers till I come to the section I'm searching for. I need to check the exact wording.

Here it is. Step 5: "Admitted to God, to ourselves, *and to another human being* the exact nature of our wrongs."

I close my eyes and inhale through my nose. Oh, Simon, dear Simon. You weren't messing about, were you? You really were following the program. You were working the steps properly. To the letter.

The question is: who did you tell?

Part Three

25

Mum bangs on the bathroom door. I flinch at the noise.

"Astrid, you've been in there for ages! What are you doing?"

I dry myself with one of her rock-hard bath towels. My skin feels raw and sensitive and every bone in my body aches from lack of sleep.

"I'll be out in two minutes."

I stare at the dark hollows under my eyes, my gray complexion. I should text Josh and tell him I can't work on the painting today. Tell him I'm ill. But what will I do if I stay home all day? Go crazy, that's what. I need the distraction. Now more than ever. Besides, I've agreed to do the painting—I can't let them down.

Back in my bedroom, I'm in the middle of fastening my bra when I see it. Or rather, when I *don't* see it. The gold juggling ball. It's missing from my bedside table.

I *knew* something was different in here. She's taken it. She's been in my room and stolen Simon's juggling ball. The only thing of his I have left. My heart thumps. I bend down to look under the bed, just in case I'm mistaken and it's rolled off, but it isn't there. I pull open drawers and rifle through them, even though I know I won't find it. I even open my wardrobe and go through all my pockets.

It isn't anywhere. It's gone.

This girl has wormed her way into the house when I wasn't here. She's had the nerve to sit on my mum's settee, drinking her tea and feeding her lies. She's left her poisonous note on the stairs and nosed around in my room. The very air feels contaminated. It's all too close for comfort now. What does she want with me?

Down in the kitchen, as I wait for the kettle to boil, a bitter anger floods through me. I can't blame Simon for working through the Twelve Steps. I'm doing it myself, or trying to. But he must have given this girl, whoever she is, my name—my *real* name. How else would she have tracked me down? My fingers curl into fists. It was *our* shameful secret—it bonded us together like glue. We said we'd take it to our graves. What were you thinking, Simon? How could you be so stupid? So careless?

Mum comes in with her arms full of dirty washing for the machine. I pretend to be reading the small print on the back of the box of teabags. There's no way I can tell her, because I know exactly what she'll say if she knows I'm being stalked and threatened. She'll tell me to go to the police. She'll insist upon it. And I'd have to tell her about that night. She'll never forgive me. Never. I can't even forgive myself.

I can't tell Josh either. This is the man who won't even contemplate staying in a beach hut overnight because it's against council rules. He'll want nothing more to do with me.

If only I'd had the sense to tell him about my past straightaway, maybe, just maybe, it would have been all right. He might have been sympathetic, willing to help me. Now, though, he'll feel duped. All the things he admires most about me: my love for my "career," taking time out to look after my "depressed" mother—it's all one great big sham. He'll despise me. I'll lose them both. Mum *and* Josh.

"Promise me you won't let that girl in if she comes back."

Mum wrinkles her brow. "You're not still on about that, are you?" Her face softens. "Look, even if she *was* casing the joint for someone, I'm sure she'll have told them not to bother. There's nothing worth stealing in here."

I force a laugh. "You're not wrong there."

But she *is* wrong. Something has already been stolen. Simon's juggling ball. And my peace of mind—what little I had in the first place.

Josh picks me up in his dad's car. If he notices how bad I look—and he must do, surely—it doesn't show on his face. The relief that I don't have to walk all the way to Mistden on my own is overwhelming. Even so, I glance up and down the street before getting in. She could be watching me right now. I sink down into the passenger seat and watch Josh's hands resting on the steering wheel. The car, a swanky Mercedes, smells of leather and newness, and I wish I could enjoy the luxury of being driven around in it, but I can't. I don't even know why I'm doing this. It's going to be impossible to get back into the painting zone.

"I had a peek at your picture last night," Josh says, eyes fixed firmly on the road ahead. "I can see all the shapes already. It's going to be fantastic."

His left hand leaves the wheel just long enough to squeeze my knee.

"You okay?"

"Yeah, I'm fine. Just a bit tired, that's all."

"Don't worry," he says, grinning. "Once you've knocked back a quick double, you'll be fine."

My stomach clenches. A quick double? What the hell is he talking about?

"A double espresso, that is. I've bought you some strong Colombian coffee to keep you going."

If I wasn't a bag of nerves, I'd be laughing out loud.

"Oh, thanks. That's great."

I stare out of the window at the houses we're passing and the people walking by. What will I do if I see her? The girl in the puffer jacket. It has to be her. Who else could it be?

My fingers ache from where I've been clenching them into fists. The moment I've dreaded for so long has finally happened. I've been found out. But why is she tormenting me like this?

As Josh turns the car into his dad's driveway, I've made up my mind. There's only one way out of this mess. I have to take matters into my own hands and find that girl myself. Make her tell me what she wants.

26

I stand in front of the easel and stare at the blank canvas. I doubt I'll be able to keep my hand steady enough to hold the brush, let alone do anything creative with it.

Josh places his hands on my shoulders and kisses the nape of my neck. I lean back into him, glad of the solidity of his warm body against mine. At least I'm safe when I'm here.

"Dad's going out later," he says. "We can have one of our long coffee breaks." His tongue flicks my earlobe and sends shivers up my spine. "Without the coffee."

I turn round and fling my arms round his neck, kiss him long and hard on the mouth. Whatever nasty little game this girl is playing, she's not going to spoil this for me. She's not going to win. I won't let her. I'm finally sorting myself out and building bridges with Mum, falling in love again, painting. Whatever I've done in the past, that part of my life is over. I'm not that person anymore.

The hours pass. Somehow or other, I manage to still my mind for short bursts of time, long enough to play around a little with the composition, to define the darker areas with a bluish gray. I can't trust myself to do anything that requires more prolonged focus. And yet, as I stand before the easel, the finished picture spreads out in my mind. Even with no added color, no detail whatsoever, the image is already there, waiting to emerge.

But now more images superimpose themselves over the canvas. A nightmarish montage that unfolds before me even when I screw my eyes tight shut. A crumpled body on the pavement. A child's face, contorted with panic. Blood on my sleeve.

I back away from the easel, almost tripping on a ruck in the dust sheet that Richard has spread on the floor. Righting myself by flinging a hand out to the wall, I run out of the room and into the downstairs cloakroom, lock myself in, and perch on the edge of the closed toilet lid, elbows on my knees, hands clasped between my legs. My mind swings wildly from one incoherent memory to another, but nothing makes any sense. Just when I think I've nailed something down, something that will make sense of it all, it slips away again.

I try to slow the rhythm of my breath, holding lungfuls of air for as long as possible then exhaling slowly through my nose, till at last the panic subsides and I feel strong enough to stand up. I run the cold tap in the little sink and splash my face. I hardly recognize my reflection in the mirror. The pale, pinched face. The puffy eyes.

Above my head comes the sound of footsteps. The cloakroom has been installed into the space under the stairs, so the vibrations follow the slope of the ceiling. I've no idea how long I've been holed up in here. It could be ten minutes; it could be twenty. I flush the toilet and wait for a few moments before sliding the bolt across and opening the door, stepping out into the hallway.

Richard is pulling on his jacket and slipping on a pair of deck shoes he's left by the front door. His blond-gray hair is flecked with white paint, his clothes too. He smiles broadly when he sees me and lifts his hand in a fixed wave.

"See you in a couple of hours, Astrid. I'm going to see a man about a boat."

When Josh appears in the doorway of the small room just five minutes after the front door closes I'm sorting my brushes out, giving myself time to summon up the courage to face the canvas again.

"Are you ready for your coffee break yet?" he says, and we both know exactly what kind of break he has in mind. At least he doesn't seem to notice how little progress I've made with the painting.

"What if your dad comes back early?"

"He won't."

"How do you know?"

"I think he's gone out to give us time alone. And no, I didn't ask him to, if that's what you're thinking."

I force myself to sound normal, to make a joke. "Maybe he's having a secret tryst of his own. He must have loads of women after him."

Big mistake. Josh looks as if I've just slapped him round the face.

"Not to my knowledge," he says.

I'm taken aback by the unexpected sharpness of his tone.

He sighs. "Look, I know you must think I'm being oversensitive. But it's taken us both a long time to come to terms with Mum not being around anymore. I just can't imagine him falling for another woman. Mum was . . . Mum was pretty special."

He takes the brushes from my hand and lays them down on the table.

"You're special too," he says softly.

I feel his heartbeat as he holds me close against his chest, and for a few moments we just stand there, our arms wrapped tightly round each other. Am I special enough that he'll still love me when he realizes I've been lying? Special enough that he'll forgive me for the things I've done in the past? For whatever it was I did that terrible, terrible night?

His voice, when it comes, is barely more than a whisper. "Let's go upstairs, Hilary Phelps."

My whole body stiffens. I shrink from his touch. How on earth does he . . . ?

He takes a step back. "Hey! You really don't like that name, do you?"

Stupid girl. I told him on the beach. He's just teasing me. But still, hearing it so soon after seeing it written on that death notice is a shock. I attempt a smile and Josh grins back at me. The noise of my own heart beating furiously is, of course, in my ears only.

He pulls me toward him again, but I wriggle out of his arms. I need time to recover. "Let me wash my brushes out first."

He pretends to look hurt. "How to make a guy feel wanted."

"Acrylic paint dries really fast and these are expensive. You have to look after them."

"Can I help?"

"If you want to. You've got to work this soap into the bristles all the way down to the ferrule . . ."

He drags his teeth over his bottom lip and takes the bar of soap from my hands. "I love it when you talk dirty."

The corners of my mouth turn up. The tension of the last few minutes is starting to recede.

"And then rinse thoroughly with lukewarm water."

"Yes, ma'am."

I follow him with my eyes as he carries my brushes and soap away. I love everything about this man: his walk, his voice, those eyes that go from kind to sexy in a heartbeat. The way his hair curls over his ears. The smell of him.

Then I think of those words on the back of the photo. *What goes around comes around. It's time to pay for what you've done.* That's karma, isn't it? Actions have consequences. I don't deserve to be this happy. That's what it means.

By the time I hear the sound of Richard's tires on the gravel driveway I'm back at my easel, trying to work on the reflections of light in the water beyond the jetty. I wanted to stay in Josh's bed forever, curled up next to his strong, warm body, pretending everything was normal. But it isn't, and the harder I try to convince myself otherwise, the more ominous the whole thing seems. The more chilling. Who would do such a thing? And why?

Richard's voice floats through the window I opened earlier. He must have walked round to the side of the house, be standing with his phone just out of sight by the garage. His voice has a low, measured intensity I don't recognize. My brush pauses mid-air.

"No. I haven't told him yet." There's a long pause. "Yes, she's here now."

My chest tightens. There's no reason to think he's found out about me—he could be talking about anything—but still, it's the first thing that comes into my head. I tiptoe into the next room and strain my ears for more, but as I'm leaning toward the window he walks farther into the garden and our eyes meet. He frowns and I dart back to the easel as if I've been caught doing something I shouldn't. A minute later the front door opens and he bounds up the stairs. He's saying something to Josh, but I can't make out what. Their voices are muffled and indistinguishable from down here.

The paintbrush slips through my fingers and onto the floor. This is absurd. I need to get ahold of myself. *She's* made me like this. That nasty fucking girl and her cruel games. Who *is* she?

I keep imagining her opening the envelope. The feeling of dread in the pit of her belly as she realizes I know her darkest secret. Scaring her is the only fun I've had in a long while. Almost more fun than actually killing her.

Almost.

But there comes a time when fantasizing about something isn't enough. The release when it happens—if it happens at all—is less satisfying. Less pleasurable. It's like a drug I've developed a tolerance for.

It's time to up the dosage.

27

I t's unbearable going back into the cottage. What if there's another brown envelope waiting for me?

The relief when there isn't doesn't last long. Because she's still out there somewhere, plotting her next move. And for the next two days, there's no chance of escaping to the house in Mistden and being with Josh, because he and his dad won't be there. They're going away for some long-standing family event in Berkshire.

I can't get Richard's face when I said goodbye earlier out of my mind. He could barely look me in the eye. Has that girl told him something? Is that what that phone call was about? If he has, he'll tell Josh while they're away. He's bound to. Why the hell didn't I tell them sooner? Why am I such a coward?

Mum's getting ready to visit Pam for the evening. A few weeks ago I'd have been delighted to have had the house to myself for once, to watch what I want on TV, or listen to music without her complaining it's too loud. But tonight, I don't want to be alone. Tonight, I need company. I think of Helen's number upstairs in my room. Maybe I could invite her over when Mum's gone.

"There's some quiche and salad in the fridge," Mum says. She pecks me on the cheek. "You look done in, darling."

"I am. I'm not used to standing up all day."

"Why don't you have a nice early night?" she says, and for once, I don't resent the suggestion. For once, I appreciate that she isn't just nagging, that she has my best interests at heart. Not that there's much chance of me getting any sleep.

Helen's voice sounds different. At first I think it's the signal, but then she laughs as if I've said something funny, and I haven't. The realization judders through me like an electric shock. She's been drinking. Of course she has. The timbre of her voice has altered. It isn't distorted from bad reception—her speech is starting to slur.

"Helen, are you okay?"

"Yeah, I'm fine. Why wouldn't I be?"

There it is, that defensive tone hovering just below the surface. It sounds like something I would have said. Back in the day, when Mum used to keep calling to check up on me.

My mind races. Loath as I am to admit it, perhaps I should have listened to Rosie. The very last thing I need right now is a friend who's still drinking. I need to disassociate myself from all that. Self-preservation, that's what's important now. In any case, we've only known each other a few weeks. We're hardly best buddies.

I'll talk to her, though, try to persuade her to stop. It's the least I can do after she's been so kind and listened to all *my* crap.

I change tack quickly and tell her about my day, about starting the painting for Josh's dad. About the house and how beautiful it is. Anything to keep her on the line, keep her talking.

"Things are really taking off for you, aren't they?" she says, but not in a snide way. She sounds sad and wistful.

I'm trying to think of how to respond when she speaks again.

"I've got nothing left, Astrid." Her voice cracks.

"Oh, Helen, that's not true. You're doing so well."

"I was, but I'm not anymore. I've . . . I've been very weak today." At last, there it is. The admission.

"Come on, Helen. It's not too late to stop. It's just a little setback. Don't have any more. Please."

"It's all right for you. You've got your mum and Josh. You're still so young. You've got your whole life ahead of you. I'm all washed up."

If only I could tell her what's happened, but I can't, can I? Not while she's drinking. Before I can stop myself I tell her to hold on and that I'm on my way round right now. She's at that dangerous self-pitying stage. I've got to be strong and help her before she loses it completely. It could quite easily have been me who broke first. When I think of how close I've come lately . . .

My hands are shaking so much it takes me ages to get my feet into my shoes and tie the laces, partly because it'll be the first time I've left the house on my own since opening that envelope, and partly because turning up at Helen's flat while she's drinking is going to test me to my limits. I'm fragile enough as it is at the moment. But if I leave her on her own, who knows what might happen?

I'm on high alert from the second I leave the cottage, walking as fast as I can without actually breaking into a run. I'm there in under five minutes, panting as I press the bell and stare up at her window. At last, the curtain twitches. A few minutes later the buzzer goes and I push open the heavy glass door and head for the stairwell. The door to her flat is ajar when I get there. The telly's on in the background.

As I move farther in, I see her in the kitchen, emptying a bottle of wine down the sink. My shoulders relax.

"Shall I make us both some coffee?" I say, trying not to look at the red wine sploshing against the stainless steel, averting my eyes from the telltale purple ring in the large wine glass still standing on the counter, like the one I saw not so long ago on her draining rack and wondered about.

She hands me the empty bottle and goes and slumps in an armchair. I push it through the flap of her swing bin as fast as I can. I don't want to hold it any longer than I need to. It makes a loud clinking noise, and I bet if I rootled around in there I'd find another empty. She probably wanted me to see her tip it down the sink—a ruse to cover up how much she's already had. I know all the tricks.

All the while I'm busying myself with the coffee-making, Helen is staring into space through dull, heavy-lidded eyes. I'm right. She's drunk a lot more than half a bottle.

While I'm waiting for the coffee to brew I pick up the empty wine glass, take it to the sink, and swill it out with water. Then I use it to rinse away the last traces of wine down the plug hole.

"Here, get this down you." I put the tray on the coffee table, then sit on the sofa opposite.

"It's good of you to come," she says, pointing the remote at the TV and pressing it wildly, impatiently, her thumbs stabbing at the buttons. Eventually, she finds the right one and turns it off.

I keep my voice as low and calm as I can. After all, I've no idea what kind of drunk she is, whether she's the type to get obnoxious and aggressive or just maudlin and sleepy. I'm hoping it's the latter.

"It's not a good idea for you to be on your own right now, Helen. And I know you'd do the same for me."

She leans forward and grasps the handle of the mug, takes a mouthful of coffee, and sinks back in her chair with it.

"Helen, what you said on the phone just now—it's not true. There's still time for you to turn things around."

She blows air through her cheeks. In the harsh overhead light she looks older, drained. It's horrible to see her like this, with her hair all wiry and unkempt and her blouse gaping open.

I want to tell her that she's wrong about it being all right for me, that however rosy it looks from where she's sitting, I could lose everything if this Laura ups her game. Laura. She's probably not called Laura at all. She wouldn't be stupid enough to give Mum her real name, surely?

Helen closes her eyes and, within a few minutes, her breathing changes. She's fallen asleep already. Whatever I say to her now, she won't remember in the morning. Gingerly, I extricate the mug from her fingers. Her eyes open briefly. Seconds later, she's dropped off again.

I stay for a while, just in case she wakes, but soon she's out for the count and snoring her head off. Then I empty her mug of coffee down the sink and pour her a large glass of water, which I leave on the coffee table. Just as a precaution, I empty out her wastepaper bin and put that next to her armchair too.

As I pull her front door shut behind me it strikes me that the whole time I've been in Helen's flat I haven't once had the urge to drink. Even with all this other weird shit going on, helping Helen has made me stronger. Maybe it's true what they say at AA. Maybe this Twelve Step thing really works.

But when I'm back on the street the panicky feeling returns. It might still be light, but that doesn't stop the tension in my neck and shoulders, the sensation that I'm being watched wherever I go. I can't get back to the cottage soon enough and, even when I do, the fear still clings to me like a wet shirt and I have to check each and every room before settling down in front of the TV. I can't concentrate on anything, but at least it's background noise.

The more I think about it, the more convinced I am that who ever's doing this to me is someone Simon met at AA. He used to make a point of going to meetings in different parts of London. Said it was good not to get too attached to one group. Spread the misery, he used to joke.

Oh, you've done that all right, Simon. You've done that all right.

28

The next morning I wake with a stifling sense of unease. It's only seven fifteen, but I need to get up and clear my head. It's a miracle I slept at all, but in the end I was so exhausted my body must have taken over and switched off my mind. That's what drinking used to do—silence the maelstrom of my thoughts.

They always come back in the morning, though—the thoughts, the regrets, the fears—they never go away for long. As I'm pulling on my jeans and sweater I think of Helen, alone in her flat, waking up with a stonking headache and the jitters. I should call her later, after she's had a chance to sleep it off. Make sure she's all right.

It's low tide and the beach is empty, save for the gulls. It's already warm and the sea is glassy and luminous. Otherworldly. The early-morning sun glitters on its surface.

For a while I just stroll along the water's edge, trying to convince myself I'm not scared. Maybe it's a good thing that Josh and Richard have gone to Berkshire. It gives me time to think, to work out what I should do, if there's anything I *can* do.

Who *is* this person who knows all about my past? Someone Simon got close to? Close enough to let her take his photo. To disclose his guilty secrets. *Our* guilty secrets.

The tide has washed up a dead eel that gleams silver in the sun. A gull makes a beeline for its glistening bead of an eye. With one stab of the beak, it plucks it out. I clap my hand to my mouth. I know it's just nature and that the eel is already dead, but the savagery of it still shocks me. I watch as the gull rinses the eyeball in the shallows, then gobbles it down.

I hurry past, suddenly afraid of the emptiness of the beach and the immensity of the sea. I know it's just words on a piece of paper, but it's a real threat this time. *You'd better not get too comfortable in sleepy little Flinstead. You'd better keep your wits about you from now on.* And to deliberately put my name on a death notice like that . . .

Soon I'll be level with the beach huts on stilts, the ones with their backs turned defiantly to the water. I set off in a diagonal line toward the wooden steps that lead up to the path in front of them, unnervingly aware of my own vulnerability. It reminds me of the time I came down here at night, how the fear crept up on me like the tide.

I squint in the sunlight. Something that looks like crockery is strewn all over the sand up ahead. I jog over there to check it out. It *is* crockery. A pretty tea set, some of it smashed, lies scattered on the ridge of pebbles and shells left by the tide. I look up and see that one of the huts' windows is wide open. The crockery must have been thrown out deliberately.

As I reach the path I see exactly what's happened. Several of the huts have had their doors kicked in, padlocks sawn off; personal contents litter the decked platforms and spill on to the path: cushions, towels, plates. A plastic bucket and spade. Green shards of glass from a broken bottle on a dark, drying stain on the concrete.

I recognize the Carter hut straightaway and it too has been damaged. The door is hanging off its hinges. I know it's only a beach hut, little more than a small painted shed, and no one has been hurt, but it's still a shocking sight. I should tell someone. Call the police. My heart hammers in my chest.

I look in both directions. Surely someone else will be along soon. Someone I can share my dismay with. Someone who'll take over and phone the police themselves. But there's no one in sight. I climb past the hanging door and step over the threshold into the hut. It doesn't seem to have been ransacked, like some of the others, but the single bed is all messed up, and two of the cushions are on the floor. Perhaps whoever's responsible got frightened off before they had a chance to do any more damage. Unless . . .

A sudden impulse makes me open the cupboard under the counter, the one I saw Josh tidying something away in. It's one of those unconscious actions I don't even question till I'm in the process of doing it. The cupboard is empty apart from a box of glasses on the bottom shelf and a blue-and-white polka-dot bikini on the top shelf. I rock back on my heels. It must have been the bikini he hid in here, because the box is large and heavy and I would almost certainly have heard the glasses clinking against each other if he'd been picking it up and sliding it inside.

I take hold of the bikini top and draw it out. It's a skimpy little thing and there are grains of sand in the bra cups. It doesn't mean anything. It could belong to anyone. A friend or relative. Or maybe it belongs to one of Josh's ex-girlfriends.

I think back to the other day, when Richard conveniently left us alone together in the house. For all I know, that's a common occurrence, an unspoken arrangement between father and son. I could end up telling him all the sordid details of my life like some shame-faced penitent when all he wants is a bit of fun over the summer. A couple of weeks ago, that's all I wanted too.

I step toward the broken door to make my way out and see if anyone else is coming along the path and catch sight of something that most definitely *wasn't* here before. A half-empty bottle of brandy and two glasses on the wide shelf that serves as a kitchen counter.

A pulse beats in my throat. There's still a drop of amber liquid in the bottom of one, and a lipstick smear at the top. Josh said his dad never used the hut, hasn't for ages. So either the vandals stopped and helped themselves to a glass of brandy, or Josh is messing around with someone else as well as me.

I lift the glass up and breathe in the fiery tang of solvent and burnt caramel and my insides fold over. I almost gag with longing. Why the hell am I worrying about what Josh may or may not be up to? Someone out there appears to want me dead. This is nothing compared to that. Nothing.

I put the glass down and wrap my fingers round the neck of the bottle, feel the comforting weight of it in my hand. I imagine unscrewing the top and lifting it to my lips, the brandy scalding my throat, searing my esophagus like liquid fire. Just a few good swigs and it will all go away. I won't care about anything anymore. Josh. Simon. The girl in the puffer jacket. The fractured events of that terrible night. Just a few good swigs and it will all start to fade.

The sound of a dog barking brings me to my senses. I lurch out into the sober glare of the sun and come face to face with two stout old ladies and their excitable Bichon Frise. They're both staring at me as if they think I'm the perpetrator and they've caught me red-handed. The stouter of the two women raises her walking stick in the air and points it straight at me.

"This is Richard Carter's hut," she says. Her tone is indignant, accusing. It doesn't help matters that I'm still grasping the bottle of brandy.

"I know. I'm a friend of the family."

She squints at me from behind thick-lensed spectacles. The little white dog strains on its lead and barks. More dog-walkers are turning up now, staring at the huts in horror, tutting and exclaiming.

One of them, a middle-aged man with a black Labrador, pulls out his phone and starts taking pictures.

"Bloody bastards!" he says. "I'd like to get my hands on them!"

Walking-Stick Woman's companion peers behind me into Richard's hut. "We should call the police," she says, giving me a sidelong glance. She clearly still thinks I'm a suspect.

I return the bottle to the hut and come out again. I need to start acting the part of concerned citizen. "Looks like they only got as far as kicking the door in on this one." I gesture with my head toward the beach. "There's crockery all over the sand back there."

She purses her lips. "It's disgraceful," she says at last. "Bored teenagers, no doubt."

I pull out my phone. I've never actually rung Josh before. He sounds surprised when he answers.

"Your dad's beach hut's been broken in to. So have lots of others. I'm here now."

"Shit!" I hear him relaying the information to his dad.

"Dad says can you let Charlie in the art shop know? He lives in the flat above the shop. He'll be able to board it up for us till we get back. Dad forgot his phone in the rush to leave yesterday, or we'd ring him from here."

"Sure."

The two women are now chatting to someone else. Seems like I'm off the hook.

"You're luckier than some," I tell him. "There's bottles of wine been smashed, and plates and cups and things." I take a deep breath. Part of me wants to mention the brandy and the messed-up bed so that he knows I've seen it. But a bigger part doesn't. Because while I've got a deranged stalker on my tail I'd much rather keep Josh on side. Besides, I'll know from his reaction if it means something, and I don't want to know. Not yet.

29

I t's raining. The vestry smells even damper and mustier than usual. It's nearly eight o'clock and Helen's still not here. I should have called on her earlier—I meant to—but what with all the business with the beach huts, I forgot all about it. And then Charlie asked me to mind the art shop while he boarded up the hut. I can't believe he trusted me, a complete stranger, with all that valuable stock and a till full of cash.

But what kind of friend have I been to Helen in her hour of need? What if she woke up after I left and started drinking again? The image of Simon twitching and jerking next to me, a drool of saliva oozing from the corner of his mouth, thrusts its way into my mind. There's something else this time, something I'd forgotten till now: his phone, chirping and pulsating in his shirt pocket like a trapped bird. Why, after all this time, has that image popped into my head?

I force myself back to the present. The atmosphere feels different tonight. Acne Man hasn't turned up, but several new people have—new to me, at least. A fat middle-aged man with pasty white skin wearing a tracksuit and cheap white trainers cracked with age. He's three seats away from me, but I can smell them from here. Jeremy, who's sitting right next to him, keeps pinching his nostrils with his finger and thumb as if he's got an itchy nose. Then there's a black man in his late twenties or early thirties. A couple of times I've sensed him glance over at me. The rest of the time he hangs over his knees and stares at the floor.

Rosie is chairing tonight. She's wearing badly applied pink glittery nail polish that looks like something a seven-year-old would wear for a special party. Her voice drones on and it isn't long before my eyelids droop. I haven't slept properly for the last two nights and, though my mind's still spinning with everything that's happened, my body craves sleep.

Rosie's voice washes through me, like the murmurings from Mum's radio that come through the wall at night. I'm sinking into a dream-like state, but every so often a particular phrase snags at my attention and drags me to the surface.

"It's more than just apologizing . . . you have to actually *do* something . . ."

My eyes flick open. Why do I always get the feeling that everything she says is directed at me and no one else? As if I'm the only person in the room. I know it's just a coincidence that tonight she's chosen to talk about Step 9, about making amends to people we've harmed, but after that horrible message I can't help reading more into it. It's as if she knows things about me I've never told her. I'm being paranoid, I know I am.

I wish I hadn't come. I could just stand up and walk out. Nobody's going to stop me. I don't have to justify my decision to any of them. But something keeps me tethered to the chair. It's the same thing that brought me here in the first place, and it's nothing to do with Mum's list of dates by the calendar, or that edginess she gets when she thinks I've forgotten a meeting and can't quite bring herself to remind me.

Rosie corners me at the end, as I knew she would. She and I are the only females in the room tonight. Is that why I tolerate her advances, because my usual ally is missing, presumed pissed?

"No Helen tonight?"

"No."

She leans toward me and lowers her voice. "I don't like to gossip, but . . ." Her eyes dart toward Jeremy, as if she doesn't want him to witness her indiscretion. But Jeremy is busy doing what he always does, overseeing the teas and coffees, as if this were a business meeting he's convened and he's keen to reward everyone for their contributions.

"I've seen her buying wine," she whispers.

I wrinkle my nostrils. Her breath smells like an old ashtray.

"She was probably buying it for a guest," I say. I'm not going to tell her about last night. It's none of her business and, besides, it feels disloyal talking about Helen when she isn't here.

Rosie makes a noise that's halfway between a sigh and a laugh. "I can see you two get along, and that's great. But if you're serious about beating your addiction, Astrid, then you really need to work with someone who's been sober for a few years. Someone who's got experience of the Twelve Steps and can guide you through them."

"Someone like you, you mean."

Rosie does her slow blink. What with that and her crinkled gray skin, she reminds me of a lizard.

She touches my arm and her voice drops to a whisper.

"This thing could kill you, Astrid. You know that, don't you? Let me help you."

I shake her off. She's gone too far. She's being intrusive. And anyway, why is she so obsessed with helping *me* and not any of the others? If she's so worried that Helen's still drinking, why isn't she trying to help *her* instead?

I'm aware of her eyes boring into the space between my shoulder blades as I leave the vestry. I don't care how many people she's sponsored in the past. I'm not going to be another one of her bloody *projects*.

30

The voice on the intercom is wary.

"Okay. You'd better come up."

Helen is waiting for me at her front door. Her face is pale and tired-looking, but at least she seems sober.

"I was worried about you," I say. "Especially when you didn't show up tonight."

A puzzled expression distorts her face. She smacks her forehead with the palm of her hand. "Shit! I forgot all about it."

"You didn't miss much, to be honest. Only Rosie droning on about making amends."

I follow her into the living room.

"I'll make some tea," she says. Her voice sounds hoarser than usual and she won't meet my eye.

"It was just a slip-up, Helen. You can get back on track."

She says nothing. Then, after what seems like an age, she starts to speak.

"I'm so angry with myself. So ashamed. I feel like I've let us *both* down. I'll tell you one thing. It's made me absolutely determined that it won't happen again. I've been reading the Big Book all day."

"If it's made you stronger, then maybe it was meant to happen."

Helen smiles at last. It feels like a cloud has lifted. She goes into the kitchen and puts the kettle on.

"Thanks so much for coming round last night," she says. "But I really wish you hadn't seen me like that."

"You weren't so bad. You fell asleep almost as soon as I arrived."

She hangs her head in shame.

A few minutes later she brings in the tea.

"How are things with you?" she says.

"Oh, Helen, the last thing I want to do is burden you with all my troubles. You've got enough of your own."

"If we focus on each other's problems, maybe our own won't seem as bad." She gives me a sheepish smile. "Maybe Rosie's right with all her little sayings. Maybe we just have to accept that this is the way it works."

"Maybe."

"So what is it? What's happened?"

I reach for my mug, then change my mind. I'm feeling sick all of a sudden.

She leans forward. "Not another photo of Simon?"

"Someone tricked their way into the house when Mum was on her own. There's a girl who's been following me. She left another envelope. Not a photo this time. It was a page from a newspaper. A death notice with my name on it." Helen covers her mouth with her hand. "And a note. A horrible, horrible note."

Helen stares at me, bewildered. "Who *is* this girl?"

"I don't know, but she's the one who's doing all this."

Helen frowns. "What makes you say that?"

"Because she took Simon's juggling ball and left me that note." My breath catches in my throat. "There's something I didn't think anyone else except Simon knew about. I've never talked about it. Not even to the counselors at rehab. It's just too . . . shameful."

"Can you tell *me*?"

"I want to, but . . . I'm not sure if I can."

"Wait," she says. "Let's do this properly."

"What do you mean?"

She gets up and goes over to the bureau, opens a drawer. "It's something I've been thinking about ever since I woke up."

She brings over a photocopied sheet of the Twelve Steps and places it on the table between us.

"Look, I know we're supposed to work our way through each step in chronological order, but the way I see it, if we both have a problem with the God thing, then maybe we should just concentrate on the ones that make the most practical sense."

Her relapse seems to have galvanized her into full-on recovery mode, but I have to admit she's looking and sounding a whole lot better than she did the other night. And if I'm going to do this step-work with anyone, I'd rather muddle through with Helen than with Rosie.

She points to the highlighted sections on the photocopy, which, now I come to look at it more closely, is full of crossings-out—the God references, mainly—and lots of linking arrows and scribbled notes.

"Step 4, for instance. Making a *searching and fearless moral inventory of ourselves*. We could do that, couldn't we? We could combine it with Step 8 and include all the people we've harmed over the years."

I try to keep my face neutral. I've heard it can take months to complete Step 4 properly, but I don't want to dampen her enthusiasm. I'm not sure Rosie and Jeremy would agree with cherry-picking only those steps we can face. Of mixing them up in this way and leaving God out of the equation altogether. Nor would some of the Twelve-Step Nazis I met in rehab.

"And then we could do Step 5," she says. "Our own version of it, obviously—and read each other our lists. That way, we'll have . . ." She leans forward to check the wording. "*Admitted to ourselves and to another human being the exact nature of our wrongs*."

I swallow hard, because that's what Simon must have done. That's why I'm in this mess in the first place. And yet she does have a point. It's got to be better than not doing it at all.

"Think about it, Astrid. If you can conquer your demons and face up to your past, what's left to be scared of?"

"Well, when you put it like that . . ."

Helen goes over to the bureau again and returns with paper and pens.

"No time like the present," she says.

For the next fifteen or twenty minutes we sit in silence, each composing our lists of shame. Is this really the way forward? Is this what I have to do to get better? Face each and every cold, hard truth about myself? Deal them out like cards on a table, picture-side up? Surely some things are best kept hidden. Then again, I've already told her what happened with Simon, so she might as well know the rest.

"Okay," I say at last. "I think I've reached saturation point."

"Me too," she says, resting her pen on her lap and rubbing her eyes.

"You first," I say, before she says the same thing to me.

She clears her throat and stares at her notepad. "These are in no particular order."

I nod encouragingly.

"So, number one. I let down my colleagues. Embarrassed them in front of an important client, lost business for the firm."

She closes her eyes and sighs. "I'm mortified, looking back on it." She clears her throat again. "Number two. I told my best friend to fuck off and die when all she was trying to do was help me. Number three. I threw up in Waterstones. All over their buy-one-get-one-half-price display table. I caused a real scene when they confronted me."

The corner of my mouth twitches. I can't help it. I look down at my lap and focus on my own sordid list. This isn't meant to be funny.

"Number four. I told my niece and nephew a secret about their mother when I was drunk. Something I promised I'd never tell a living soul. My sister hasn't spoken to me since."

Just like Simon promised me, I think, and once more, the piece-meal memories of that night parade behind my eyes.

Helen looks up at the ceiling for a few seconds before continuing.

"Number five," she says, and takes a deep breath. She's saving the worst for last. It's what I've done in my list too.

"I destroyed the love of my life. He gave me another chance but I pushed him away from me."

Her eyes swim with tears and for a few seconds she hugs her chest and rocks to and fro in her chair. My eyes fill up too. Nothing about any of this is the least bit amusing.

I don't suppose it matters how I respond. The important thing is that she's said these things out loud, that she's shared them with me.

"So have you thought about how you can make amends?" I ask her. I know I'm skipping ahead, but I'm not ready to read my own list out yet.

Helen consults her notepad. "I suppose I could send a letter of apology to the partners in my old firm. Perhaps I could offer to do some unpaid work for them. They'll probably say no, but at least I'll have offered."

"Sounds like a plan."

For the next ten minutes we come up with one action she could complete for each item on her list. Some will be trickier than others, of course. She doesn't think her husband or her best friend or her sister will want anything more to do with her, but she can at least try.

Now the time has come to read out my own ghastly bullet points. I can't help feeling that mine are far worse than hers, but of course everyone's journey is different. Everyone has their own rock bottom.

As I read, I'm reminded of the nightmare I had a while back, the one where Richard Carter read out this same list in the Flinstead and Mistden community hall, and I find myself adopting a vaguely similar tone of voice. So "fucking a friend's boyfriend in the back-seat of his car while she was visiting her parents" takes the form of a somewhat unorthodox liturgical chant. Although by the time I get to "asking my dad for help with a deposit on a new flatshare and then blowing the whole lot on a three-day bender in Bruges," my voice has become a little more halting and awkward.

"You know the next one because I've already told you. I made Simon start drinking again."

Helen gives me a sad little smile.

And now here it is. The last one.

"Go on," Helen says. "It won't seem as bad when you say it out loud."

"Believe me, it will."

"Say it anyway."

So I do. I tell her everything I can remember, try to stitch the disconnected memories together.

"I wish I could make sense of it all, but I can't. The only thing I know for sure is that something bad happened that night. We hurt an innocent young mother in front of her child. And for what? Thirty fucking quid, or whatever it was."

I can't believe I'm doing this. This secret's been locked away for so long it's like I've convinced myself it didn't happen, that it was just a bad dream I once had. It feels like I'm betraying Simon by telling her. And yet he must have told someone too. He must have betrayed *me*.

Helen's right, though. Telling her hasn't made it any less shocking or shameful, but the tightness in my chest does seem to have loosened slightly. There's a little more space to breathe.

My eyes swim with tears. "She might have been badly injured." I gouge my left thumb into the palm of my right hand. "And even if she wasn't, who knows what psychological harm we caused, to her and the child?"

I don't tell her what else goes through my mind in the dead of night: that she might even have died. There's a knot in the pit of my stomach. I'm sure we'd have heard about it on the news if she had, but it's still a possibility. I know it is.

Rosie's voice plays over and over in my mind like a broken record. "It's more than just apologizing . . . you have to actually do something."

If Simon really was working the steps before he met up with me again, could he have got as far as Step 9? Could he have somehow tracked down that young mother and tried to make amends? Maybe it backfired and this is some kind of revenge for what we did to her.

Except that doesn't make sense. Why would she have his photo? You don't take photos like that of someone smiling into the camera unless you really, really like them. No. It has to be someone he formed a relationship with, someone connected to his recovery.

But now that the seed has been planted it won't go away. What if his attempts to befriend her didn't backfire? What if they succeeded only too well? Simon could be very persuasive when he wanted. Even more so when he was sober. Maybe she even fell for him. And if she did, how much would she hate me when she found out what led to his suicide?

What goes around comes around. It's time to pay for what you've done.

Helen leans forward. Her mouth is moving, but I don't hear what she's saying.

At last, her words filter through. "Talk to me, Astrid. Talk to me. What are you thinking?"

I'm thinking of Mum all alone in the cottage, oblivious of the danger I'm in. Oblivious of the danger she could be in. The danger I might have put her in because of the stupid, thoughtless things I've done. I should have gone straight home after the meeting. I could have told Helen all this tomorrow.

"I'm sorry, Helen, I've got to go."

31

Mum's brushing her hair when I peer round her bedroom door, my chest heaving from having run all the way home. She looks up in surprise, her face etched with concern, and I know in that instant what I've always known, deep down—that her love for me is fierce, protective. That she loves me as only a mother can. And I love her.

Dad's old cardie is lying on the bed near her pillow. My eyes stumble over it and back to her face. It's unbearable to think of her holding on to it at night, her tears melting into the woolen fibers.

"Why are you so out of breath?" she asks.

I rack my brain for a suitable response. "I fancied a run. I'm too embarrassed to do it in the day."

Mum narrows her eyes. "Are you all right, Astrid? Has something upset you? You haven't been . . ."

She checks herself and walks over to her dressing table, unscrews a pot of Nivea, and starts applying it to her face.

"I'm fine, honestly. Just a bit out of condition, that's all. You have locked the back door, haven't you?"

She gives me a look that's a cross between amusement and surprise. "Yes, I'm sure I have. I don't know why you're so jumpy lately.

This is Flinstead, remember? We've got one of the lowest crime rates in the country." She puts the lid back on the cream. "And since when have you cared whether I lock the back door or not?"

"Since you started letting random strangers look round the house."

"Not that again."

Her cheeks are pale and greasy in the low-energy light and the circles under her eyes look darker than ever.

"Night, Mum."

"Goodnight, darling," she says.

Downstairs, I can't resist trying the handle of the back door. When it opens onto the cold, black night a frisson of alarm goes through me. Anyone could have got in while Mum was upstairs, all alone. She's always been relaxed about security. I have too. It was Dad who used to do the nightly round of locking up. Dad who looked after us.

I shut it quickly, lifting the handle up and turning the key as fast as I can. This is ridiculous. It's a terraced cottage. The only way someone could get into the house is via the garden, and that would mean climbing over all the other garden boundaries first, and they're not likely to risk their own safety by doing that. Not when they can harm me in other, more insidious ways.

Even so, I roam the house like a restless ghost, checking I've pulled the bolts across the front door and that all the windows are tightly shut. I make myself a cup of coffee. I shouldn't, not at this time of night, but the chances of me falling asleep are slim. What difference will a bit of caffeine make?

Josh sends me a text. Even the beep of my phone makes me jump.

Dad's driving back tomorrow to sort the hut out, but I'm staying on here for another day with my cousins and getting the train back. Dad says feel free to drop round in the afternoon and work on the painting if you want. Xxx

I tap out an upbeat reply. It's stupid to feel upset that I won't see him for another day, but I am. Things seem so much more bearable when I'm with Josh.

I take my coffee into the living room, not putting the light on until I've drawn the curtains across. That's another thing Mum hardly ever does. I've told her that you can see right in from the street, but she never seems to care. Maybe she would if she knew that someone was stalking her daughter. Possibly stalking *her* too.

That girl crossed a line by coming in here under false pretenses. Invading our personal space, touching our things. It took guts, though, I'll give her that. Which makes me wonder what else she's capable of.

The next day dawns cold and gray. I've been tossing and turning all night long, trying to make sense of the riot in my brain. If I slept at all, it could only have been brief snatches here and there. One thing that occurred to me as I thrashed about is that I haven't yet spoken to the other Oxfam volunteer—the one Rosie said must have sold the Cranberries T-shirt. He probably won't remember who donated it and, even if he does, I doubt he'll tell me, but it's worth a try. He may not even be there, but I need to do *something*.

I don't like leaving Mum on her own, but the thought of spending the whole day cooped up with her in this cottage fills me with gloom. Besides, I've made her promise she'll be on her guard. The story about the burglars doing the rounds seems to have hit home at last. She's decided to start locking the porch door from now on.

It's the first time I've needed my coat in ages, and after the gorgeous weather we've been having it seems like an omen. What if it's that girl who brought the T-shirt in? She had Simon's photo, after all.

I look both ways before setting off in the direction of the shops. Who knows how many times she's been waiting for me to come out of the house? Waiting and watching. Following my every movement. I won't be stalked like prey any longer. I won't be drawn into her mind games. If that's what they are. The picture with the bloodied hand was one thing. Thinly veiled death threats and tricking my mother are quite another.

And now that I've made the decision to actively look for her, I feel a bit braver. More in control. I'm the stalker now.

Flinstead Road is quiet. It's too early and miserable for visitors, and even the hardy pensioners, who like to get their shopping done before everyone else, are fewer in number this morning. The Oxfam shop isn't open yet, so I wander up and down to kill time. I haven't quite worked out what I'll say when I do go in, but I'll wing it when I'm there. That's if he's even working today.

I make a point of crossing the road every so often so I can glance in both directions without looking shifty. But I'm sure I still do. Who zigzags down a street for no apparent reason at five to nine on a weekday morning? I should have brought a shopping bag—that would have stopped me feeling so self-conscious.

A girl wearing jeans and a hoodie gets out of a car up ahead and I freeze. She's not wearing a puffer jacket, but she's exactly the right shape and size. Mum said she was small and slight with dark hair, which certainly fits the description of the girl I nearly tripped over that time. The girl I keep seeing.

I quicken my pace. I've never been close enough to study her face in any detail. Apart from the time I nearly fell over her, but then I was so fixated on thinking I'd just seen Simon's ghost that I didn't register it in any detail. I'd be a useless witness. Still, I might as well check her out, just in case.

She hesitates outside the newsagent's and, since I'm gaining on her, I slow down. Then she picks up speed again and I'm off. I'm so busy keeping her in my sight that I almost walk straight into one of those damn mobility scooters. But even though I only took my eyes off her for the few seconds that it took my feet to disentangle themselves from the front wheel, she has somehow managed to disappear. I hurry toward the spot where I last saw her, outside the bakery. As I draw level with the window display of cakes and scones, I move nearer the curb and glance swiftly inside as I pass. She's there, in the queue.

My heart thumps, and for a moment I just stand there, staring at her, unsure of my next move. It *could* be her. If only I could see her hair. As she approaches the counter, she pulls her hood down to reveal a short blond bob. Deflated, I carry on walking. What the hell am I doing? Following random strangers doing nothing more villainous than buying a loaf of bread.

I retrace my steps toward the Oxfam shop, which is now open. But when I go inside the only assistant in sight is Rosie, reaching for a little china plate that a woman is pointing to. I turn to leave before she sees me, but it's the woman she's serving who calls out.

"Hello, Astrid. How are you?"

I stare at her, trying to work out who she is and how she knows my name. Then it dawns on me. It's Mum's friend Pam. The one who couldn't wait to phone her and tell her she saw me going into the pub. She's the last person I want to speak to but, if I don't, she'll probably tell Mum I was acting weird and I'll have to face an inquisition all over again.

"I'm fine." *No thanks to you,* I'd like to add.

"You wouldn't do me a favor while you're here, would you? I've just seen a lovely jacket I think my Christine would love. You're almost exactly her size. Will you try it on for me so I can see what it looks like?"

She hands me a soft leather jacket that's been folded over her arm and holds my coat while I slip it on. Then she takes a step back to get a better look. Rosie's eyes are on me too. I sense them raking me from top to bottom. I turn round so Pam can see what it looks like from the back and eventually she's satisfied that, yes, Christine will love it.

I'd love it too. It's got that lovely lived-in feel to it and it fits perfectly. But it's £18 and, though that's ridiculously cheap for a leather jacket, even a second-hand one, it's £18 more than I've got or am likely to have anytime soon.

When I step outside again, a sea fret has rolled in and cloaked the street in a cold, gray haze. What few shoppers there were have disappeared and the whole place has an eerie, haunted feel to it. Like a scene from a horror movie.

What goes around comes around. It's time to pay for what you've done. The words echo in my mind like an ominous voiceover. Except this isn't a movie. This is really happening. I pull my collar up and hurry home.

32

I've done what Josh suggested in his text message and come to Mistden to get on with the painting, or try to. Mum will only get suspicious if I start hanging around the cottage keeping tabs on her. But when Richard Carter opens the door to me I wish I'd stayed at home. Gone is the relaxed, amiable grin he usually greets me with. It's ever since that phone call I overheard in the garden, I'm sure it is. Something about him has changed.

He steps aside to let me in.

"I really appreciate all your efforts yesterday with the beach hut, Astrid," he says. There's an awkward formality about him. His words sound all clipped. He follows me to the easel. "Charlie tells me you minded the shop for him."

"Yes, it was fun. I . . . I really enjoyed it."

He meets my eyes at last. "Actually, I think he might be looking for someone part-time. I'll have a word with him, if you like. Although I expect you're itching to get back to your life in London."

My life in London. It sounds so cool. So glamorous. And yet, is it my imagination or did he emphasize that phrase in a weird way, almost as if he knows it was anything but? I think of my last squat. The stained mattress on the floor. The pungent smell of mold and mouse.

"As soon as your mother's better, of course," he says, giving me a strange little smile.

I busy myself squeezing more paint onto my palette so that he can't see my red face. I don't have to respond. I can't, anyway. What would I say that wouldn't stick in my throat? If he knows I've been lying to his son—lying to both of them—surely it's only a matter of time before he says something to Josh. That's if he hasn't already. Why the hell haven't I been honest with them? They're decent people. They'd have understood, I know they would. But now, after four whole weeks . . . how will they trust me?

I force myself to look at him. "I was between jobs anyway."

"Just like Josh," Richard says. "I'll miss him when he goes back to London and starts work again."

The words "so will I" are on the tip of my tongue. Because if I'm right and Richard has somehow found out about my past, who knows if Josh will stay in contact? I unwind the cling film from my brushes, aware of Richard still hovering in the doorway.

"It's been very difficult for Josh, losing his mother, as I'm sure you'll understand."

His words seem weighted. Weighted with something he's not saying. "It's taken us a while to get used to it being just the two of us. I . . . I wouldn't want him to be hurt again."

My heart sinks. He *does* know something. He must do, or why would he be saying that? Who was he talking to on the phone the other day? Who's told him about me?

The doorbell goes. "That must be Jez," Richard says, but still he doesn't move from the doorway. There's something else he wants to say—it's written all over his face.

"One of my yacht-club buddies," he explains. "He's been helping me with a few legal bits and pieces. You never know when you'll need a good lawyer, and Jez is as honest as they come."

The word "honest" reverberates in my head. Was that some kind of coded message?

At last he leaves the room, and I roll my shoulders back to ease the tension in my neck. I could cry. I've grown so attached to this new version of myself. The helpful, responsible girlfriend. The selfless daughter. What started as a veneer is now seeping into my flesh and bones. I don't want it to end, any of it.

After all those years of kidding myself I needed excitement and danger, the edgy glamour of a big city, it's been a revelation to discover that a gentle, ordinary existence with kind, generous souls like Josh and his dad and the daily routine of my painting is just what I need. And now I've gone and ruined everything by not coming clean with them sooner.

I recognize the voice in the hallway instantly, and freeze. But before I have a chance to dive into the downstairs loo, Richard is leading him into the room.

"Jez, meet Astrid, my son's new girlfriend. She's a very talented artist, as you can see. She's painting us a *trompe l'œil*."

Jeremy from AA looks directly into my eyes. My chest constricts. It must have been him. He must have said something to Richard. He's betrayed my confidence. Broken the AA code. How *could* he?

He extends his well-manicured hand. "Delighted to meet you, Astrid."

"M . . . me too. Delighted to meet you too, I mean."

Jeremy's right eye twitches in what might be a wink. It's some kind of reassurance, I think. Maybe I've got it all wrong and he hasn't given me away. Isn't going to. Maybe Richard doesn't even know that "Jez" is an alcoholic and I'm just imagining a change in his behavior, in which case I'm safe.

But for how long?

Jeremy steps closer to my picture and leans in toward it, hands clasped behind his back. "It's the shadows that make it seem so real, isn't it?" he says, scratching his chin.

My heart beats in the back of my throat as he takes a step back and tilts his head to one side. "The clever art of deception, eh?"

"Are you having fun with your family?"

There's a slight pause on the other end of the line. Oh God, I wasn't wrong. Josh knows.

"Yeah, it's been great catching up with all my cousins. You're going to meet them soon."

My shoulders sag with relief. I'm being paranoid, as usual. It's okay. There's still time to make things right. Josh's voice sounds all crackly and faraway. I walk into the kitchen and out through the back door. There's a better signal outside.

"Really?" I make my way to the end of the garden, out of earshot of Richard and Jeremy, who are in the living room, heads together over some papers and with the French window wide open.

"Yeah, it's Dad's sixtieth in a couple of weeks. He thinks we should have a party, a sort of birthday–cum–housewarming do. We talked about it on the journey up here. It's a bit last-minute, but that's how he is. He's going to send an email invite round to everyone this evening."

Visions of this beautiful, empty house filled with people crowd into my mind. Noise and laughter echoing off the walls and floorboards. The popping of corks and the flowing of champagne. The chink of glasses. It'll be like being in the Flinstead Arms all over again. I feel weak just thinking about it.

"Sounds great."

"You can be our artist-in-residence," Josh says. "I can't wait to show you off. Oh, and Dad says to invite your mum as well, if she's feeling up to it."

The thought of Mum, here in this house, fills me with dread. I doubt if Richard or Josh would say anything to her about her "depression." Most people shy away from that topic, especially in social gatherings, but what if they did? Mum would be absolutely furious that I'd lied about her. It'd set us right back to how we were when I first came out of rehab. And even if that doesn't happen, she might let something slip about my past, answer a question a little too truthfully. She never lies about anything. Ever. It's not the Quaker way.

"I'll ask her tonight," I say, knowing full well I won't.

Jeremy's words come back to me. *The clever art of deception.* Maybe he *was* just talking about the *trompe l'œil*.

Even if he was, this can't go on. I can't lie to them forever.

33

Five minutes after I've said goodbye to Richard and Jeremy and set off for home it starts pissing down. A soaking deluge that drenches me within seconds. The rain sweeps the pavement and plasters my hair to my head. By the time I've reached the end of the lane and turned left onto the main road, the potholes are brimming and cars splash through them, sending great arcs of water into the air. But there's nowhere to take cover until the bus shelter at the top of the road, so I have no choice but to trudge on through it.

I don't take much notice of the car at first. I assume it's just slowing to avoid the ever-expanding puddle at the side of the road, but then I realize that it's coasting along beside me. Instinctively, I move away from the curb, my fear returning.

I slide my eyes to the right. It's still there, hugging the curb. When the window on the passenger side slides down I break into a run. I don't know anybody round here with a car except Richard, and this isn't a Mercedes.

Somebody calls my name—a man—but I don't stop running. The second time they say it, the voice sounds familiar and I force myself to slow down and look properly. Jeremy's face peers at me through the lashing rain and I feel like a fool. He's beckoning me to get in and, though sitting in a car with Jeremy is one of the last things I want to be doing, my clothes are now sticking to me uncomfortably and I can hardly say I'd rather walk. Not in this weather and not when I'm still a good twenty minutes from home. Besides, I don't really want to be on the street for any longer than necessary, not with the threat of that death notice hanging over me.

Reluctantly, I open the door and slide in.

"We can't have you walking home in this," he says in his posh, affable voice. He waits while I put my seatbelt on. Except I can't pull it out far enough to reach the buckle—it keeps stopping.

After a minute or so of trying and failing, Jeremy says, "May I?" and leans across to help. I wish he wouldn't.

There's an embarrassing moment when his upper body swivels in front of me so that his head is perilously close to my neck, like a clumsy lunge after a first date. He grasps the metal tongue and draws it out.

"It's a little temperamental, this one," he says. His breath smells of garlic and I try not to breathe so I don't have to smell it. "You have to draw it out slowly or the retractor mechanism locks."

At last, he clicks it into the buckle and he's back on his own side again. I breathe out in relief.

The indicator ticks as he waits for a break in the traffic and I wonder whether he's going to say anything about what happened earlier. Pretending not to know each other in front of Richard. I hope he doesn't. Because I don't want to talk about it. I just want to be home and get out of these wet things.

"Which street do you live on?" he asks as we join the flow of traffic.

The windscreen wipers swish backward and forward but, even on full speed, it's difficult to see through the torrential rain.

"Just drop me off at the top of Warwick Road," I tell him.

"No, no, I'll drive you all the way home."

"That *is* home," I lie. Even if I have to walk up someone else's driveway till he's gone, I will. I know I'm being overcautious. But that's what being stalked does to you. It makes you suspicious of just about everybody.

When we reach Warwick Road and I'm about to open the car door, Jeremy places his hand on my forearm. Just briefly, enough to make me pause. Oh no, he's chosen now to start talking.

"There's a Buddhist quote I'd like to share with you, Astrid."

Bloody hell. This is all I need.

He looks at me from under his steel-gray eyebrows, like a headmaster admonishing a wayward pupil.

"Three things cannot be long hidden: the sun, the moon, and the truth."

My fingers fumble to unclick the seatbelt, the word "truth" running through me like an electric shock. As the belt unclicks and recoils, it's as much as I can do to mumble my thanks for the lift, open the passenger door, and climb out. He takes ages to drive off and I know he's waiting on purpose because he knows I don't live in this large Georgian house with the immaculate flower beds and the Mazda convertible parked up on the driveway. But I walk all the way to the front porch anyway, pulling my phone out of the back pocket of my jeans as if to make a call.

Eventually, he puts me out of my misery and drives away. The rain has eased off a little now and I slip my phone into my coat pocket, retrace my steps to the pavement, and continue down Warwick Road toward Mum's cottage in a state of heightened awareness till I'm safely behind the front door. I stand for a few seconds in the dark hall until my breathing returns to normal. He was only making a point about coming clean with Josh and Richard. He doesn't know anything else. Of course he doesn't.

Mum takes one look at me and laughs. "I was wondering whether you'd get caught in the downpour. Come on, get out of those wet things and I'll hang them up to dry. You look like a drowned rat."

She bustles off to unfold the clothes horse she keeps in the back room while I shrug off my coat and slip my hand in the pocket to retrieve my phone. But it's the wrong pocket. My fingers close over something else. Something I don't immediately recognize. Curious, I pull it out. It's a little package secured with an elastic band. My heart skips a beat because I think I know what's inside. With trembling fingers I ease the band off and unfurl the piece of paper it's wrapped in. My throat closes.

It's a miniature bottle of vodka.

With blood pounding in my ears, I race upstairs to my room. If Mum sees this, I'm done for. I drop the paper on the floor and stare at the bottle nestled in the palm of my hand. It's cold and smooth against my skin. Absolut Blue Vodka, 50ml, 80 proof. How the hell did this get in my pocket? Someone must have put it there. But that's impossible. I'd have felt it, wouldn't I?

"Astrid, are you bringing those clothes down?"

The sound of Mum's voice makes me start. I can hardly breathe.

"Just coming."

I stuff it into one of my socks and ball it up, tuck it right at the back of my drawer. I need to get it out of here as soon as I can. Mum searches my room sometimes—she pretends she's looking for dirty mugs, but we both know what she's really looking for.

I think of all the people who've had access to my coat today. It's been hanging up in Josh's dad's house all afternoon, but why would Richard Carter slip a bottle of vodka into my pocket? It doesn't make sense.

Unless it was Jeremy. He's had ample opportunity to do it, both at the house and just now, in the car. He could have dropped it in when he was leaning over me to sort the seatbelt out. But why would he do that? He wouldn't, surely. All he wants me to do is come clean with Josh and Richard. To tell them I'm an alcoholic.

I took my coat off in the Oxfam shop this morning, gave it to Pam when I was trying that leather jacket on. But Pam's hardly likely to have done it, and she'd have noticed if Rosie had, wouldn't she? It was folded over her arm the whole time and, anyway, it couldn't have been Rosie. She might just as well have the Twelve Steps etched into her soul like letters carved in rock.

The fact is, it could have been anyone. I was pickpocketed once, in broad daylight. Didn't feel a thing. And it must be a lot easier to put something *into* a pocket than take it out.

I take one last look at my closed drawer and imagine myself unscrewing that little silver cap later tonight. Slugging back 50ml of Swedish pure-grain vodka. My mouth waters. Whoever did this knows exactly what they're doing.

I pick the paper off the floor from where I've dropped it and go to put it in the bin. Looks like it's a promotional flyer for a local business.

Oh no. Please, no. I stare at the printed words till they swim before my eyes: "P. Hollingford & Sons, Funeral Directors." And then the slogan in large black letters. **"It's never too early to start planning your own funeral."**

34

All the time I'm eating supper with Mum, or pretending to, pushing the food around on my plate and hiding as much as I can under the mashed potato, I'm thinking of the words on that flyer. And I'm picturing the vodka wrapped up in my sock and wondering what would happen if I just had a couple of sips. If ever I needed some Dutch courage, it's now.

I can't help thinking of how, not so long ago, I nearly bought a bottle myself. But I didn't, did I? I found the strength to say no, just as I'll find the strength to get rid of the one upstairs. I'll do it after supper. Tell Mum I'm going out to get some chocolate.

A horrible thought drops into my head. Sly and swift, it pierces through the incessant mind-chatter like an arrow heading straight for its target. What if it was there all along, nestled in the lining of my pocket, just waiting to be discovered? I haven't worn my coat for a couple of weeks, haven't needed to. It's been hanging up in the porch all this time.

The porch. Oh my God! That girl could have dropped it in when she came round. I look at Mum, squashing peas against the back of her fork with quiet determination, oblivious of the turmoil churning in my mind. She could have found it at any time. It's a miracle she didn't.

It takes me ages to get out of the house. Mum's got a migraine coming on and by the time I've cleared the supper things away and taken a cup of tea up to her it's already getting on for half past eight. Then the bloody phone rings and it's my great-aunt Dorothy wanting a chat. I tell her Mum isn't feeling too good, but that doesn't stop her bending my ear for almost forty-five minutes. Still, at least Mum can't quiz me about where I'm going. She's taken a couple of her Sumatriptan tablets and, by the sound of her breathing just now when I put my ear to her door, she's already fast asleep.

It's not raining anymore, but the streets are still wet and it's almost dark. The bottle is back in my pocket. It's still wrapped up in the sock but my fingers won't leave the little bundle alone. I can feel the shape of it through the cotton. I think of that flyer in my bedroom and the hairs on the back of my neck stand up. "**It's never too late to start planning your own funeral.**"

The fear returns in one sickening blast. As does the voice in my head. The one that's telling me to slug back the vodka right now and chuck the empty in a bin. It'll take the edge off my fear, and what harm could fifty measly milliliters do? It won't even touch the sides.

Except that's the trouble. It'll just make me crave more.

I swing from fear to rage to paranoia, flinching at shadows, my eyes darting from side to side as I walk. What was I thinking, coming out alone at night? I could have just tipped the vodka down the sink and got rid of the bottle in the morning, chucked it in a bin on the street somewhere. If anything happens to me, Mum won't even realize I'm missing till she wakes up, and that won't be for hours. Sumatriptan always knocks her out.

I have to get rid of that bottle. If I'm not prepared to go to the police, I have to deal with this my own way. I'm not going to lose my mind over this. I'm not.

I make my way to the greensward, where there's less chance of one of Mum's friends spotting me and reporting back, and, as I do, my fingers work to free the bottle from the sock. Now it's clasped in my hand, my thumb on the cap. A small grenade. I'm holding it so tightly I'm surprised it doesn't break. I imagine the small explosion in my pocket, shards of glass digging into my palm, wetness soaking into the lining fabric.

I've passed three litter bins already. What's wrong with me? Why don't I just throw it away and go home?

You know why, Astrid. Because then you won't have it anymore. You'll have lost your chance to drink it.

That's right. As long as it's still here, in my pocket, I can fantasize about drinking it, kid myself I could get away with it. But the rational part of my brain knows that's not true. There's another bin a little farther down. I'll throw it in there.

Except I don't. I walk straight past it. This is crazy. How can one tiny bottle exert so much control over me? But it's not the bottle, is it? It's me. My addiction. She knows that. That's why she put it there.

This time, I do it. I toss it into the next bin I come to, hear the soft little thud as it lands.

I take a lungful of night air, enjoying the sweet scent of rain-soaked earth and the salty tang of the sea. I've done the right thing, even if it did take me this long.

By the time I get home I've made a decision. I won't live like this anymore. Whatever I did when I was drinking, I wasn't in my right mind. It wasn't the real me. It changes now. No more lies or prevarication. If I've got any kind of future with Josh, he needs to know everything. Mum does too. It's like Helen said the other day: if I can conquer my demons and face up to my past, what's left to be scared of? Besides, if I don't do it soon, my stalker might tell them first.

What if she's already told Richard? It would certainly explain why he was acting so weird with me today.

35

After yesterday's rain the sky is a perfect eggshell blue, the clouds little more than white wisps. Not that I've seen much of the weather. I've spent most of the day pretending to work on the *trompe l'œil* while Josh and Richard got on with the decorating upstairs. I've been rehearsing my speech in my head the whole time.

Now, at my request, we're taking the circuitous route back to Flinstead. One last futile attempt at procrastination.

"I was going to suggest this myself," Josh says, his right elbow resting casually on the open window. "It's a lovely afternoon for a drive."

For a moment or two, I almost change my mind about telling him. It would be so easy to sit here, driving along with the windows down and the warm breeze tickling our skin, chatting and laughing and flirting like we normally do.

Josh indicates left and turns into a narrow country lane bordered with hedgerows covered in frothy white blossom. I've never been down here before; it's beautiful.

"Let's open the sunroof," he says, and presses a button on the dashboard. As it slides open the sweet smell of hawthorn comes wafting in and with it the promise of summer. A world alive with new possibilities. If only I could stay in this car forever, cocooned from the harshness of the world, suspended in this moment before everything changes.

"Mum loved this time of year," Josh says. "Everything coming into bloom."

A large green verge is coming up on the left, with a weeping willow spilling over it, the tips of its leaves almost touching the ground. Josh pulls over and parks as close to the trunk as he can get so that we're partially concealed by the green canopy of the tree.

He unclicks his seatbelt and shifts position so that he's looking right at me.

"I'm so glad I've met you, Astrid."

I clench my fingers into the palms of my hands. Every second that passes without him knowing the truth feels like an even worse betrayal of his trust. Maybe I should do it right now, in the car, before he says anything else.

But there's really only one place to come clean with him, and that's where it all started. Down on the beach. Whatever happens next, the sand and the sea will still be there. The tide will still turn.

He leans in to kiss me and, of course, I kiss him back. How can I not?

When the kiss finally comes to an end, Josh refastens his seatbelt, checks his wing mirror, and pulls out onto the lane.

"Shall we stop off at the Old Schooner before I drop you back home?" My heart turns over. "It's a hundred times nicer than the Flinstead Arms," he says. "And it's got a beautiful garden."

I know I should respond, but I can't. Even if I could think of what to say, I doubt I'd be able to speak, my mouth is so dry. All I can see is a tall glass of lager. I imagine it sliding down the back of my throat, crisp and cold, slaking my thirst.

"I . . . er . . . Actually, I think I'd rather just buy a can of Coke and go and sit on the beach. Do you mind?"

"Of course not." He goes quiet for a while, then says: "I make it a point never to drink more than half a pint when I'm driving. If that's what you were worrying about."

"It wasn't, no." How I wish I could live up to this image he has of me. "I just need some sea air after being indoors all day."

"You are happy to do the painting, aren't you? I hope you didn't feel like you had to say yes. Dad can be a bit—how shall I put it?—persuasive."

"I *love* doing the painting."

His shoulders relax. We're heading toward the beach now. In a few minutes we'll stop at the shop for a couple of Cokes and then we'll be there and I'll have to tell him. Plunge straight in and get it over with. The truth and all its repercussions.

"I've got something to tell you."

We're sitting on the sand, our backs against the sea wall. Josh does that crooked little smile I've grown to love and pulls me closer. "Should I be worried?"

The smile fades when I don't respond. "Astrid, what's wrong?"

A Jack Russell on one of those extendable leads comes up to us and puts his paws on my knees. I fondle his soft ears and gaze into his eager brown eyes. If only the owner wasn't hurrying straight toward us, her face one big, indulgent smile, I could have told this little dog the whole story and Josh could simply have listened. But now we're smiling too, saying hello and chatting about the weather.

At last, it's just the two of us again, and Josh is looking at me with questioning eyes.

"I haven't been entirely honest with you," I say. Understatement of the year.

Something in Josh changes. He doesn't say anything and he doesn't move. But the energy between us shifts.

"There *is* someone back in London. I *knew* it."

"No. There's no one else, I swear."

"What was his name?"

I breathe out. "This isn't about him."

"What was his name?"

"Simon. His name was Simon."

"Are you still in touch with him?"

"I told you, this isn't about him."

"You haven't answered my question," he says.

"No. I'm not still in touch with him." I stare at the sea. It's unusually still and calm today. Eerily so. It looks like a painting. "Simon's dead. He . . . he killed himself."

"Shit." Josh runs his hands through his hair. "I'm so, so sorry."

"Simon and I, we . . . we used to drink. A lot."

The silence tingles between us. "I started drinking heavily when I was fifteen." I knead the palm of my right hand with my left thumb, really gouging into it. "I'd like to say there was a reason, one key event that started it all off, but there wasn't. I was a difficult teenager. It just kind of . . . crept up on me."

I wait for Josh to say something, to ask another question, but that's not the way this is going to happen. Of course it isn't. It was never going to be a normal conversation.

"I was stupid and selfish and I let people down. My parents, my friends. I let myself down. Over and over again."

Somewhere in the distance a siren wails.

"Simon wanted to stop. He started going to AA." Now that I'm actually saying the words I feel strangely removed from them. As if this is somebody else's story. Which in a way it is.

"You have to understand that I'm different now. I haven't had a drink in over six months."

"What happened? With you and Simon?"

A small flare of hope ignites inside me. He isn't ranting and raving about having been lied to. He's still right here next to me.

"Simon tried to persuade me to stop too, and I tried, for a while. But I was drinking in secret and he found out. Simon left me."

Why does it feel so bad, admitting that? After all the things I've done and the people I've hurt, why does admitting that Simon left me make me feel so humiliated?

I tell him the rest. About meeting up with him again, about the beer in my rucksack and the binge back at the squat. I tell him how it ended.

"And that's not all. Oh, Josh, I did something else once. I . . . I might have hurt someone when I was trying to steal her bag." A wave of nausea rolls through me. "I wish I could remember what happened, but I can't. I just know it was bad."

Josh hasn't moved the whole time I've been speaking, but now he shifts his weight forward and crosses his arms over his knees.

"I wish I'd told you right at the beginning. I wanted to, but I didn't know *how*. The longer I put it off, the more impossible it seemed."

His face is closed, unreadable.

"I almost told you, that day we made lunch together. But then you started telling me about your mum and I . . ." I stifle a sob. "I just couldn't . . ."

I reach for his hand and hold it in mine. "I'm telling you now because I need you to know. I don't want there to be secrets between us."

He withdraws his hand. Slowly, calmly. A deliberate and considered separation that's a hundred times worse than an angry shrugging-off.

"Say something, please. I can't bear this silence."

But still he won't speak.

"It's not as if you've been entirely honest with me."

Josh's face is incredulous. Appalled.

"Come again?"

"I know you've been sleeping with someone else. In the beach hut. After *we'd* been there too." I can't believe I'm saying this, but I have to know the truth.

"What the hell are you talking about?"

"The red lipstick on the brandy glass. The bikini. I saw them, Josh. I saw them that day the huts got vandalized."

Josh stiffens. The muscles in his jaw are tight where he's clenching his teeth.

"But it doesn't matter. We can start again now, can't we? Please say we can start again."

I want to reach out and touch him, but the silence stretches between us like a wall. An impenetrable boundary I daren't cross. It's like a force field keeping us apart. Instinct tells me that only he can break it and, right now, he can't. Or won't. I don't know how I expected him to react, but this glacial silence is unbearable.

"I love you, Josh." There, I've said it. I've said it out loud. "That's why I'm telling you all this. Because meeting you and your dad and all the rest of it—the painting, the swimming—it's been the best time I've ever had. It's made me realize what I want from life. What's important. I'm so sorry I didn't tell you before, but I was frightened you'd hate me for it."

Josh straightens up and blows air through his cheeks. He turns to face me. There's a coldness to him, as if he's already cutting off. "So what you said about being here to look after your mum, I suppose that was a lie too?"

I force myself to hold his gaze. Now that I've started, I can't give him half the story. I have to tell him everything. No holds barred.

"Mum paid for me to go into rehab. I had nowhere else to live."

"So what you're saying is, she's been looking after *you*."

I close my eyes and nod. There's no mistaking that tone.

"I've been going to AA. That woman you saw me with, she isn't Mum's friend, she's someone I met there. We've been supporting each other. I go every week. I'm making it work, I—"

"Shall I tell you why Dad and I went to Berkshire? What I was doing with my cousins?"

Something weird has happened to his face, as if his features are set in stone. His eyes darken.

"We were visiting my mum's grave. We do it every year on the anniversary of her death. I've never told you *how* she died, but maybe now's the time." He takes a deep breath and looks me straight in the eye. "She was killed by a drunk driver."

My gut recoils as if I've been punched.

"The car mounted the pavement and plowed straight into her. She never stood a chance."

He balls his fists on his knees. His upper lip distorts in a sneer. "The guy who did it was released last year. Only served eight years of his twelve-year sentence."

"Oh, Josh, I'm so—"

"Don't. Please don't say anything else. Astrid, you've got to understand that I'm finding all this a little hard to deal with right now. I need time to process what you've told me. I'll ring you."

And with that, he gets up and walks away.

36

I sit on my hands and rock till he's out of sight, the urge to run after him even more powerful and all-consuming than the urge to drink. But I won't give in to either of them. I pull my phone out of my jeans pocket and speed-dial Helen's number.

My voice is thick with tears. "I've told Josh everything. He hates me."

"Give him time, Astrid. Give him time. It's a lot for him to take in."

"His mum was killed by a drunk driver."

Helen's silence says it all. "Where are you?" she says at last.

My mouth seems to have stopped working. I can't answer her.

"Where are you?" she repeats.

"At the beach."

"I'll meet you on the greensward."

I'm crying so hard that I don't even see her at first.

"Oh, Astrid," she says, linking her arm into mine and guiding me across the grass and toward the pavement. "I'm so sorry he took it badly, but you've done the right thing. You *know* you have."

I stare at my feet as we navigate the parked cars. Sockless in their sandy plimsolls, still damp from the wet sand, it's like being a little girl again, hanging on to Mum's arm while we cross the road.

"Do you want to come back to mine and talk?"

"I don't think I *can* talk. Not yet. I just want to crawl into bed and never wake up."

Helen stops in her tracks. She looks horrified. "You don't mean that, Astrid. Tell me you don't mean that."

"I don't mean that," I say.

But I do. I *do* mean that. Right now, the thought of falling asleep and not waking up again sounds like the perfect solution. I might have done the right thing, but that doesn't make it any easier to bear.

"You'll feel better about things in the morning," Helen says. "I'm sure you will. And so will Josh. He'll probably have phoned you by then. You'll see. It was just a shock for him, that's all."

But he doesn't phone. Minutes bleed into hours. Hours into days. For long swathes of time I stay in bed, dimly aware of Mum coming in at intervals with mugs of green tea and crackers with cheese. Chicken soup that cools in the bowl then disappears.

If I consume any of these offerings, I don't remember how they taste. My bladder swells uncomfortably. Ignoring it for as long as possible becomes a form of self-punishment. When I get back to my bed, the duvet and pillow have been plumped, the bottom sheet smoothed out. A cup of green tea is on the bedside cabinet, a chocolate biscuit on the saucer. The window has been opened and a sweet draft of fresh air billows the curtains.

Mum's willing me to get better, I know she is. But it's like I'm dead inside. I'm not even scared anymore, just numbed by everything that's happened. Nobody can hurt me any more than I've already hurt myself.

I check my phone. A whole string of messages, but they're all from Helen:

Astrid, I'm worried about you. Phone me. Please.

Why don't you come over? I've made a lovely curry.

I toss the phone onto the floor. There's only one name I want to see flash up on my screen right now and that's Josh.

When the noise of my thoughts won't let up, I paint continuously in my head. Not the picture I've been working on at the Carters' house but something wild and abstract. Mad brushstrokes and garish colors merge into dreams of tequila. Me and Simon necking shots till we slither to the floor in a tangle of sweaty limbs and sour breath. Josh watching me, contemptuously, from a corner of the room.

All the years I've wasted. All the chances I've squandered in the past. I'm not surprised someone's sending me hate mail. I hate myself too. I've hurt people. Dragged Simon back down when he was doing so well. Attacked an innocent young woman on the street. A mother with a child. I don't deserve to live. Maybe that girl, whoever she is, is right. Maybe I am better off dead.

Mum tries, in vain, to persuade me to see the doctor.

"We don't want you falling into depression," she says, and I picture myself teetering on the edge of a vast black chasm. Will I fall, or will I jump? What's the difference, in the end?

My eyes snap open. It's the middle of the night and there's been none of that hazy period between sleep and wakefulness. I reach for my phone, but he *still* hasn't texted. It's been over a week now.

There's another message from Helen.

I take it there's been no word from him yet. He's not
worthy of you, Astrid. xx

She's wrong about that. I'm not worthy of *him,* but he could at
least contact me, say that to my face instead of ignoring me for days
on end.

The only positive I cling to is that he must be serious about me if
his reaction is *this* bad. If I'm just another summer conquest, surely
he wouldn't care so much. But when I said all that stuff about him
being with someone else in the beach hut, he didn't deny it. If it
wasn't true, why didn't he say so?

Oh God, I hate this! When did I become so needy? Since I
stopped drinking, that's when. Why the fuck did I throw that vodka
away?

I get up and go downstairs, trying to step lightly so that the stairs
don't creak and wake Mum. But when I reach the hall, I see a strip
of light at the bottom of the living-room door. She's never up this
late.

Her head shoots up from the notebook she's been writing in.

"What are you doing?" I ask.

"Just making a list, dear, that's all. It helps sometimes, when I
can't sleep."

"Why can't you sleep?"

She gives me a funny look. She's worrying about me; of course
she is. I sit down beside her and she closes her notebook, but not
before I've seen the words: "Try not to react to everything she says."

For the first time, I realize something profound. That mixed in
with all her anger and hurt at my behavior is frustration at her *own*
behavior, her failure to be a different parent, one who might somehow have prevented my lapse into darkness or, at the very least,
dealt with it in a more effective way.

"You look different," she says. "A little brighter."

"Yeah. I decided not to fall." She looks puzzled. "Into depression."

"I'm very proud of you, Astrid. For telling Josh the truth and . . ." She presses her lips together. "And for not drinking. It must be so difficult."

"It's like a fight that never ends."

"I know," she says. "I mean, I don't know, but I can imagine. I . . . I read things. Articles. Websites." She points to a copy of the Big Book on the coffee table. "And that, of course. I should have read it before." She sighs. "When you first started drinking too much, I thought it was just a phase you were going through. There I was, seeking solace from the Quakers, when all the time I should have been getting you professional help."

"But . . . but I thought you only became a Quaker after Dad died."

Mum does a sad little smile. "No, Astrid. I started going to meetings when you were seventeen. It was the only way I knew how to cope."

The lump in my throat swells. I can't believe I didn't know that. Can't believe I've been so blind to her suffering all these years.

"Has he been in touch yet?" she asks.

"No."

"Well, then, he's not worth bothering over, is he?"

Everything's always so black and white for Mum, so obvious and clear cut. And yet she does have a point. If Josh can't bring himself to forgive me, if he can't cope with who I really am, then maybe he's not the man I thought he was.

"I'm meant to be going away this weekend," Mum says. "To a Quaker retreat in Cambridge. But I've decided not to go."

"Not because of me, I hope."

"I don't want to leave you on your own."

"I'm not going to drink, Mum. I'll be fine, I promise. I'm feeling better now."

But even as I say the words I know that I don't want her to go. I don't want to be alone. Not anymore.

37

My appointment at the job center is this afternoon. If it weren't for Mum reminding me, I'd have forgotten all about it. It's a half-hour bus drive away and it's the first time I've traveled beyond Flinstead and Mistden since I arrived here after rehab. It's also the first time I've left the house since telling Josh. The first time I've been out on my own since disposing of that vodka.

I rang the number on that flyer the other day. P. Hollingford & Sons doesn't even exist. My stalker actually went to the trouble of creating a fictional funeral directors', just to freak me out. But there've been no more brown envelopes while I've been stewing in my bed. No more sinister packages. Perhaps she's lost interest by now. Probably thinks she's succeeded in driving me insane.

Even so, when the bus finally arrives, I go right to the back and press my shoulders into the seat. I read a story once about a woman who was almost strangled by someone in the seat behind her. A complete stranger. He even used her own scarf to do it. Maybe that girl has mental health problems too. Well, she must have. In fact, the more I think about it, the more I keep returning to my original theory, that this is someone Simon met through AA, and nothing to do with the mugging. He should have chosen his confidante a little more carefully. If he weren't already dead, I'd want to kill him for blabbing. Tears spring to my eyes. If only he were still alive and I could give him a piece of my mind.

Half an hour later, I'm in the larger, brasher seaside town a little farther along the coast from Flinstead. Funfairs and bingo halls and takeaways. Everything Flinstead is not. I'm early for my appointment so I kill time by strolling down the high street. It's good for me to be in a new environment, seeing people going about their business. I can't wallow in bed forever, feeling sorry for myself, and I can't allow myself to be scared.

I'm just about to go into WHSmith to have a look at the paperbacks—I decided this morning that I really need to start reading again, to lose myself in a good book—when I spot a familiar figure disappearing through the doors of M&S. Tall. Messy hair. Red shoes. It's Helen.

I check my watch. The job center's only round the corner, and I've still got a bit of time. I'll go and say a quick hello, let her know I'm up and about again. All those texts of hers I've ignored—I need to thank her for being so supportive in my hour of need.

I cross the road and make my way through the glass doors into the women's clothing section, but I can't see her anywhere, which means she's probably walked through to the food hall. Knowing Helen, she's stocking up on chocolates and cakes. That goodie cupboard of hers was looking a little depleted last time I went round.

I never know where anything is in M&S, so I wander up and down the different aisles, looking for her. She must be here somewhere. And then I see her. Standing in front of the red-wine section. Oh no. I hang back, transfixed, as she reaches for a bottle and examines the label, puts it into her basket. Then she puts another one in, and another.

After everything she's said about staying sober, all that step-work we've done. How could she do this? I should have responded to her texts. I've been so wrapped up in my own misery I didn't stop to think that maybe she needed help too, that all those messages of support were actually cries for help. She wanted to talk. Not just for my sake, but for hers too. Helping me would have helped her.

I watch, appalled, as she puts yet another bottle in her basket and makes her way to the tills. Maybe if I had more time I'd approach her, persuade her to put them back on the shelf. Who knows how she'll end up if I don't? But my appointment's in less than five minutes and I can't afford to miss it. I just can't. You can lose your money for turning up late. I don't want to start off on the wrong foot, and how do I know she hasn't been drinking this whole time in secret? She won't thank me for barging up to her in a public place and confronting her. I know I wouldn't, if the tables were turned.

I hurry out of the shop and back up the high street toward the job center, wrestling with my guilt at not being selfless enough to miss my long-awaited appointment and help her.

The fact is, I've only got the strength to help one person now, and that's me. Rosie's right. I've made friends with the wrong person.

38

It's Friday, and Mum is about to leave for her retreat. It's the first time since I've been here that she's trusted me to be on my own overnight and, though neither of us has actually said as much, we both know it's a big deal.

She hugs me, perhaps for a second or two more than usual, or maybe it's me who takes longer to release her, and our lips graze each other's cheeks. Then I watch her walking down the path to the street, a small, sprightly figure in her navy raincoat, belted far too tight round her waist, the wheels of her overnight case bumping and rattling over the uneven concrete.

I have a sudden urge to run after her and tell her not to go. But Mum deserves a break, doesn't she? A break from me. I wouldn't mind one of those too.

The decision makes itself. I'm going to the house in Mistden, to see if I can speak to Josh. The very least he can do is tell me to my face that we're over.

Dusk is coming on and the birds are gathering in the trees, tuning up for their evening chorus. I close the front door behind me and set off in the direction of Mistden. It's a warm June night and there are lots of people about, visitors and locals, enjoying the fine weather. If ever there was a time for new beginnings, a time for forgiveness, it's now, but after my self-imposed confinement I feel like an alien, displaced in a foreign land. Too raw and vulnerable to let the warmth in.

I go through my options as I walk. If Josh isn't there, then I'll speak to his dad. If Richard won't talk to me about Josh, then surely he'll talk to me about the painting. After all, he commissioned me to work on the project, didn't he? He'll have to pay me for my time, for the work I've already put in. He might be angry with me about lying, but instinct tells me he's a fair-minded man. A good man.

I think of my unfinished painting on the wall, the paints and brushes and all the other paraphernalia lying there waiting for me. A still life of abandoned art materials. I could finish the job, couldn't I? It'll be awkward, for all of us, but once I'm shut away in that room, immersed in the moment, I know I can do it. And when Josh sees how committed I am, when he sees the finished piece, he'll forgive me—they both will—and we can go back to how we were. We can start all over again, only this time there'll be no more lies.

By the time I reach the turnoff to the Carters' house, night has fallen. The quiet country lane is unusually full of parked cars tonight. I'm halfway along when I realize why, but still a part of me clings to the hope that I've got it wrong, that all these people are, in fact, visiting someone else.

The hope gutters and snuffs out like a spent candle as I approach the familiar curved driveway. Music, light, and laughter spill out into the surrounding darkness. Richard's sixtieth birthday–cum–housewarming party is in full swing, and I haven't been invited. What with everything that's happened, I'd forgotten all about it. I've never felt so lonely.

I shrink back into the shadows of the large shrubs and watch the bodies move about inside. Then I grow braver and step a little closer to the house. Nobody can see me out here. The windows at night will be mirrors. It's like watching actors on a brightly lit stage. Revelers in a party scene, oblivious to all but their own chatter and laughter.

Most of the noise is coming from the back of the house so I presume the French windows must be open and people are taking the party into the garden. I have an overwhelming urge to look, to seek out Josh and Richard in the throng, even though I know I shouldn't. I should turn round and go straight home before one of them sees me and it's too late. I couldn't bear to be spotted like this, to see the awkwardness and embarrassment in their eyes. The uninvited guest, spying on them from the bushes.

I move stealthily up the driveway and round the side of the house by the garage. If I stay close to the boundary hedge and don't venture too far, I'll be all but invisible. Why am I doing this? It's absurd. An act of pure masochism. And what am I hoping to see? A forlorn and lonely Josh, sprawled on a deckchair, nursing a beer and resisting all attempts to join in the merriment? Maybe it would be better if I saw him laughing and having fun, chatting up a pretty girl. Leading her into the shadows at the end of the garden. At least then I'll know where I stand.

The garden looks magical, meltingly beautiful, as if it's hosting an open-air production of *A Midsummer Night's Dream*. All twinkling fairy lights and candles in Mason jars hanging from trees. There are people sitting on wicker chairs with cushions, or milling about with drinks and cigarettes. There are even a couple of sofas on the lawn. A glamorous black woman is sinking into one of them now, stretching out her long legs and tapping away on her phone while Nina Simone sings "My Baby Just Cares for Me." A couple in their forties are standing close together, swaying gently in time to the music right in front of her.

I hear Richard's voice before I see him. The deep baritone boom of it, resounding in the still, balmy night. He's exactly as I imagined he would be in this kind of milieu. The charming, magnanimous host. The life and soul. Then I see Josh.

I exhale slowly. He's in earnest conversation with a rather beautiful woman who reminds me of one of those pre-Raphaelite models, all flaming hair and bright-red lips. I think of the red lipstick on the brandy glass and crumple against the hedge. I wanted to see sadness in his eyes. To know he's missing me as much as I'm missing him, but he's smiling. Laughing. Touching her arm.

More guests fill the garden. The music gets louder. I must leave before I do something insane, before I walk over to Josh, fling my arms round his neck, and bawl my eyes out. But just as I'm about to creep away Richard approaches the two of them, a tray of nibbles in his hands. Josh helps himself to whatever is on there, then slips away and gets swallowed up by a group of happy, shiny young people. His cousins, maybe? The ones he couldn't wait for me to meet?

Richard rests the tray on a table and whispers something into the redhead's ear. She throws back her neck and laughs prettily. Now I see that she's older than I thought, in her forties or early fifties, even. Richard's hand rests gently in the small of her back. He leans in toward her and, for one brief moment, their foreheads touch. Now his hand slips a little lower. All of a sudden, Josh reappears. Richard grabs hold of the tray and disappears into the throng of guests.

Back in the darkness of the lane things fall into place. What I overheard Richard saying on the phone the other day, about not having told him yet and that he would do, soon. At the time I'd been so paranoid I thought he was referring to me, that he'd found out about my past and was waiting for the right moment to break it to Josh. But maybe he was talking to this woman, discussing when to tell Josh about their relationship. I'm no expert on body language, but they're clearly much more than good friends.

The bottle of brandy in the beach hut. The red lipstick on the glass. The discarded bikini. It all makes perfect sense now. He's been meeting this woman in private, keeping their relationship a

secret. Hardly surprising, considering Josh's reaction when I made
a joke about his dad being a bit of a catch. All that stuff Richard said
about not wanting Josh to get hurt again. I thought he meant hurt
by *me*, but he must have been worried I'd seen the brandy and the
two glasses in the beach hut. And didn't I see him talking to a redhead once on the street? He was trying to warn me not to say anything. Of *course* he was.

I've been such a fool, doubting Josh. He really was serious about
me and now I've gone and fucked it all up. First by lying to him all
this time, and then by trying to justify it by accusing him of being
some kind of player. No wonder he didn't want me at his dad's
party.

How I don't get knocked down as I stumble home in the darkness I don't know. There are no lights on these country lanes and
whenever a car whizzes by at what seems like death-defying speed,
I shrink into the hedgerows in case their headlights don't pick me
out. I've forgotten to charge my phone, so it isn't long before it dies,
and with it the torch function I've been relying on. The only good
thing about having to blunder along, half blind, is that all my mental resources are focused on keeping myself at a safe distance between the dangerous part of the road and the ditch at the side.

But I'm exhausted from the effort and soon my focus disinte-
grates. All this time I've been trying to convince myself that I don't
care, that losing Josh isn't the end of the world, and that I'm better
off on my own, but now that I've seen him there in the garden I
know I'm just fooling myself, because I want him more than ever.

By the time I smell the aftershave, it's too late. The footsteps are
right behind me. My heart thuds painfully in my chest. I've been so
consumed with self-pity I've pushed all thoughts of my stalker to
the back of my mind. I've let my guard down, and in the worst possible place. I'm all alone in the middle of a country lane in the dark.

I brace myself for the thrust of a blade somewhere soft and unexpected. In the periphery of my vision I see a shadow, but when
my eyes dart to the right it's gone. I reach into my pocket for my

house key, gripping it by my side like a small, sharp knife. It could be used as one. A jab in the face. In the eye.

My jaw clamps tight. My whole body stiffens. This has gone too far. I won't be bullied like this. I won't. I've got nothing to lose anymore. Nobody gets to scare me like this. Nobody gets to send me fucking death notices and poke around my room and steal my things. Nobody gets to terrorize me on the street at night.

I spin round, still clutching the key. "What do you want with me?"

My voice slices into the night air, shrill with rage. It's her, the girl in the puffer jacket. She freezes, like a startled deer. Her face is moon white, her eyes like dark saucers. She visibly shrinks under the glare of my gaze. Her hands, I now see, are empty. My breath returns.

I step forward to exploit my advantage, but she's already rearranging the features of her face. There is a condensed fury about her that threatens to erupt at any second. My fingers tighten round the key.

"Astrid Phelps." She spits my name out as if it's the worst kind of insult.

I stand my ground. "Who *are* you? Why are you following me?"

She glares at me. "Because I have something to say to you."

39

She's smaller than I thought, but I have the impression that behind that little-girl façade are nerves of steel.

"Well, get on with it, then." My voice sounds a hell of a lot braver than I feel.

"I know all about you," she says. "The things you've done."

I step back. So I'm finally face to face with the person who's been tormenting me all this time, the person who knows things about my past that nobody else should know.

"Who *are* you? Why did you go to the house? Why did you trick my mother into letting you in?"

She narrows her eyes. "We were going to get married, Simon and I. Did you know that? We were childhood sweethearts."

I stare at her, my brain tying itself in knots, trying to process her words. This must be the girl who had a crush on him, who wouldn't take no for an answer. The girl he finished with when he met me. She's lying. She must be.

A small laugh explodes in my mouth. "Married? No, I don't believe you. He only went out with you for a few weeks. You're lying."

She smiles, but there's nothing friendly about the shape of her mouth. "Well, that's where you're wrong. He came back to me, when he gave up drinking. When *you* wouldn't. I took him back."

"Took him back?"

"Didn't he ever tell you about me?" She gives a bitter little laugh. "Of course he didn't. You only knew him when he was drinking. He was a completely different person when he was sober. That's when he contacted me again. We used to be an item back in the day, before you turned up."

A car whips by and we shrink into the hedge as it passes.

"Come on," she says, and before I can gather my thoughts I'm doing as she says and walking alongside her. How did I let this happen? How has she managed to reassert herself so fast, to take the upper hand?

"He was doing so well," she says. "Until he met *you* again." Her voice is icy. Unforgiving. "You were a selfish, drunken bitch."

I don't say anything in my defense, because there's nothing I *can* say. She's right.

"I knew who you were as soon as you answered his phone."

I stop walking and stare at her. "What do you mean? I don't remember anything about that." Except now that she's said it I realize that I've had that memory before, seen the image of his phone vibrating in his shirt pocket. Did I really answer it?

There's that bitter little laugh again. "Well, you wouldn't, would you? You were off your head. Who do you think called the ambulance? It took me ages to get any kind of address out of you." She pauses. "Not that it made any difference in the end."

Tears spring to my eyes. I thought that calling the ambulance was the one good thing I managed to do in that whole sorry episode and now it turns out that I didn't even do that.

"What do you want with me?" My voice rings out louder and more aggressively than I intended. I mustn't aggravate her. I don't know what else she's capable of.

"If it was up to me, I'd have nothing whatsoever to do with you. I'm doing this for him. For Simon."

WHO DID YOU TELL?

"What do you mean? Doing what? Simon's dead."

She stops and eases her arms through the straps of her rucksack. She puts it on the ground in front of her and crouches down to undo the buckle. At last she finds what she's looking for and draws out a long brown envelope.

My knees begin to tremble. What else can she possibly taunt me with?

She straightens up and looks at me, the envelope still in her hand. There's a strange, wistful expression on her face. "Can't believe I'm finally handing this over. So many times I nearly tore it up, but something always stopped me. I guess it was the thought of him watching me from wherever he is and hating me for it."

I stare at her, bewildered by the sudden change in her behavior, her voice. Maybe it's all some horrible trick to lull me into a false sense of security. Maybe this envelope she's still clutching as if she can hardly bear to pass it over contains something so terrible I've wiped it from my memory.

"Deep down, I knew he didn't love me. Not the way he loved you." Her voice is so quiet I have to strain my ears to hear her.

"I kept thinking he'd get over you and that he and I would . . . I don't know, live happily ever after." She laughs, but it's not the bitter little noise she made earlier. "Like that was ever going to happen."

"I don't understand."

She stuffs her things back in her rucksack and stands up with the envelope. She holds it out toward me and I see my name, the familiar slope of Simon's handwriting. "Then you'd better read this."

For a few seconds we're each holding one end of the envelope. I can't bring myself to take full possession of it and she can't bring herself to release it. Eventually, her fingers loosen and the envelope is mine. My heart is racing. Can this really be a letter from Simon? A letter to me?

"I think it's what's commonly known as a suicide note." She looks away. "I know I shouldn't have opened it, but I couldn't help myself. I had to stop reading after the first couple of paragraphs. It was too painful."

She tilts her head back and sniffs.

"I've been trying to give it to you for ages, but every time I came anywhere near you I changed my mind. I didn't *want* you to read his lovely words. I was jealous of you, don't you see? All I ever wanted was for Simon to love me the way he loved you." She sniffs again. "You were the one he was thinking of, right up to the end."

I stare at her, open-mouthed, my mind still trying to catch up, to recalibrate. Is this what it all boils down to? All these weeks of wondering who the hell has been stalking and persecuting me like this, thinking I'm in real danger, thinking my own mother might be at risk. I feel like grabbing hold of the wretched girl by her collar and shaking her.

"Is that why you've been trying to freak me out all this time? Because you were jealous?"

She pinches her lips together. An angry little frown puckers her forehead.

"I wasn't just jealous, I was angry with you. Furious. Still am, if you must know."

She's walking away from me now, striding off toward the main road. She's picking up speed. No, she doesn't get to walk away from me that easily. Not after everything she's put me through. I'm the one who should be furious.

"Laura, come back!"

She stops and turns, her face streaming with tears. She wipes them away with her fingers. Mascara streaks her cheeks. Even when it's blotchy with tears, I can see that she has a beautiful face. High cheekbones and pale, almost translucent skin. She's like a tiny porcelain doll. How could I ever have been scared of her?

"So you told Mum the truth about your name, at least."

She looks down at her feet. "I don't really know why I went to your house. Maybe I was hoping I'd find some evidence that you didn't deserve to have Simon's letter. But when I saw your room, it looked so . . . empty and sad. I saw you were reading the Big Book and then I saw . . ." She glances at me from the corner of her eye. "Then I saw the gold ball and I knew. I knew you still loved him."

She reaches into her jacket pocket and takes it out, stares at it. "Here, have it back. I've got the other two at home. I shouldn't have taken it."

She fumbles around in her pocket for a tissue and blows her nose. She's given up trying to wipe away her tears. Oh, for fuck's sake, I'm starting to feel sorry for her now. And I can hardly take the moral high ground, can I? Not after the things I've done.

"Keep it," I tell her. "They belong together."

She puts it back into her pocket. "If only I hadn't let him go."

"What do you mean?"

Her shoulders sag. "When he gave me this letter to give to you, he told me there was something else he had to do. Something that would make everything all right." She gives me a helpless look. "I should have gone with him. I should never have let him go off on his own like that. It was too soon. If I'd had the slightest suspicion he was going to . . . to do what he did, I'd have told one of the nurses. I'd have *made* him stay in hospital."

She stares at her feet. "He was so persuasive, though. So calm and determined. I had no idea."

"There's nothing you could have done," I tell her. "When someone's made the decision to end their life, they don't usually talk about it."

Laura looks up at me then. "I miss him so badly."

"So do I." My words come out all muffled because now I'm crying too. "And anyway, it's my fault he started drinking again. My fault he died."

She turns away. "I wanted to kill you when I found out what had happened." She faces me at last. "But I don't feel like that anymore. Not now I've met you."

"Tell me, Laura, why do you wear his aftershave?" But even as I'm asking her the question I already know the answer.

"It's my way of kidding myself he's still with me. I'd have looked after him, Astrid. I'd have stayed with him forever."

"You couldn't have stopped him, you know, even if you'd tried." She nods. "I know that really, but I still torture myself about it."

We've reached the main road now. She looks at her watch. "The last train leaves soon. I've got to run."

She races off, rucksack bumping against her back, her dark hair flying out in the wind.

"Wait!" I shout after her. "I'll come with you."

But she doesn't slow down and after a few minutes trying to catch up with her, I stop, exhausted, and hang over my knees to get my breath back. It's not as if the two of us are ever going to be friends, not after all that's happened, so what's the point? She's done what she came here to do and now she's gone.

She's gone. After weeks of dread weighing me down like a heavy cloak, I feel lighter. As if I've finally come up for air. As I walk back to Mum's cottage, my heartbeat returns to normal. I'm safe. At last.

My fingers curl round the envelope in my pocket. A letter from Simon. I'm going to need every single ounce of my strength if I'm to read his final words. How will I cope, hearing his voice in my head after all this time, as if he's back from the dead after all?

There she is, letting herself into her mother's house, like a sad little wraith. All alone in the dark with her guilt and her shame and her fragile sense of hope that maybe, just maybe, she'll get another chance at love.

I'd laugh out loud if the very thought of her didn't make me want to retch.

I think it's about time I stopped messing about with hate mail and bottles of vodka in her coat pocket, fun though it was. About time I stopped playing games. I've wasted enough time here as it is. The little bird is weakened now. It's time for the cat to pounce.

Like I told you before, bitch, what goes around comes around. Some mistakes can't be corrected. Some mistakes you have to pay for.

40

I close the front door behind me and go into the living room, curl up on the end of the sofa. But before I've even drawn the envelope from my pocket the craving starts. A delayed reaction to everything that's happened since Mum left for her retreat. The implications of not being invited to the party. The confrontation with Laura. The words I'm about to read.

I draw my knees to my chest and hug them tight, rock backward and forward. I want a drink so badly I can barely breathe. All this time, I've been running scared and I've managed to keep it together, but now, now that I'm finally safe, I'm on the verge of throwing it all in.

I get as far as opening the flaps of the envelope and holding the edge of the folded paper between my forefinger and thumb when the feeling swells till it's all there is. I focus on my breath. It's fear, that's all. Fear of the emotions I'll experience when reading it. I might not have to worry about Laura and her nasty games anymore, but my memories will always stalk me. The grief. The guilt. And now I've lost Josh too—the one person who might have saved me from the worst of myself.

I glance at the clock. The Co-op will be shut—it's past ten. But there's a little Asian shop that sells food and wine, isn't there? That might still be open.

No. It's crazy to give in now.

Suddenly, I'm back on my feet and in the hall again. I'm just minutes from buying what I need. From pouring it down my throat and drowning out the noise in my head. Mum won't be back till Sunday evening. I'll have time to sort myself out by then. It'll be just this once, to get me through tonight. She'll never know. How am I supposed to read this letter without a drink inside me?

Now I'm opening the front door, going back out into the night. My feet move faster and faster. Slapping rhythmically against the pavement, they've got a life of their own. They're not listening to that small voice of reason. The one that's getting quieter by the minute. The one that's fast losing the battle.

I've almost reached the shop now, but, oh no, I'm too late. Tears of frustration stream down my cheeks as I stare at the dirty gray shutters. It's fate, I know it is. I should be relieved. I *am* relieved. Because the decision has been taken out of my hands. There's nothing for it but to go back home and ride the yearning out. Drink coffee and smoke. Eat biscuits. Bang my head against the wall and scream if I have to. Smoke some more. I should never have left the house in the first place.

I'm walking home when a memory worms its way into my head. Helen in M&S, placing bottles of red wine in her basket. My stomach twists and churns. I glance over my shoulder toward her apartment block at the end of the street, on the verge of heading straight for it, but now another memory pushes through. Mum's face, saying goodbye to me before she left. The worry in her eyes. The knowledge that she was taking a huge risk by leaving me on my own. And I know that I can't let it happen. I can't let her down all over again. There'll be no going back if I do.

With a sickening sense of inevitability I realize that there's only one person who truly understands what I'm going through right now. All those times she's tried to reach out and help me and I pushed her away. All those warnings she gave me about Helen still drinking, and what did I do? I ignored every one.

The Oxfam shop is closed, of course, as I knew it would be. I peer into the darkened interior, hoping by some miracle I'll see her inside, but I don't. Of course I don't. If only I'd kept hold of her number. It was stupid of me to throw it away. Stupid and arrogant.

But what about the sleeping bag and flashlight I saw in her cloth bag that day I tried the dress on? Is it possible that she really is sleeping in the shop overnight? Maybe she's there right now, all alone in that smelly back room, huddled down on the floor. It's worth a try, isn't it? Okay, so she's annoying as hell, but she's managed to stay sober for eight long years. She must be doing something right. And it's not as if I have any other options, not now I've remembered what's in Helen's flat. If I take one look at a glass of wine tonight, I'll be all over it.

I dart down the alleyway that leads to the access road behind the shops. I've never been down here before and it takes me a while to work out which is the right door. For all I know, she won't even be here. She might have found somewhere else to stay by now.

I squeeze past the rubbish bins, bracing myself for the sight of a rat scavenging for food. I've seen a fair few in my time, especially when I stayed in squats, but I never got used to it. They always freak me out.

I raise my fist and rap sharply on the door with my knuckles. I wait, then rap again. Louder this time.

If anyone can help me stay off the booze tonight, it's Rosie.

41

At last, I hear a shuffling noise from inside, then the sound of bolts being drawn back and the rattling of keys. The door opens a fraction of an inch and two suspicious eyes peer out through the gap. When she sees it's me, her eyes soften and something akin to pleasure passes across her face. She knows she's got me and, for once, I don't care. I need to be saved. From myself.

The door opens a little more, wide enough for me to edge sideways into a cramped, dark space full of boxes. She sticks her head out of the door and scans the street in both directions before closing and locking it behind us.

"How did you know where to find me?"

I follow her into the back room. "I saw your sleeping bag. I guessed."

The inner door that leads through into the shop is closed and there's a paraffin lamp on the table. Of course. That's the smell I recognized before but couldn't identify. Her red sleeping bag is unfurled on top of a makeshift mattress of old curtains and blankets piled on top of each other. It makes me think of the fairy story I loved as a child. "The Princess and the Pea."

Rosie leans across the table to adjust the wick of the lamp and dim yellow light expands in the windowless room. Shadows dance on her face. She looks grotesque. As far removed from a fairy-tale princess as it's possible to be.

"I'm trying not to use too much electricity," she says. "In case they notice the bill's higher than usual."

She gestures to a chair. "You can shove that stuff on the floor and sit down if you want."

She takes hold of a kettle and disappears with it into a recess. I hear her filling it up.

"I thought Helen was your go-to friend in times of trouble." She sounds defensive, as well she might. I've spurned her advances too many times.

"I don't think she's very well."

"Hmm."

Rosie comes back into the main space of the room and goes over to a stained Formica shelf that passes as a kitchen area. An assortment of chipped and dirty mugs is stacked up next to a large box of value teabags and a catering-size jar of cheap instant coffee. A small pyramid of used teabags congeals on a saucer.

"Tea or coffee?" she says.

"Coffee, please. Black."

"Don't worry, it will be. I've used the last of the milk."

I shiver. It might be warm outside, but in here it's distinctly chilly. Rosie grabs a cable-knit sweater from the top of one of the donation bags and tosses it toward me. I catch it by the sleeve and give it a quick sniff. Time was I wouldn't have cared less about putting someone's dirty sweater on, but with sobriety comes a more refined sense of smell. I'm more discerning all round now I'm not permanently shit-faced. Rosie watches me with interest.

"You've been crying," she says.

"No shit, Sherlock."

Rosie laughs through her nose. She turns her attention back to the kettle and soon she's sloshing hot water into two mugs.

"Sugar?"

"No, thanks."

She spoons three heaped teaspoonfuls into her own mug and hands me the other. Then she crosses her ankles and sinks, effortlessly, onto her sleeping bag.

I sniff. "Aren't you going to ask me why I'm here?"

Rosie smiles. There's a smugness about her that infuriates me. I'd get up and leave right now if I didn't know for sure what I'd do if I did.

She holds her mug close to her chin so that steam rises up in front of her face. "I knew you'd show up, one of these days. It was just a matter of waiting."

A tear rolls out of the corner of my right eye. I don't want to break down in front of her because I know, as soon as I do, I'll tell her everything, just like she wants me to. Like she's wanted me to from the very beginning. And yet there's something about the way she's sitting there, that patient, resigned expression on her face, as if she'll sit there forever until I do, that acts like a valve inside me, and the words judder out.

"My boyfriend died. He killed himself and it's my fault and now I've got his suicide note and I can't read it. I just can't. Not without a drink."

Rosie puts her mug on the floor. She's looking at some place I can't see, some private region inside herself. In a terrible flash of insight, I see in her a future version of me, or how I might end up, eking out my interminably dry days sifting through other people's rubbish, squatting in a shop that smells of death and decay.

Rosie returns from wherever it is she's been. "A letter? From Simon?"

I'm amazed she knows his name. I don't even remember telling her. I must have let it slip during one of my shares. "Yes. I only got it tonight."

She narrows her eyes. "How come?"

"His ex-girlfriend gave it to me."

Her eyebrows flicker. "I thought *you* were his ex-girlfriend."

"I am. I mean, I *was*. It's a long story."

"You've got a new boyfriend now, haven't you?"

I shake my head. "Not anymore. I finally did the right thing and told him the truth, and now he doesn't want anything to do with me." I stare at my feet. "I should never have allowed myself to get involved with him in the first place. It was too soon after Simon. But I *am* involved. I've fallen in love with him."

Rosie tugs at her sleeves and pulls them over her knuckles. "Tell me about him."

"He's here for the summer. Helping his dad renovate an old house."

"No. Not him. Simon."

I stare at her. She's got a really weird expression on her face, as if she's trying to bore into my mind and extract my thoughts. But she's right. I *do* need to talk about him. Exorcize his ghost once and for all.

"I used to think he was the only man I could ever love. The only man who understood what it was like to be me."

Tears flow down my face. Sitting in the back room of an Oxfam shop with a mug of revolting instant coffee and baring my soul to an AA zealot like Rosie is the very last thing I want to be doing. Is this really my last refuge? Because I know what's going to happen if I stay. She'll start talking about God and how I need to surrender to His will. How I need to go back to Step 1 and start all over again. We'll probably end up praying together.

"And yet now you feel the same way about this new man?"

"Yes, but it's *different* now. Because I'm not drinking anymore. When I'm with Josh I feel safe. He's uncomplicated. Kind, responsible."

"And Simon wasn't?"

Rosie's stare is intense. All these questions about Simon! She's probably done a counseling course or something. Still, it sounds as if she knows what she's doing, as if all this is leading me somewhere I need to be.

"Well, he was kind when he wasn't off his head. But uncomplicated? Responsible? Those aren't words you associate with addicts. You of all people should know that." I close my eyes. "I can't explain why I loved him. I just did. It was an intense kind of love. It was . . . visceral."

Rosie shifts her sit bones. She gazes at a point beyond my right shoulder and frowns. "When someone we love dies before their time, it's so much harder to bear, isn't it?" she says.

I nod. It's hard to tell in this light, but I think there are tears in her eyes. Maybe she's thinking of her mother. I drain the last of my coffee. It might be foul, but it's warm and wet and drinking it gives me something to do.

"I don't suppose we can smoke in here, can we?"

Rosie shakes her head. "It'll set off the smoke alarm. You can stand on the lav and stick your head out the window if you want." She laughs. A deep, throaty chuckle I've never heard before. "I've managed to cut right down since I've been dossing here."

She's not so bad, really. If we'd met each other when we were both soaks, we'd have had a right old laugh. Christ, just thinking about that makes me want a drink. I get my fags out of my pocket and go and lock myself in the loo before I start blubbing again. I don't want to end up like Rosie, pushing sixty and squatting in a charity shop, having to balance on a toilet seat with my head shoved up next to a fanlight every time I want a smoke. What would Josh think if he could see me now? What would Richard?

When I've smoked it down to the butt, I pinch it out between my fingers and drop it out the window. Then I do a wee. I unlock the cubicle door and, just as I'm about to wash my hands in the basin, something catches my eye. The familiar face of Dolores O'Riordan staring up at me from the top of Rosie's cloth bag.

A chill runs through me. I look over my shoulder, but Rosie can't see me from here. I run the tap, then slowly, carefully, I lift the Cranberries T-shirt out and hold it up in front of me. My stomach knots in dread. It's the same one I saw on the mannequin. The one

I thought I must have imagined. The one Rosie denied all knowledge of. Except I didn't imagine it. Because here it is, in my hands. Tentatively, hardly daring to breathe, I work my fingers round the edge of the hem till I find it. The small, round bleach stain that tells me, beyond a shadow of a doubt, that it's Simon's.

42

With trembling hands, I refold the T-shirt and replace it in the bag. As I do this, I catch sight of some paper folded in half and stuffed down the side.

"Astrid? Are you okay?" Rosie's voice makes me flinch. I whip the paper out and stuff it into my back pocket.

"I'm fine, yeah, just drying my hands." At least, that's what I try to say. What actually comes out is a strange little croaking noise.

"Did you turn the light off in the loo?" Her voice is right behind me now. I spin round to see her looming in the doorway. Her eyes flick toward the bag on the floor. The swiftest, most subtle of glances, but I saw it. I saw it.

I nod, barely trusting myself to speak. She knows I've seen it. The space between us prickles with tension.

"You lied to me." My voice is high and squeaky. I clear my throat and try for something on a lower register, something that carries more weight. But the same reed-thin warble betrays me. "You said it must have been sold."

She shrugs, as if it's nothing.

"Okay, so I lied. I had a feeling it might be worth something. Special-edition T-shirts often are. So I looked it up and one just like it was sold on eBay for eighty quid."

She steps forward and plucks the shirt from the bag, shakes it out in front of her, and stares at it, as if she can't quite believe what she's saying. Of course she can't. Because she's lying through her teeth.

"We're not supposed to siphon stuff off for ourselves. Things that might fetch a bit more for the charity are auctioned online. But as you can probably tell, I'm not exactly flush at the moment." She tilts her chin back and gives me a defiant stare. "But I changed my mind. I wasn't going to do it."

I nod as if I believe her. Until I know for sure what I'm dealing with here, I need to tread softly, let her think she's fooled me.

"Simon came close to selling it once," I say.

Her fingers tighten round the fabric.

"The Cranberries were playing the night we met. Not that he was particularly sentimental, but . . ."

She's still clutching the T-shirt, as if she daren't let it go, as if she suddenly needs it to be as close to her skin as possible.

With trembling fingers, I reach into my back pocket and pull out the piece of paper. My palms are damp with sweat. Rosie tenses as I unfold it. It's a photocopy of a story in a newspaper with one small paragraph ringed in red. It's headed "Young man commits suicide at Seaford Head, West Sussex."

I've been a fool. An idiot. Ever since Laura gave me Simon's suicide note, I've convinced myself that the only thing tormenting me is myself. My inner addict struggling to get out. But what if it wasn't Laura sending those messages? She apologized for scaring me, yes, but what if she just meant following me around and coming to the house under false pretenses? Lying to Mum? She never actually admitted to sending them. I just assumed it was her.

The memory of Rosie reaching for his gold juggling ball when I

WHO DID YOU TELL?

emptied my pockets that time flashes into my mind. The way she squeezed it into the palm of her hand and went into that semi-trance. It makes me think of how I used to hold it close to my chest at night and draw comfort from it, as only a lover could.

A lover . . . or a mother.

My legs turn to jelly. A tide of nausea swells up inside me and black spots swim before my eyes.

She moves as if to touch me, but I step aside, out of reach, move back into the storage room. My brain struggles to compute. I remember Simon once telling me his mother had "issues," that she hated him having a life of his own. But he never said she was an alcoholic. How can she be *here*, in Flinstead? It doesn't make any sense. Unless he told her about me. But they were estranged, weren't they? Had been for years. I must have it wrong. Yet how else would she have his T-shirt?

If I hold my nerve, I can make a dash for the back door and get away from her. I need to work out what this means. Panic rushes through me in an icy flood. Rosie locked the door behind me. I saw her do it. Didn't even question her motives.

My eyes roam the room for a set of keys, but I can't see any. What I do see is the PC, and my mind picks at a memory, sees it open on the Windows template screen when I was trying that dress on. I think of the fake flyer wrapped round the bottle of vodka. She must have created it in here. Used the shop's printer to run off a copy.

Then I catch sight of the keys. She's slung them onto her sleeping bag. Rosie sees me looking at them and her jaw tightens.

"I'm sorry, Astrid, but I can't let you leave."

Strategies charge through my head. She wants to talk, so we'll talk. It's what she's wanted all along, isn't it? Sidling up to me at every opportunity, trying to engage me in conversation, pressing her phone number into my pocket. And to think I thought Helen and a couple of bottles of red wine might be a danger to me tonight.

"Sit," she says, inclining her head toward the chair I was sitting on before.

Fear roots me to the spot.

"Sit," she says again, and I find myself obeying, because what else can I do?

Think, Astrid. Think!

I lower myself onto the chair.

Rosie picks up my empty mug. "I'll make you another one," she says.

Still holding the T-shirt, Rosie moves toward the recess we've just come out of. I consider making a dash for the front of the shop and hammering on the glass door to attract a passerby's attention, but no sooner does this idea come into my head than I dismiss it. The chances of anyone walking by at this time of night are slim. I need to get hold of those keys and make it to the back door.

I wait till I hear the sound of her rinsing my mug in the sink before getting up as quietly as I can and enclosing the entire bunch of keys in the palm of my hand so they don't jangle. Then I creep as fast as I can to the door at the back. The top bolt slides across smoothly and noiselessly. So far so good. But the bottom one is stuck fast. I pinch the barrel between my thumb and forefinger and yank it across with all my strength. The metal gouges into my flesh as it shoots back with a loud clank.

"Astrid? Astrid, what are you doing?"

With fumbling fingers, I stick the first key in the lock, but it won't turn. I try the other one on the key ring, but my hand's shaking so much I drop it. Now I don't know which one I've just tried. By the time I've got the right key in the keyhole, she's behind me. Her hand grips my shoulder, pulling me back.

"I'm sorry, Astrid, but I can't let you leave."

I twist the key, but it won't fully turn. There's some kind of obstruction. Rosie tries to push me out of the way.

"Stop it!" she hisses. "You'll break the lock. Give me the keys!"

I grab the handle with my left hand and pull the door toward me at the same time as twisting the key as forcefully as I can. At last, it works and the door springs open. I elbow Rosie sharply in the side of her chest and run away from her into the night. She's shouting after me, but I'm back up the alleyway now and on Flinstead Road, my chest tight with panic, adrenaline coursing through my veins.

43

I don't stop running. I don't even glance over my shoulder. I daren't. I don't care if Helen's been drinking. I don't care if she's mad at me for turning up in the middle of the night. She'll *have* to let me in. She'll just have to.

I reach her block of flats and hold my finger on the buzzer. What if I can't rouse her? What if she refuses to get out of bed to open the door? But just when I'm on the verge of giving up, the intercom crackles into life.

"Helen, it's me."

"Astrid? What are you doing here?"

"For God's sake, Helen! Let me in. Please! I'll explain when I come up."

At last she buzzes me through.

I take the stairs two at a time. It's a good job it's not the holiday season yet or this block would be fully occupied. I'd have disgruntled residents threatening to call the police, the racket I'm making. Helen is standing at her front door in her pajamas.

"What on *earth*'s the matter?"

"Rosie," I gasp, hanging over my knees in her hallway to catch my breath. "It's Rosie!"

My chest is tight with pain. I've never run so fast and so far in such a short space of time. Years of drinking and not looking after myself properly have taken their toll. I could have given myself a heart attack.

I reach into my jeans pocket and pull out the folded photocopy. "Look what I found in her bag. She's got his T-shirt too."

Helen takes the paper and walks away from me into the living room.

"Where did you get this?"

"I told you. From Rosie's bag. She's his mother, don't you see? Rosie is Simon's mother!"

My knees give way. Helen rushes forward and steers me toward the sofa.

"Where is she now?"

"In the shop. That's where I've just come from."

"But Astrid, it's one thirty in the morning. How could you have been in the shop?"

"She's got nowhere to live. She's sleeping there."

Helen stares at the piece of paper. "Did Rosie say anything? About Simon? About . . . this?"

"Just a load of weird shit about needing to talk to me, but I was so freaked out by then I wasn't really concentrating on what she said. My mind was too busy working out how to get away from her."

"Did she try to come after you? Does she know where you are?"

"I don't think so. I didn't hear anyone behind me. I didn't look. I just kept running."

"Does she know where I live?"

I think of the gray blur that rushed past the flats the first time Helen brought me here. The one I thought might be Rosie.

"I don't *think* so. I mean, I've never told her. Have you?"

"No." Helen takes a long, deep breath through her nostrils. "Which means as long as you're here, you're safe. But what about your mother? Won't she be worrying about you?"

"Mum's on a Quaker retreat. She won't be back till Sunday evening."

Helen nods. "Well, that's sorted, then. You'll stay here tonight and we'll work out what to do tomorrow." She rests her hand on my arm. "You must be terrified, you poor thing. And exhausted. You need to sleep."

"I can't imagine falling asleep anytime soon."

"Has Josh been in touch yet?"

Josh. Richard. The party. Ever since finding Simon's T-shirt, the pain and humiliation have been squeezed out. Now they come surging back. Tears well up in my eyes as I explain.

"Seeing him there, it made me realize how much I've hurt him by not telling the truth. It made me realize how much I've got to lose if he decides he doesn't want me. I can't bear it, Helen. And now all this, with Rosie. I mean, why is she *here*, in Flinstead? What's she going to *do*? She could ruin everything." I sniff back the tears. "If it's not already ruined."

And then I see it, sitting on the kitchen counter. A three-quarters-full bottle of red wine and an empty glass. My heart sinks.

Helen sees what I'm looking at. Her whole body stiffens. "It's not what you think," she says. "I had a friend round earlier."

"Oh, Helen, surely you don't expect me to believe that?"

For a second I think she's going to continue with the pretense, but then she hangs her head and sighs.

"Okay, okay. I was going to tell you," she says, her voice suddenly low. "You're right, I *have* been drinking again." She stares at the floor.

"I know, I saw you in M&S the other day."

Her head jerks up. "I've just been having one glass, every now and again."

"Stop it, Helen. You're deluding yourself. You know you are."

She shakes her head. "I'm not. I'm honestly not. I haven't wanted any more than that, I promise. I know what they say in AA, that it's impossible for people like us to just have one. But it is possible.

WHO DID YOU TELL?

After everything I've been through and all the soul-searching since, I've found a new resolve. And it's working, Astrid. It really is. It's called moderation management."

I can't believe she's saying this. I can't listen to it anymore. I can't. It's the same old rubbish I used to say to myself. The endless rules I kept setting—no more than two glasses a night, no drinking before 9 P.M.—they were all just excuses not to stop for good. Because the prospect of *never* having another drink was unthinkable. Still is.

"So why did you buy so many bottles? You must have put at least four in your basket."

She won't meet my eye. "They were on special offer." She gets up and goes over to it. "I have one small glass every day, and that's it. I can do it now. I can manage my drinking." She looks down. "Apart from that one little slip before."

I have to stop her doing this. I need her sober. Tonight more than ever. I shake my head in despair.

"Soon it'll be two glasses, then three, then the whole bottle. You know it will. You can't do this, Helen. Please, listen to me. You're trying to normalize your drinking, but nothing about people like us is normal."

Her hand is on the neck of the bottle, her fingers almost caressing it. Suddenly, she twists off the screw cap and pours the wine into the glass. My stomach flips at the familiar glugging noise. A dangerous, glorious sound.

"Please, Helen. Don't do this. Not now. I need your help. I need you sober."

But it's too late. The glass is already at her lips.

44

I watch the sinews in her neck contract as she swallows. Something inside me stretches taut, then sags. Josh doesn't want me anymore. What he said about needing time to process things—it was just a polite way of telling me to get lost. He hates me. And even if he does agree to see me again, Rosie and her twisted vendetta will put paid to any future we might have together. She's not going to sit back while I start again with somebody else. As far as she's concerned, I'm responsible for her son's death.

Helen licks her lips and places the glass on the counter.

"Don't be taken in by the cult of AA, Astrid," she says, her voice soft and low. "You are *not* powerless over alcohol. You never were. You just lost your way for a bit. You're a different person now. Just like me."

She picks the glass up again and holds it in front of her face. I see the light reflected in the ruby-colored liquid, imagine the rich, grapey smell of it in my nostrils. The way it will taste on my tongue. The smooth, velvety feel of it sliding down my throat.

"If Josh really loved you, he wouldn't be putting you through this," she says, and takes another measured sip. There's nothing wild or reckless about her. Nothing remotely alcoholic. Quite the opposite, in fact. She looks more in control than I've ever seen her. "How long is it since you told him?" she says. "Two weeks now, isn't it?"

I dip my head. Helen's right. Josh doesn't love me. She's right about AA too. It *is* a cult. If alcoholism is what they say it is, if it's a medical condition, a *disease,* then why the hell is God the only cure? And how can I trust in it when the person so keen on peddling its diktats at every meeting was lying to me all along?

I raise my eyes. Helen's still there in front of me, poised and reasonable, the wine in her glass barely touched.

The last piece of my resolve finally snaps. If she can do it without falling apart, why can't I?

"So," I say, my mouth watering in anticipation. "Are you going to pour me a glass or not?"

The wine blazes a path from my mouth to my gut. The sensation is so familiar. So right. Like coming in from the cold to a room filled with warmth and long-forgotten comfort. Before I know what I'm doing, I've downed several mouthfuls, one after the other. I can't believe I'm actually doing this. What the hell's wrong with me? This is madness. I've got to stop before I drink the lot.

I lean toward the table and put my glass down next to Helen's. It feels wrong at first, like lighting a cigarette and letting it burn out in an ashtray. What's the good of wine if it's all the way over there on the table and not right here in my hand, where I can swig from it whenever I please? But it's different now. It's not going to be like before. I'm going to moderate myself. I'm just going to have one glass. That's all. If Helen can do it, so can I.

"What are we going to do about Rosie?" she says.

I'm so grateful for that. The way she says, "What are *we* going to do?" It makes the whole thing seem manageable, somehow. Less scary.

"I don't know."

I lean forward to reach for my glass, then change my mind at the last moment. It's too soon. I've only just put it down. I've got to get used to this new way of drinking. I've got to get used to being normal.

"What I can't understand is how she found me here. Simon couldn't have told her where my mum lived—he didn't talk to her anymore. He *hated* her. And anyway, I didn't move in with Mum till after he'd died and I'd come out of rehab."

I reach for my glass, resisting the temptation to slug it right back. I've got to be sensible about this and savor each and every sip.

"He didn't talk about her very often. From the little he *did* tell me, it sounds like she used him to fulfill her own emotional needs after his father died."

Helen nods. "I read an article about that once. I think it's quite common. They end up treating their own child like a surrogate spouse."

"But why didn't he tell me she was an alcoholic?"

Helen has suddenly gone very still.

"What? Helen, what's the matter? What are you thinking?"

She picks up her glass and takes a sip. "Maybe she isn't."

"What do you mean?"

"Maybe she's just pretending."

"What, pretending to be an alcoholic just so she could attach herself to me at meetings? Bloody hell, Helen. That's really creepy. Mind you, it explains why she was so keen to work with me on my recovery."

Recovery. My recovery. The words reverberate in my head. I stare at the wine in my hand and the glass starts to shake. Oh no, what have I done?

It's not too late, Astrid. It's not too late. You can stop right now.

But my mind is already starting to become fuggy and there's a funny, bitter taste in my mouth.

Helen eyes me over the rim of her glass. Her face looks all blurry. "Did he tell you that?" she says.

"Tell me what?"

"That he hated her?"

Helen stretches her legs out and rests her bare feet on the coffee table. She has the biggest feet I've ever seen on a woman. They're veiny, like her hands, and there's a disproportionately wide gap between the big and second toes. Simon had that too, but somehow it didn't look so bad on him.

I start to giggle.

"What's so funny?" she says.

"Your feet."

"They're not funny, they're—"

"Tragic," I say. "Your feet are tragic."

She lifts each foot in turn and circles her ankles. "So you don't think I could make a living as a foot model, then?"

Now we're both laughing hysterically.

"I'm so glad I met you," I say, when our laughter has subsided into long sighs and occasional snorts.

Helen hands me my glass of wine and I take another mouthful. Maybe it's because I haven't drunk anything for ages, but it's gone to my head already. I'm starting to relax at last, the sinking dread of the last couple of hours now fuzzy and weightless. Still there, somewhere, but too far away to matter. This is what I've missed. The sweetness of not caring.

"I never realized a glass of wine could last so long." I chink my glass against hers. "Not that I'm complaining."

"No indeed," she says, giving me a strange little smile. "But what are we going to do about Rosie?"

Rosie. Fuck! How could I have forgotten about Rosie? I rub my eyes. It's hard to make sense of it all. I can't get my head round the facts. What they mean. My brain feels like cotton wool. Something scary happened earlier, but I can't quite remember the sequence of events.

"Fuck Rosie and fuck Josh!" I shout. "Fuck both of them!"

Helen clinks her glass against mine. "Foul-mouthed little slut," she says.

I laugh. She's good at the old banter is Helen. Except her voice sounds different. There's a tone to it I haven't heard before. Something snags at the very edge of my conscious mind. Why is she looking at me like that?

My head slumps to my chest and suddenly I'm awake. I must have dozed off. Shit, I've got the spins. I rest my head on Helen's shoulder and close my eyes, but that only makes things worse.

"Need to puke." My voice sounds all weird and disembodied.

Helen plonks the wastepaper bin on my lap and I wrap my arms round it. I can hardly keep my eyes open. Something isn't right. It's all spiraling out of control. I'm ill. I need to get to the loo.

I try to stand up but lose my balance and fall down again. How the hell did I get so pissed on half a glass of wine? I stopped, didn't I? But wait, there are *three* empty bottles on the coffee table. What the fuck? Where the hell did they come from? This wasn't meant to happen. I wasn't going to drink any more. I can't believe I've been so stupid. And yet, the evidence is here. My spinning head. The empty bottles.

I slump over my knees and retch in disgust. I've lost control. After all those months of staying sober, I've ruined everything.

I'm curled up in an uncomfortable position, and I'm cold. So cold. The room is pitch black and my head is throbbing with pain. Feels like there's a creature trying to punch its way out of my forehead. I struggle to sit up, but a wave of nausea forces me back down.

I don't know where I am. Oh yes, I'm on Helen's sofa. But where are my clothes? Oh no. I haven't, have I? I have. I've been sick. I can smell it.

"Just look at the state of you."

The voice startles me. It's coming from the other side of the room.

"Helen? Is that you?"

"Of course it's me. Who did you think it was?" Her voice is unusually bitter, her face cold, immobile. She switches the main light on, blinding me with its harsh glare. "You just couldn't stop yourself, could you?"

It's several minutes before I can keep my eyes open long enough to see anything. When I do, I wish I couldn't. I'm lying here in my underwear, my vomit-covered clothes in a heap on the floor next to me. Four empty bottles of red wine on the coffee table and . . . a pair of Helen's brown tights, discarded on top of them, hanging limply down like the shed skin of a snake. What the hell is happening here?

I roll off the sofa onto the floor, shaking and sweating. Then everything goes black.

45

When I come round the tights are gone but the bottles are still there. There's only one glass, though. Daylight streams in through the large window. How could I have let this happen? After all the promises I've made. How many times do I have to make the same mistake before I learn?

I rack my brain to work out what day it is. It must be Saturday morning already. But then I hear church bells. Sunday. How can it be Sunday? I take a long, deep breath to steady my nerves. If I can just get myself home in one piece, I have the rest of the day to sober up before Mum comes home.

Oh God. Mum. She won't forgive me. Not this time.

I heave myself into a sitting position. A mouthful of bile shoots into my mouth and I shiver uncontrollably. I'm in serious trouble here. I reach for my sodden T-shirt, still lying on the floor with my jeans. And that's when I realize I'm not alone. Helen is sitting in the armchair by the window, watching me. She's fully dressed and she looks so different. Smarter, more fashionable, her hair unusually sleek, as if she's just styled it with straighteners. She's holding something on her lap, something soft, caressing it with her fingers.

"I . . . I don't understand." My voice is so hoarse I barely recognize it. It hurts to speak. My neck feels tender, bruised. "Why aren't you . . . why aren't you as hungover as I am?"

Helen laughs through her nose. A mean, dismissive exhalation. "Because I have something called self-control. Because I'm not a pathetic excuse for a human being like you."

"Helen, you're frightening me. What happened last night? Why did you let me drink so much?"

"I didn't have much choice," she says. "You're quite something when you're pissed, do you know that?" She unfolds herself out of her chair. "That wine would have lasted me weeks if you hadn't turned up and bullied me into opening it all." She laughs then. A horrible, sarcastic laugh. "I don't think moderation management's quite your thing, is it, Astrid?"

She walks toward the bureau and takes hold of a framed photograph sitting on the top. I've never seen it there before. Now she's thrusting it in front of my face and I see that it's a gap-toothed child, grinning from ear to ear. A little boy. But before I have a chance to ask her who it is she whips it away and returns to her chair. She holds the photo in her lap and gazes down at it, stroking the glass in the frame.

"My darling boy," she says, her voice suddenly so low I have to strain my ears to hear it.

Then I see what it was she was holding just now and my gut heaves. It's a woolen trapper hat draped over the arm of her chair. It looks exactly like the one Simon used to wear. Fear twists and coils in the pit of my stomach as the terrible truth dawns. The child in the photo is Simon. Oh God, I've been a fool.

Helen looks up slowly, her face a mask of hatred. "He came back to me. Did you know that? He was getting better. Until he met *you* again." She spits the words out. She's done it on purpose. Helen *made* me start drinking. She saw how low I was, how close to the edge, and she seized the chance to get her revenge. To do to me what I did to Simon. All the things I've told her. She knows everything. Everything!

Gingerly, I reach for my stinking clothes. My hands are shaking so much I can barely get hold of them and lift them toward me. Helen is out of her chair in a flash, the photo falling to the floor in her haste to yank the clothes out of my hands. She kicks them across the room. Then she slaps me, hard, across the face. The force knocks me back onto the sofa and I cower into the cushions, my cheek burning from the sting, my head spinning from nausea and the strength of the blow. I'm pouring with sweat.

She picks up the photo and wanders over to the window with it, talking to me as if nothing has happened.

"Whenever I think of him as a child, he's always the age he is here, in this photo. Seven years old. A gangly little thing with a cheeky grin." Her voice is soft now, indulgent. "Reading his science books, asking impossible questions, making up silly jokes and giggling before he reached the punch line."

She shakes her head. "He could have done anything, been anyone." The softness in her voice has gone. "That's what hurts the most. The waste. The sheer waste of a life."

I shift position on the sofa and another wave of nausea washes through me. If I can summon up the strength, maybe I can launch myself at my clothes, grab them, and make a run for it. But just as I'm about to move she turns round again.

"I hadn't seen him for years. I'd had to distance myself, you see? I'd told him I couldn't spend the rest of my life bailing him out, dreading every phone call, every knock on the door. I'd told him I only wanted to see him if he stopped drinking. For good. It was the hardest thing I've ever done, but it was the only way."

For a second I feel a pang of sympathy. This is what it must have been like for Mum. Oh, Mum. I'd give anything to be safe at home with you right now. Sitting in your cozy living room in front of the telly, cradling mugs of hot tea in our hands. All those mind-numbingly tedious moments I never truly appreciated but which right now seem like a blessing.

"But after six months of silence I couldn't stand it any longer. I had to know how he was. *Where* he was. I was desperate. I contacted hospitals, the police, visited homeless shelters. He'd completely vanished, and it was all my fault. I was too strict with him, thought I could stop him drinking from sheer willpower alone."

She clasps the photo to her chest and rocks in grief. I shuffle to the edge of the sofa. If I'm going to make a run for it, I need to do it now. While her defenses are down. "So when he turned up on my doorstep one day, looking like the walking dead, I welcomed him back with open arms. My boy had come home to me at last. He needed me. And this time I'd see to it that he got better, once and for all. I'd never let him out of my sight again."

She turns sharply and, in that instant, I know that it's me she's not going to let out of her sight now. She's seen me looking at my clothes and she walks over to them, stands right next to them. There's no way I'll have the strength to overpower her, not in the state I'm in. She's at least six feet tall. Of course! It was her I saw by the beach huts that time. I wasn't hallucinating. She must have dressed herself up in Simon's old things, been wearing his hat! Maybe I should forget my clothes and just make a run for it. My coat must be hanging up in the hall. I could grab it on the way out, or grab anything that's hanging there. Just to cover myself up enough to get home and lock myself in the house. Phone Rosie for help.

Except I don't have her number. I threw it away. All Rosie wanted to do was help me. She's always been trying to help me, right from the start, and I was too stupid to listen. She's never trusted Helen. Never.

Helen walks toward me, almost as if she knows what's going through my mind. "He told me all about you. How the two of you lived."

She leans forward and strikes the glass-topped coffee table with the flat of her hand so that the empty bottles crash down and roll onto the floor. My empty wine glass has fallen onto its side and cracked, a dribble of red wine seeping out like blood. I know beyond a shadow of a doubt that if I dare to make a move she'll strike me too. And harder than before.

Her eyes spark with hatred. "The last thing he needed was a girl like you. He needed his mother. He needed *me*. I brought him into this world and I was going to keep him in it, for as long as there was breath in my body."

She takes a step closer. I flinch. Now she's sitting on the coffee table right in front of me, so close our knees are almost touching. All I can think of is that cracked wine glass still lying on its side. I daren't look at it again in case she sees me and reads my mind, but I know it's there and that I'll use it if I have to.

"I contacted AA," she says. "They put me in touch with a local group. I went to one of their meetings and two of them came back with me to the house, spoke to Simon while he was still in bed. He was sick for weeks. I gave up my job and started doing freelance work, working from home as much as possible. I didn't want to leave him too long on his own. I cooked him lovely meals and bought him books to read. I cut his hair, like I used to when he was little. Bought him new clothes. The stuff he'd brought with him was so disgusting I threw most of it away.

"I kept some of it, though," she says. "His jacket and his hat. They're all I have left of him now. I kept one of his T-shirts too, but it must have got mixed up with some bits and pieces I took to the charity shop."

Her face hardens.

"I took his phone away. Didn't want all my good work to be undone, didn't want him going back to you and sinking back into his old ways. It was me he really loved. He left you and came back to *me*. So much for all that garbage you told me the other night, about him hating me. He came back to me because he *loved* me and he knew I'd look after him."

"I'm sorry I said those things, Helen. I'm sure he didn't mean them—"

"Shut up, you little bitch. I'm sick of the shit that comes out of your mouth, do you hear me? I've had to steel myself to listen to it these last weeks."

After what seems like an eternity she starts to speak again.

"They talked to him for hours, those men from AA. They talked and he listened. When he was well enough he started going to meetings. I'd drive him there, wait in the car outside, and drive him home afterward. He was working the program, doing it properly. Not like you and your halfhearted attempts. He *knew* it was his only chance. He *understood*.

"His sponsor used to come to the house and I'd hear the things they used to say. I read the Big Book from cover to cover so I could help him, so I could bring him back from the hell he'd been in since meeting you."

"But Simon used to drink *before* he met me, he was—"

"It was meeting you that sent him down the wrong path. My boy would never have mugged a defenseless young mother and left her to die. Not *my* boy. Not Simon."

A cold sweat breaks out on my back. Left her to *die*? What's she saying? What does she mean?

"He tried to pull you off her, but you just kept tugging and tugging at her handbag. They thought she was just concussed when she fell, but she died a few days later from a torn blood vessel in the brain. That poor child of hers. That poor, poor child. All the lives you've destroyed."

I stare at her in horror. "You're wrong. She couldn't have died. We'd have heard about it if she had. It would have been on the news."

"How would you know what was in the news and what wasn't?" Her spit flies through the air toward me. "You were out of your head. You're a drunk, remember?"

It can't be true. It *can't*! She's lying. She must be. And yet how *would* I have known what was on the news? I might have thought I was checking, but I'd have been pissed most of the time.

"Simon knew, though. He knew what you'd done. That's why he

left you. And he was doing so well. Eight months he'd been sober. He was like a different man. The man he was always meant to be. But the stronger and healthier he became, the more arguments he started. Why didn't I trust him? Why was I taking all his money? Why couldn't I treat him like an adult? If I didn't stop acting like a jailer, he'd leave, he said. He'd find somewhere else to live."

She leans toward me, and I shrink back into the cushions, my gut knotting with fear.

"I couldn't let that happen. Because I knew, I knew that as soon as he was on his own, he'd be back to his old ways. Maybe not straightaway, but bit by bit. So I relented. If I wanted to keep him at home with me, I knew things had to change. I started taking less of his money, gave him more freedom. Gave him his phone back."

She shakes her head and sneers. "I'd deleted your contact details, but I should have deleted hers as well. That lovestruck little fool he'd known at school."

Laura. She must be talking about Laura.

"He was always popular with the girls. Went out with loads of them." She sneers at me. "Far, far prettier than *you*. All through his secondary-school years, he kept Laura dangling on a piece of string. Sometimes he'd take pity on her and take her out. I never imagined for a minute that she'd be the one he rang after all that time, but then, maybe he knew she was the safest bet."

She clenches her hands into fists on her thighs. "She came round to the house. I was furious, but what could I do? If I made a fuss, I knew he'd leave. So I kept quiet. I figured it was better him being friends with her than going back to you."

My toes curl as she clenches and unclenches her fists, over and over again. If I could just reach that broken glass . . .

Helen's voice drones on. "Little did I know what they were planning up there, the two of them. She was helping him pack his bag. The next thing I knew, a taxi had arrived and they were piling his things into it and driving off."

She leans in toward me, her voice scarily low. "You know the rest, of course. Within a few weeks they'd had a row and he'd hooked up with you again. Two weeks later he was dead."

She squeezes her eyes shut and bites down on her bottom lip. Her body sways and for a second or two I think she's on the verge of collapsing. Then she's staring at me again, her face pinched with rage. "You saw to that, didn't you?"

Something beeps from the windowsill. It sounds like the text-notification sound on my phone. Helen walks calmly across the room to pick it up.

"I charged it up for you," she says, a faint smile twitching the corner of her mouth. "That's probably Josh, thanking you for those lovely selfies you sent him."

Now she's openly smirking. "Quite the little sex kitten, aren't you?"

46

"What are you talking about?"

I lurch to my feet, trembling and weak. This can't be happening. I don't understand.

"Get dressed, you pathetic creature."

"Give me my phone!"

"Get dressed first."

With shaking hands, I pick up my smelly clothes from the floor and struggle to get into my jeans. My legs are all sticky with sweat and the jeans are damp. I pull on my T-shirt, almost gagging at the smell of vomit that's soaked into it.

Helen watches with disdain as I tug it down over my hips, trying to cover the horrible wet patch at the crotch. Her eyes travel slowly from my face to my feet and back up again.

"At least he knows the real you at last," she says, and tosses the phone toward my face, forcing me to swerve sideways to stop it hitting me. It lands on the sofa and I grab hold of it, heart racing.

I've waited over two weeks to see Josh's name flash up on my screen and now here it is. Four text notifications, and they're all from him.

"*Stop sending me these,*" says the first one I read.

I close my eyes. Now I know what happened to that poor young woman, now I know for sure what kind of person I really am, a couple of inappropriate selfies are the least of my problems, but I have to know what I've done. See it with my own eyes. I go into my messages and there they are. I have no recollection of doing this. None whatsoever. I must have been out of my head.

Well, duh, Astrid. Of course you were out of your head. You've drunk so much you blacked out. Welcome back, loser.

They're worse, far worse, than I could ever have imagined. Me sprawled on the sofa, bottle in hand, red-wine stains splattering my T-shirt, an inane grin plastered over my stupid face. Then a shot of my purple-stained teeth and my nostrils as I leer at the camera I'm holding too close. I look horrendous. Ugly. Revolting. And—oh no, please no—not this. Not this. I've actually hoicked up my T-shirt and pulled down the cups of my bra. And there's vomit on my chin.

I force myself to look at them again. This is what happens when I drink. I'm embarrassing. Beyond embarrassing. I'm monstrous. I killed a woman. Left a child without a mother.

Tears streaming down my cheeks, I read his replies.

I can't believe you're drinking again, not after everything you said in your letter.

What's he talking about? What letter?
I read the next one:

I thought we had something. I thought it would be okay. That sooner or later we'd get back together. But all the lies and the drama. These disgusting pictures. I don't need this in my life. I don't want it.

His words claw at my heart, but the last one, the one that's just arrived, is the worst of all. Just four blunt words:

Leave me alone, Astrid.

Helen takes a step toward me.

"I might have helped you take the photos, but you got yourself into that state all on your own."

What does she mean, she *helped* me take them? Oh my God! She must have positioned herself somehow so it looked like it was me holding the phone.

Suddenly I'm reaching forward and snatching the stem of the cracked wine glass. I smash it into the table and run at her with it clenched in my fist, but somehow she manages to grab hold of my wrists and hold my hands up high.

She laughs in my face. "He won't want anything to do with you now. A nice clean-living boy like Josh Carter. Not that he would have come back to you anyway. Over two weeks and not a single phone call. Not even a text. It's hardly love, is it?"

I ram my knee hard into her crotch, slam it up against her pubic bone. She lets go of my wrists and doubles up in pain. The broken glass falls to the floor and I push her to one side and run out into the hall. There's no sign of my shoes—I'll have to make my escape barefoot.

But before I can open the front door she's back on her feet and pulling me down onto the floor, kneeling on my stomach. She's got another wine bottle in her hand—an unopened one this time. She raises it aloft, a look of such hatred on her face that I know it's only a matter of seconds before that bottle comes slamming down on my head.

"All the deaths I had planned for you . . . What right have you to go on living, when my boy is dead? And that poor young mother too. I should have strangled you while I had the chance. I came so close. So bloody close. One more twist round your neck and you'd have gone."

I think of those tights, draped over the table earlier. Oh God. I shut my eyes and brace myself. With Helen's full weight kneeling on top of me I'm powerless to roll away.

"Simon didn't love you. He might have *said* he did, when he was drinking. But if he loved you so much, why did he leave you? Not once, but *twice*. He left you for good. Forever." Her face changes. "He chose *death* over you."

I can barely breathe with her kneeling on my stomach, but somehow I manage to force the words out. "He chose death over you too."

She starts to shake. At first I think it's fury. Then I realize she's crying, her whole body heaving with emotion.

"He didn't. He *didn't*! You think you know everything, but you're wrong! *You're wrong!*"

She rocks back on her heels and hurls the bottle at the wall with all her strength. Shards of wet glass shower down over both of us.

I take my chance. I scrabble to my feet and wrench the front door open, launch myself down the stairwell without looking back. I've reached the bottom now and I catch sight of myself in the glass door. A bedraggled, filthy mess. I smell my sweat and the stench of stale booze and vomit wafting off me. I've got to get away from here, get myself cleaned up before Mum gets home. Or I'll lose her as well as Josh. I'll have nothing left. Nowhere to go.

I run out onto the street, the concrete cold against the soles of my feet, bits of grit digging into them and making me wince, but I don't stop. I run until I can't run anymore and I'm crouching at the edge of the pavement, throwing up into the road, people shaking their heads and tutting as they walk past.

"Disgraceful," says an old lady.

The only thing that keeps me going is the thought of shedding these vile clothes straight into the washing machine, of sinking into a long, hot bath. Then I'll drink as much water as I can pour down my throat, make a large mug of coffee, and climb into bed with it. I doubt I'll be able to sleep, but if I can just rest and get my head together before Mum comes home, maybe she won't realize I've been drinking. I can pretend I've got the flu.

At last I'm at the front door of the cottage, and my hand reaches up for the key round my neck. My insides fall away in a sickening thump. Where is it? Where's my key chain? I grope under my T-shirt, hoping by some miracle that it's still there, caught in my bra or under the waistband of my jeans, but even as I'm scrabbling around, I know it isn't. The key is gone. She must have pulled the chain off when she tried to strangle me with her tights.

I slump against the porch door, defeated. I'm going to have to wait here like this till Mum gets home this evening, and she'll see the state of my clothes. The state of *me*. She'll know straightaway I've been drinking and that'll be that.

I make one last, futile attempt to check for the key, pulling out the pockets of my jeans, even though I know it can't be there. Tears stream down my face. Why is this happening to me? How is it possible that I'm standing in my mother's front garden, in damp, vomit-stained clothes, with no keys, no money, and no phone, with no shoes or socks and filthy, bleeding feet?

Think, Astrid. Think. I'll have to go back to the shop and find Rosie. It's Sunday, but the charity shops stay open in the summer months, to catch the tourist trade. What the hell am I waiting for?

Dizzy and trembling, I set off back toward Flinstead Road. People are staring at me as I pass, at my stained clothes and dirty bare feet. Some of them actually stop in their tracks and glare at me as if I'm some kind of criminal. Every so often I have to stop and retch into the road. Not one single person asks if I'm okay. Of course they don't. I stink of booze and vomit. I look like a tramp.

By the time I get to the shop I'm breathless and light-headed. I think I'm going to faint. I push open the door of the shop, praying that Rosie will be there behind the counter, that she'll take one look at me and usher me straight to the room at the back. I'll be able to wash at the little sink outside the toilet and find some clothes to put on, something to put on my feet. But Rosie isn't there. It's a woman

I've never seen before, and she's looking at me as if I'm something the cat's just dragged in. So are the other customers. They're literally moving out of my way, as if I'm contaminated.

"Please, I need to see Rosie. Is she here?"

"No. It's not her day to come in." The woman's nostrils wrinkle in distaste. She makes darting glances at the other customers.

"Can you ring her for me? It's really urgent I speak to her."

"I'm sorry, but I don't have her number."

"But you *must* have. Please."

"Do you need any assistance here?" The voice is familiar. I look round and see, to my dismay, that it's one of the stout women I met at the beach huts the other day, the ones who saw me climbing out of the broken doorway with a bottle of brandy in my hands.

"You again," she says, shaking her head. "I'm going to phone the—"

"But I'm not doing anything. I just need to see Rosie. I've been . . . I've been . . ."

"You've been drinking too much, young lady. That's what you've been doing. Now stop bothering this poor woman and—"

"Please, you don't understand. I'm the victim of . . ."

I gulp for air. What am I the victim of? What can I tell them that would make sense? Whatever I say is just going to sound preposterous. And why would they believe a dirty, smelly drunk like me anyway? I blunder past the racks of clothes and the other customers and back onto the street. The weekend tourists are out in force. I can't bear the way they look at me, the way they nudge their companions, the comments they make under their breath. I see myself through their eyes. A dirty, half-clad woman, reeking of drink. I might just as well be naked.

The bossy woman with the walking stick is now shouting after me. I have to get away from her. Get away from all of them. But I've nowhere to go. No money in my pockets. No phone. No way of contacting Rosie, or anyone else. This is all my own fault. I've brought everything on myself. Helen deceived me, yes. She

pretended to be my friend, my confidante. She waited for an opportunity to hurt me, and she did. She has. But she didn't pour that
wine down my throat. I drank it myself. She might have encour-
aged me, but I could have said no. I could have walked away, and I
didn't. I didn't.

And this is how I've ended up. How I always end up when I've
been drinking. Out of control. Sick. Disgusted with myself. A
woman is dead because of me. Simon too.

I head for the beach. It isn't a conscious decision, more a case of
my legs taking over and carrying me away. Muscle memory. Where
else can I go?

47

Weak with exhaustion, I hunker down on the sand, my back pressed into the curve of the sea wall, arms hugging my knees. Somehow, I've made it to the farthest end of the beach, where, apart from a solitary walker heading back toward town, it's deserted. Thoughts bang about in my head, one in particular. I try to push it away, but the more I do, the louder and more insistent it becomes, till it roars like the waves and demands my attention.

Drowning. It's meant to be painless if you're brave enough to do it right. To take a deep breath as soon as the water closes over your head. Except that's not what people do. They struggle and panic and hold their breath till their lungs burn. We're programmed to cling on to life till the last possible second. To survive at all costs.

Well, I don't want to survive. I don't want to struggle. Not anymore. I've gone and done it again. After all the promises I've made. To Mum. To myself. This is my pathetic life. It's always going to be like this. And how can I live with myself now I know what I've done?

I'm worthless. Despicable. Incapable of holding on to anything of value. I take a deep inhalation. The wind has picked up. The tide is on the turn, heading out to sea. My hangover will retreat too, in time. In a while, I might feel well enough to walk back to the house and sit on the step to wait for Mum. She'll give me time to wash and pack. She might even cook me a meal and let me sleep it off. But in the morning I'll have to leave. There's no question about that. No question at all.

I see her face as clearly as if it's right in front of me. The grim set of her mouth. Those disappointed but determined eyes. The time for hysterical threats has gone. She's loved me as only the mother of a broken child—a damaged child—could. But everyone has their limit, and this will be hers.

All the times she's picked me up when I've fallen. But not this time. This time will be different. She's changed, grown stronger.

But I haven't. I deserve everything that's happened to me. Like a pinball, I've ricocheted from one crisis to the next, and here I am again. I can't do this anymore.

The walker is long gone now. This section of the beach is empty. Just me and a few gulls wading in the shallows. The sea has an inviting, milky sheen to it. The wind is whipping it up into drifts of froth that cling to the wooden breakwaters. I imagine walking into it and not stopping, soft, wet sand soothing the grazed soles of my feet. Walking all the way out until my head goes under, or the undertow drags me down, whichever is soonest. Until my lungs fill with water and my ears ring and the last shreds of memory and thought peel away and dissolve. Forever. The bliss of oblivion. Only this time there'll be no shame in the morning. No sickness. No self-loathing.

And now I'm on my feet and walking to the water's edge. Because I'm too tired not to. Too tired to walk home and wait for Mum. Too tired to see that mouth, those eyes. Too tired to stuff my tatty things into a backpack and start all over again, someplace else. Because wherever I go and whatever I do, I'll still be part of the package.

The water is cold, but I'm used to it now. I like the way it chills my bones and makes me shiver. I wade through it in my jeans, not daring to slow down. The deeper I get, the harder it is to walk. It's almost at my hips. Soon it will rise above the top of my jeans and hit the mottled flesh of my belly as it creeps icily under my T-shirt and up toward the swell of my breasts. It feels like I'm moving toward something better. Something peaceful. The sweet pull of the outgoing tide.

The water heaves sluggishly toward me, undulating against my chest, rocking me gently in its sway. The farther I walk, the more slippery it becomes underfoot. There are more hazards to negotiate. Embedded rocks and stones, the slimy fingers of seaweed clinging to my ankles and twisting round my toes.

The spray hits my face. I lick my lips and taste the salt. Dying is easy; it's life that's so hard. Simon must have felt the exact same way I'm feeling now. I think of him standing on the edge of that cliff, swaying in the breeze in the last few seconds of his life, the swoosh of the sea below. I miss him so much.

The sudden swell of a large gray wave appears from nowhere. It rolls implacably toward me. I steel myself for the impact, just as he must have steeled himself for that final step. The one that sent him plummeting down. I've never felt closer to him than I do right now. The wave engulfs me, knocks me sideways. Water rushes up my nostrils and down the back of my throat. I splutter and gag. My ears pound. This is where I should give in, let the sea consume me, but it's not as easy as it looks in films. Something inside me's still fighting, and my body takes over. Muscle memory again. The will to live.

Another wave strikes me and down I go again. I raise my head, try to breathe, but water fills my mouth. I tread water and tilt my head back, gulp for air. So much for the long, slow walk into oblivion, the water closing above my head like a trapdoor. The waves are more powerful out here. Moving walls of water, one after the other. I'm being pushed back at the same time as being dragged out. It's chaotic and terrifying. A relentless battering. My sodden jeans cling to my legs like wet cement, dragging me down.

So this is it. This is how it ends. Josh's words come back to me. "You'd be a fool not to fear the sea, Astrid. It can turn on you in an instant."

And it has. It's swallowing me whole, sucking me down to my watery grave. Cold, brown water. The stench of brine and sulfur, the searing burn of salt at the back of my throat and nose.

No! I can't die like this. If I drown, Helen's won. Simon didn't blame me for anything. Simon loved me. I know he did. He wouldn't have written me a suicide letter if he didn't. What did Laura say? That she didn't want me to read his lovely words, to know that I was the one he was thinking of, right up to the end. If he hated me so much, if he thought I'd killed a young mother just to get hold of her purse, he'd never have written me a letter. Why should I believe what Helen said when she's been lying to me all along?

Oh, Simon, I should have been brave enough to read it. You wanted me to, and I didn't. I have to get back to shore. I have to stay alive.

With one almighty surge of adrenaline, I kick my legs behind me and propel myself into motion. I can't see which way I'm headed. The waves are too big. They seem to be coming in both directions now. I mustn't panic. I try to remember everything Josh has told me about surviving in the water.

But a current is coming at me from the side, forcing me back out to sea. I roll onto my back to rest and take a breath but, as I do, a wave comes crashing down on top of me. I'm spinning like a doll in a washing machine. Which way is up? I can't get my balance. I can't breathe. I can't . . . breathe.

My chest is bursting. I have to take a breath, but I'm still under-water. *Don't panic. You'll rise in a minute. Keep faith, Astrid. Keep faith.* And here it is. The surface at last. I gulp air into my lungs, but now I'm under again. Something's dragging me down, sucking me deeper. It's no good. I can't hold on any longer. The pressure in my chest is crushing me. I'm going to have to breathe soon or I'll . . .

Water floods my mouth, my throat. I'm breathing it in. Sinking,

sinking. My eyes stare blindly at the greenish-brown murk. Light's coming from somewhere, but I can't gauge the direction. The noise in my ears is deafening. My limbs dangle uselessly. I'm spinning in a dream. Water everywhere. Above me, below me. In my eyes, in my mouth, in my nose. So salty it burns. Whirling round and down, round and down. So this is what it's like. This is how it ends. It's all a terrible mistake, but it's too late now. It's all too late. I see Mum's face. Her beautiful, kind face. Dad's too. Simon's. They're crying. They're crying for me. All the things I haven't done. The dreams that alcohol stole from me.

The ringing intensifies. The light fades.

Then hands are under my shoulders. Strong arms lifting me up. My head breaks the surface and water rushes out of my mouth. Water and puke, all mixed up together. I'm choking on it. Strong forearms are levered under my armpits, towing me back to shore. But I can't get enough air into my lungs. Just tiny, useless gasps. I'm still going to die.

My eyes snap open. I'm lying on my back on the sand. Josh's face is peering down at me. He looks scared. Voices are shouting. A siren wails. I don't know what's happening. My eyes close. My head spins.

The next time I open them, more faces bob in and out of focus over Josh's shoulder. It looks like the woman who shouted at me in the shop. Except now she looks more frightened than frightening. And, oh, there's Rosie.

"Hang on in there, Astrid," she says.

Josh wipes his mouth with the back of his hand. "Stay with me," he says.

I want to stay, I really do, but I'm fading into blackness. He's spinning away from me.

48

Behind my closed eyelids colored shapes and geometric designs shift and slide like the kaleidoscope I had as a child. They zoom in and out of focus—my very own psychedelic light show. Rising through layers of sleep, I have a moment of clarity. Am I seeing the shadows of blood vessels in my eyes? They're so intricate and beautiful, like ancient Aztec patterns.

I'm awake now, but only just. Clinging to consciousness like a drowning woman. The patterns scare me. How can such timeless art forms be swirling around inside my own head?

I open my eyes and blink in the light. Consumed by thirst, I reach for the glass of water on my bedside cabinet, the one I always put there at night. But my hand's caught up in my headphones, and something tight is pinning me down. Sheets. Tightly tucked sheets. Wait, this isn't my bed, and these aren't my headphones, it's the tubing of a drip. My left hand is connected to a drip.

Oh shit, not again. I'm in hospital. What's happened this time? What have I done? Mum's going to kill me.

A slow trickle of sensations and images seeps into my head. The fragments of a dream. A nightmare. I close my eyes against the light, willing myself to sink back down into sleep. But now that I've started to remember, the trickle turns into a steady flow and then a wave. A colossal wave that breaks over me and leaves me gasping. Because it wasn't a dream, was it? It really happened.

Someone places a hand on my forehead.

"Astrid? Can you hear me?"

The light seems even brighter now, and it takes a huge effort to peel back my eyelids. When I do, the first thing that comes into focus is Josh's face peering down at me. Blond, tousled hair. Green eyes flecked with gold.

"Astrid," he says, his voice breaking on the second syllable. "Oh, Astrid!"

Now there's another face next to his. Anxious and drawn, but full of love and as familiar to me as my own.

Mum is here too.

Over the last couple of days it's taken us all quite a while to piece everything together. Helen put a drug in my wine. Flunitrazepam. Brand name Rohypnol. The hospital found traces of it in my blood and urine. Not much alcohol at all, as it happens. She must have been saving those empty wine bottles just to deceive me. To make me think I'd lost control and drunk the lot.

"There's no way of proving it's an actual crime, though," Josh says. "She's told the police you found it in her bathroom cabinet, that you took it yourself to increase the high."

Mum shakes her head in disbelief. That kind of thing is way beyond her comprehension. If she only knew a *fraction* of what goes on in the world of recreational drug use, she'd be shocked to her very core.

"And it's not as if she got it off the internet or anywhere dodgy—apparently, it was a private prescription she had years ago, for insomnia. She told the police she never got round to throwing it away."

"What about all the rest of it, though? Sending horrible threats through the post? Lies? Manipulation?" Mum closes her eyes, then opens them again. "You could have drowned, Astrid." She turns her face away.

"But it's my word against hers, especially since I got rid of half of the evidence, and of course she won't admit to sending them. Hardly enough to warrant an arrest, is it? The police aren't going to waste their time on something like that. I'm just a former 'addict with issues' to them."

Josh squeezes my hand. "If only I'd ignored that letter and got in touch with you sooner. I was so sure I was doing the right thing."

I couldn't believe it when he showed me, when I read the words she'd written in my name. In my handwriting too, or near as damn it. She must have kept hold of the pieces of paper I wrote my confessions on and copied it.

If you respect me at all, please, Josh, don't contact me. Telling you the truth was a major step forward for me. Now I've got to give myself a chance to heal. Our relationship may compromise my recovery. I should never have let it happen—it goes against everything they say at AA. I know you'll understand.

Those endless days I spent crying under my duvet, waiting for him to contact me, to tell me I was forgiven and put me out of my misery, and all the time he thought he was doing the right thing. Thought he was following my instructions. Helping me get better.

Mum makes her cross little harrumphing noise. "I've always tried to believe that all human beings contain at least *some* element of goodness and truth, however bad they might appear to others. And I sympathize with her about losing her son. Of course I do. But what she did . . ."

"She didn't pour that first glass of wine down my throat, though, did she, Mum? There's only one person to blame for that, and that's me."

A lump forms in the back of my throat. Because accepting this means I also have to accept that I'm not responsible for what happened with Simon. I never was. I close my eyes and take a deep breath. I do have a death on my conscience, though. It's impossible to make amends now, but I'll do whatever I can to trace that young woman's family and make them see how sorry I am, how I'll regret what happened for the rest of my life. If they press charges, then so be it. I need to take whatever punishment comes my way. I won't be able to live with myself otherwise.

Mum gathers up our empty coffee cups and puts them into the rubbish bag at the side of my bed. "I still don't understand why Rosie kept her suspicions to herself for so long. If she *knew* Helen was a fraud, why on earth didn't she tell you? Why did she let you leave the shop and go round there?"

"I didn't give her much of a chance. I basically pushed her out of the way and ran off."

Rosie came to visit me this morning. We talked for ages. I try to explain to Mum what she said.

"She didn't tell me because she didn't know for sure. It was just a hunch. She gets these . . . *feelings* about people."

Mum raises an eyebrow.

"She senses things from objects too. It's something to do with picking up their energy. I know it sounds weird, but it *is* a thing, apparently. It's called clairsentience. She says she doesn't usually say anything about it because most people take the piss."

"I'm not surprised," Mum says, and I can't help smiling. Mum and I, we're more alike than I realized.

It was why Rosie wouldn't let go of his juggling ball, that time in the shop, and why she kept Simon's T-shirt, the one Helen accidentally gave away. The photocopied news report about Simon's suicide was folded up at the bottom of the carrier bag Helen dropped off at the shop. Helen couldn't have realized it was there.

Right from the start, Rosie never trusted Helen. All she felt when she was anywhere near her was this terrible, hateful anger. Plus, she's been around the block a few times. She's worked with loads of addicts in the past and she said that something about Helen just didn't add up. She had no proof that Helen was connected to Simon, but some instinct kept nagging away at her.

I wriggle my toes under the bedclothes and try to loosen the top sheet. I can't wait to get home and have a duvet again.

"I couldn't stand Rosie at first. Had her down as one of those annoying types who think God's the answer to everything."

Mum shifts in her chair.

"Actually, she's nothing like that. She's just worked out that God's the only thing keeping her sober. She's tried everything else, and nothing worked. She was only ever trying to save me the trouble of finding that out for myself."

When Rosie came to visit me in hospital she offered Simon's T-shirt to me as a keepsake, but it's time to let go of the past. T-shirts, juggling balls. They're not Simon; they're just things.

"I wonder where she's gone," Mum says. "Helen, I mean."

"Back to London, I suppose. I don't expect she ever sold her house. That was another lie. She just took out a short-term lease on the flat when she worked out where I was."

Visiting time is almost over and, although part of me doesn't want them to go, another part does. There's something I have to do—something I should have done by now—and I have to be alone when I do it.

Josh leans over and gives me a kiss. Not a proper one, not in front of Mum, but it's enough to feel his lips on mine and to know that whatever happens between us now, he knows the truth.

"Dad's new girlfriend's coming by tonight. We're getting an Indian takeaway."

I smile. He's still a bit uptight about it, I can tell, but he'll come round, in time, and if he doesn't, well, that's his problem, not Richard's. Everyone deserves a second chance at love. Even me.

I kiss Mum goodbye and watch the two of them leave. Yesterday, Josh asked me what was going to happen when summer's over. Would I go back to London with him?

I couldn't answer him at first. Because being with Josh is what I want more than anything in the world. But then Mum wants me to stay here, with her. And according to Richard, Charlie's offered me a part-time job in his shop. Everyone's been so kind. Even that bossy old woman with the walking stick turned out to be on my side. She remembered me saying I was a friend of the Carter family, that time at the beach huts. If she hadn't, she might not have rushed over to Charlie's flat and asked him to ring Richard. And if Charlie hadn't rung Richard, Josh wouldn't have known I was in trouble. He wouldn't have driven like a madman to the beach. He knew I'd be there. He just knew.

That's the thing about living in a small town like Flinstead. Everyone knows everyone else and, even if that gets a bit tiresome sometimes, a bit claustrophobic, you're never completely on your own. People look out for each other. People care. Well, maybe not everyone, but lots of people. Lots of people care.

Like Rosie. She's going to help me with my recovery. She's moved out of the Oxfam shop at last and into the spare bedroom of one of Richard's many friends, a nice old bloke with Parkinson's who needs a bit of help with housework and cooking.

And then there's Jeremy. Or Jez, as Richard insists on calling him. He can't promise me anything because these situations are notoriously difficult to prove, and it's probably going to take a hell of a lot of paperwork, but he's working on getting some kind of restraining order put on Helen. Just in case she decides to try anything else. I'm lucky to have him on my case. He used to be a hotshot lawyer in the City before the drink got to him. Oh, well, London's loss, Flinstead's gain, that's what I say.

So what I said to Josh was this: "We'll see each other at weekends and see how things go."

"One day at a time, eh?"

"Yes," I said, burying my face in his chest. "One day at a time."

49

Finally, the moment has come. I open the door of my bedside cupboard and stare at the brown envelope Mum brought in for me earlier.

Before I can change my mind, I take it out and open it up, unfold the paper inside. My hands are trembling and Simon's voice fills my head as I try not to cry.

Dear Astrid,

I'm writing this from hospital. I don't have your number anymore. Mum must have deleted it from my phone. I didn't tell you that I'd been staying with her, that she took me in when I had nowhere else to go.

Even now, I still can't get my head round Helen being Simon's mother.

The nurses say she was here the whole time I was out of it on a drip.

I picture her at his bedside, waiting for him to wake up. Just like Mum was there for me, and, crazy though it is after everything she's done, I can't help feeling a pang of sympathy for her loss.

It was a mistake going back—I know that now—all she does is try to control me. It's all she's ever done. I really regret opening up to her, telling her things about my life, about you, because it didn't take her long to start on at me again. We had a massive argument yesterday, the worst we've ever had, and I flipped. Told her to get the hell out of here and leave me alone. Told her it was her fault all this happened in the first place. If she hadn't tried to keep me as a prisoner, I might not have felt the need to escape. Might not have bumped into you that day in the park.

I take a deep breath. Reading this was never going to be easy.

I love you, Astrid—you know that. I always have, right from that very first time you came up to me in the pub and started talking bollocks about the shape of my head. I've never met anyone like you.

I squeeze my eyes shut. This must have been where Laura stopped reading.

I like to think that, if things had been different, we could have stayed the course. We could have ended up an old married couple with kids and grandkids. But you and I—we're not made like other people, are we? When I woke up in this bed and listened to Mum going on and on, blaming you for making me drink again, I started blaming you too, but that was wrong of me. I could have walked away when I saw you on that bench, but I didn't. I chose to sit down next to you because I wanted to. Just like I chose to take that can of beer.

And this decision I've made now—I'm choosing that too, and it's got nothing to do with you, or anything you did or didn't do. And it's got nothing to do with us either, or how we were with each other. It's about me and me alone.

This is the end, Astrid. It really hurts me to say that, to imagine never seeing your face or hearing your voice again. But I've made my decision and it's final. There's nothing you or anyone else can do to change my mind.

The lump in my throat swells. I'm not sure I can read any more of this, but I have to. I owe it to Simon to read his last words.

Like I told Mum, I've got to cut all ties with my past. With her. And with you too. I've got to make a new start.

What's he talking about, a new start? My toes clench on the floor. This sounds more like a break-up letter.

I've no idea where you are right now, but I'm guessing there's a strong chance you're in Flinstead, with your mum. I've no idea what her address is—Warwick Road, is it? So I've given this to an old friend of mine from school and asked her to track you down. I'm guessing she won't have too much trouble finding you. Everyone knows everyone in Flinstead, right?!

I try to swallow. He's making jokes. Jokes about Flinstead. This isn't a suicide note. It can't be.

Her name's Laura and we're together now.

My fingers grip the paper so tight I nearly tear it.

She's good for me, Astrid. I don't love her like I love you—I don't think it's possible for me to love anyone that way—but she's kind and sweet and she isn't a drinker and she's been good for me. I think it might actually work between us. I really do.

My whole body feels like it's encased in cement.

But in return for delivering this letter to you, she's made me promise I'll do something for her. Well, a couple of things, actually. A Facebook friend of hers has shared a post by a young woman about how she's still nervous going out on her own after having her handbag snatched on the street. I must have read that post a million times, and it's definitely her, Astrid. The woman I mugged. Everything fits. The date it happened, the location. Right down to the bit about some girl with braids trying to help her. You see, I lied to you, Astrid. I made you think we'd done it together. It was cowardly of me to take advantage of your blackout, but I couldn't handle the guilt on my own. I needed you to share the burden. The truth is, you tried to stop me, to pull me off. And you tried to go back to see if she was okay, but I wouldn't let you. I wouldn't let you, Astrid, and I'll never forgive myself for that. Luckily, she was okay, apart from a few cuts and bruises from when she fell. I'm hoping I can make contact with her and tell her how sorry I am, how much I regret scaring her like that in front of her kid.

I read that last paragraph again, but the words don't fully register. I read it a third time, the meaning slowly sinking in. The relief, when it comes, is overwhelming. I'm laughing through my tears. So she isn't dead. She's alive and well and posting Facebook messages. Helen was lying about that too. Making me think I'd killed an innocent young mother. The laughter dies in my throat. How could she? How *could* she?

Laura also wants me to do one last thing for my mum. Mum's been texting her nonstop ever since our row. More of her emotional blackmail, of course, but this one's harder to resist. Tomorrow, it will have been 25 years since my dad died and Mum wants us to go back to the place in Sussex where we scattered his ashes into the sea. Seaford Head. A sort of pilgrimage in his honor, I suppose. It was one of Dad's favorite places.

An icy feeling spirals in my chest.

> *I know it's just her way of getting me to agree to see her again, but I'm determined that it'll be the last thing I ever do with her. And anyway, I'm doing it for Dad, not her.*

The tremble starts in my hands and spreads up my arms, until my whole body is shaking uncontrollably. What was it Helen screamed at me in those last few seconds before I wrenched myself free, when I told her that Simon had chosen death over her?

I hear her words in my head all over again. "He didn't. He *didn't*! You think you know everything, but you're wrong! *You're wrong!*"

I fold over my knees, clutching my stomach.

Helen was at Seaford Head with Simon. She must have been there when he died.

Monday, July 15, 2019

There isn't a word for a parent who's lost a child. There should be, but there isn't. Children who have lost a parent are called motherless or fatherless. If they've lost both parents, they're called orphans. But I can't call myself childless, because that's untrue. That would imply I never had a child to start with. And I did. I had the most beautiful little boy in the world. His name was Simon and I loved him from the very first second I held him in my arms.

They don't tell you what it's like, do they, being a parent? They don't tell you how it makes you feel when your child is sad and troubled, how you'll do anything to take their pain away. And it gets even harder when they grow up. If they lose their way, it's worse, far worse, than your own suffering. Because you can't make it better anymore, not if they don't let you.

If you knew all that before having them, you might think again. But that's nature's greatest trick, isn't it, the biological imperative? Making us yearn to reproduce, filling our fertile years with all that time-wasting nonsense.

I'd have been a lot happier if I'd never had him in the first place. I was never really cut out for mothering. I know that now. But the fact is, I did have him. And that's the other thing they don't tell you, that whatever your children do, however much they throw it all back in your face, you can't stop loving them. You might hate what they've become but, deep down, they're still that little gap-toothed child you smothered in kisses and they always will be.

Once, a long time ago, I knew how to comfort my darling boy. How to make him giggle through his tears. Oh, I wasn't dumb enough to think it would never change. I knew he'd grow up, move away. Of course I did. I just didn't know how much of him I'd lose. Or how I'd lose myself in the process.

That's why I'm here. Because I'm lost. They've suggested I start keeping a journal. So here I am, sitting at a desk in the library, a nurse watching me from a discreet distance. Journaling. That's what they call it—one of those silly, made-up words. Apparently, it doesn't matter what I write, as long as I write something. Anything that comes into my head. Nobody except me will read it, they said, although I don't believe that for a second. There's no privacy in this place. One of them probably reads it when I'm in the shower, or when I'm in group therapy, which isn't that dissimilar from an AA meeting. Except it isn't in a drafty old church and I don't have to make stuff up.

When he met me at Seaford, I knew. I knew straightaway that it was the last time I'd see him. I wasn't good for his recovery, he said. Not good for his recovery! That's rich, I said. If it weren't for me, you'd be dead by now. Prophetic words, eh?

But it was what he said next that did it. The words no parent ever wants to hear. "I don't want you in my life anymore."

How could he say that? How could he take his love away after everything I've done for him? All the sacrifices I've made. All the misery he's caused. When a child disowns you, it's the ultimate rejection. A million, zillion times worse than being left by a lover or a spouse.

And that's why I ran toward the edge. I ran because I had nothing left. Suddenly, more than anything, I wanted it all to be over.

The pain. The guilt. The worry. The constant ache in my soul. I wanted it gone.

And although he'd kept on saying I had to let him go, when it came down to it, he couldn't let me go. He had to run after me and pull me back. Why? Why did you do that, Simon? Why did you try to save me? I didn't want to be saved.

I can hear him yelling all over again, feel his hands as they clutched at my sweater, me pushing him away, then losing my balance and crashing down on my back. And I can feel the vibrations, the ground crumbling under his feet as they scrabbled for purchase, his arms clawing at the air. And then he was gone. He's gone. My boy. My darling little boy. My Simon.

Why didn't I throw myself after him? That's what I can't understand. All I know is, when I crawled to the edge and peered down, saw him lying broken on the rocks below, the unnatural angle of his neck, I couldn't do it. I was so wrapped up in my horror and grief. It should have been me lying there, not him.

When a child is gone, they're gone. They're gone forever, and nothing will fill the gaping hole they leave behind. Nothing.

Blaming Astrid gave me something else to think about. Blaming Astrid made me stronger because anger is a fuel. It fires you up from the inside and propels you forward. Stops you facing the grief. Stops you sinking.

But you know what? She could have died a thousand deaths, each one more gruesome than the next, and it wouldn't have made a scrap of difference. Not in the end. Because I would still be alive, and Simon would still be dead.

Perhaps one day, when I'm a little stronger, I'll send her a copy of this journal, so she can understand that just because you imagine yourself doing something and enjoy the way it makes you feel, it doesn't mean you actually want to do it. It doesn't mean you're going to do it.

Murder, suicide, it's much harder than you think.

I'd like to say I'm over all that now. I'd like to say I wish her well, I really would.

But the fact is . . . I don't wish her well. He loved her more than me and I can't forgive her for that. So if, in my head, I'm still killing her for being here when he isn't, it doesn't mean that that's what I'll do. It doesn't make me a bad person just thinking about it. It's normal to have the odd violent fantasy about someone you hate so much that every muscle in your body contracts when you think of them. I mean, everybody does it sometimes, don't they?

Don't they?

Acknowledgments

Although *Who Did You Tell?* is my second published novel, I actually wrote it before *The Rumor*. I entered a competition with the opening chapters and was lucky enough to be selected as one of the runners-up, so special thanks must go to Alison Bonomi for "finding" me in among all those envelopes, and to Luigi Bonomi, Selina Walker, Sandra Parsons, and Simon Kernick, who were on the judging panel.

Thank you to Amanda Preston for representing me and being the best agent I could ever have hoped for, and to Sarah Adams of Transworld and Anne Speyer of Ballantine in New York, for your insightful editorial comments and suggestions. This novel is immeasurably better as a result of the input I received from all three of you. Huge thanks also to everyone else on the teams at Ballantine and Transworld for your passion and professionalism, and for making the whole experience of being published an absolute joy.

Credit must also be given to my writing posse and dear friends, aka the Frinton Writers' Group, and to early readers Dawn Brown, Fiona Parkin, and Jane Hellebrand, who gave me encouraging feedback on my first draft.

Elisabetta Massimi: thank you for telling me why you love working in scenic design—you may notice that Astrid's feelings on this topic are uncannily similar to your own!

I would also like to acknowledge the important work carried out by Alcoholics Anonymous and other organizations devoted to supporting sufferers and their families all over the world.

And last but not least, thanks to Rashid, for keeping me sane and feeding me at regular intervals.

PHOTO: CHRISTIAN DAVIES PHOTOGRAPHY

LESLEY KARA is an alumna of the Faber Academy "Writing a Novel" course. She lives on the North Essex coast. Her first novel, *The Rumor,* was a *Sunday Times* Top 10 bestseller.

lesleykara.com
Facebook.com/lesleykarawriter
Twitter: @LesleyKara
Instagram: @lesleykarawriter

ABOUT THE TYPE

This book was set in Albertina, a typeface created by Dutch calligrapher and designer Chris Brand (1921–98). Brand's original drawings, based on calligraphic principles, were modified considerably to conform to the technological limitations of typesetting in the early 1960s. The development of digital technology later allowed Frank E. Blokland (b. 1959) of the Dutch Type Library to restore the typeface to its creator's original intentions.